Just Friends

Just Friends

Lucy Keeling

Book 2 – Friends

Where heroes are like chocolate – irresistible!

Published 2021 by Choc Lit Limited
Penrose House, Crawley Drive, Camberley, Surrey GU15 2AB, UK
www.choc-lit.com

ISBN 978-1-78189-461-3

To my amazing sisters, Charlie and Abi, the very first people I would go to if I needed to plot my revenge.

Acknowledgements

Thank you to you dear reader, I am so grateful to you for taking the time to read this book. I hope it has given you a little bit of escapism and some amount of joy. It's not been easy to write and edit during lockdown, but we need lovely stories now more than ever.

Thank you to my amazing husband for giving me the most precious resource of all, time, but also for the support, encouragement and belief every step of the way.

Thank you as well to my amazing family and friends that allow me to go on about my imaginary worlds, whilst also plowing me with wine, beer, food and cake. So cheers to you, Brenda, Gwen, Abi, Charlie, Helen, Michelle H, Clare R, Nic Nic, Michelle B, Sarah, Terri, Emma, Kim, Claire (Twin) and Yvonne. Thank you as well to the gorgeous Big Red for inventing the best lockdown game which has made all the difference in these weird times, and to Andi for compiling the playlist that I listened to non-stop whilst writing this book. Special mention to Gozey who knows how much these acknowledgements mean to me.

My online writing and reviewing families are incredible, and I wouldn't have been able to write a word without their support and cheerleading. So thank you to all at #UKRomChat, Chick Lit & Prosecco, and ChocLit. An extra special thank you to those that have been so supportive of me and so many other authors, Anita Faulkner, Sue Baker, Laura (Tangents and Tissues) Jayne Heywood, Lucy Mitchell, Sandy Baker, Rachel Dove, Lucy Flatman, Leonie Mack, Sharon Ibbotson, Kiley Dunbar, Rachael

Stewart, and Emma Jackson. They are all amazing and I am so very grateful for their support and encouragement.

Thank you to the fabulous team and panel at Choc Lit for allowing me to continue to share these stories that mean so much to me. It can't be easy pulling together these stories during a lockdown, and I really am grateful. A big thank you to my amazing editor who knew exactly what this story needed to make it even better.

A special thank you to the Panel for finding something in my stories, that was worth telling: Bee Master, Shalini G, Lucie Wheatcroft, Dimitra Evangelou, Carol Elizabeth Dutton, Jo Osborne, Alan Roberton, Gillian Cox, Sharon Walsh, Fran Stevens, Shona Nicolson, Hilary Brown and Deborah Warren.

Chapter One

'I need to talk to you both about my wedding,' Sophie said as she picked up her phone, turning the camera on to check her make-up, and absolutely not to avoid watching to see how her friends would react. Making sure her brown curls were in place, she put down the phone and turned to look at Mya sat on the bar stool next to her. Paige was stood behind the bar, the earrings lining her ear glittering in the overhead lights, her side cut recently shaved.

'Oooookay. And you're nervous because?' Mya asked, with a raised eyebrow at Paige.

'It's about the maid of honour position.'

Mya and Paige both tried on a smile, but it didn't quite conceal their frowns.

'Why do you already look like that?' Sophie said.

Paige cleared her throat, giving Mya a quick 'Don't worry I've got this' nod. 'No offence, Sophie, but we have reason to believe that you'll probably go a little bridezilla on us, and now that you've decided to do it all within three months, we're pacing ourselves, but obviously we're desperate to hear about the maid of honour position.' Paige's beaming smile at the end of her speech took Sophie off course so that it took her longer than she cared to admit to process the actual message.

Eventually, Sophie's jaw dropped. 'What?'

'Admit it, you're highly organised and fastidious. This is going to be hell on us, your long-suffering but highly loveable friends.' Mya had the courtesy of at least removing the 'smile' from her face into a somewhat more palatable grimace.

'I'm going to ignore everything you've just said and carry on anyway.' Sophie shook her head and scowled at her so-called best friends.

'Shouldn't Polly be here if we're talking wedding shop?' Mya asked, spinning her head around to look for the last member of their quorum.

'If you'd just let me finish, I'll explain why she's not here yet and what I wanted to talk to you both about. You know I love you all equally, but I was thinking that it would be a good opportunity for Polly and Bailey to, you know, get a bit closer if Polly was my maid of honour. Plus she is Marcus's sister. But I didn't want you both to think that I was picking one over the other. You'll both be bridesmaids, of course. So, what do you think?' Sophie finally let go of her own hand, not realising she had been twisting her engagement ring round as she spoke.

Paige and Mya looked at each other again before bursting into huge smiles, too big actually.

'We think that's a genius idea!' Mya literally threw her hands in the air, before reaching over the bar to embrace Paige in a victory hug. 'Dodged a bullet there.'

'Guys, you know at some point I'm going to get really offended.' Sophie eyeballed her friends in turn.

'We're only messing with you, whatever you need, we're there.' Mya put her arm around Sophie and kissed the top of her head.

All the name-calling and micky taking aside, Sophie believed her; they always had each other's backs, no matter what.

'Thanks, guys. But the Polly thing? Do you think it's too forced, like I'm trying to set them up? I mean really it's not any of my, or our, business, is it?'

'Well,' Mya paused as she ran her hands through her long shiny vitamined hair, then continued, 'we all know that they would be perfect together, especially after their blazing hot kiss last year—'

'And if it means that Polly and Bailey have to spend more time together because they are maid of honour and best man,' Paige cut in, 'well, that's just the way it goes. You can sleep soundly.' Paige gave a carefree shrug and a quick glance at the baby monitor she kept behind the bar for her cat Mr Higgins.

'OK then. Yes, when you put it like that I've done no meddling whatsoever.' Sophie's shoulders lowered.

'Drinks!' shouted Mya. 'We need to celebrate the fact that Paige and I are free.'

Sophie punched Mya on her arm. 'It's a title only thing. You're still bridesmaids.'

'In that case, I definitely need a drink,' Mya muttered.

Paige nodded at Belle, her new barmaid who was currently on trial as a possible replacement for Sophie. As Belle came over towards the quiet end of the bar, she looked up at Paige expectantly.

'Are you still shadowing Clare and India or are you all settled in now?' Paige asked.

'All settled in, boss,' Belle said and turned to the two women sat across the bar. 'What can I get you, ladies?'

'Espresso Martini for me, please, Belle. I've got a long night of work ahead of me.' Mya smiled warmly.

'Rhubarb gin and tonic for me, please,' Sophie said as Mya and Paige raised their eyebrows.

'What? It's nice.' Sophie shrugged.

'Make sure these guys pay. They're here all the time and they are nearly drinking me out of business.' Paige's face was deadpan.

Mya groaned. 'Your last barmaid used to give us free drinks all the time.'

'I know and that's why I have a new one,' Paige said quickly.

'You have a new barmaid because I am an official social media goddess with millions of subscribers who hang on my every word.' Sophie smiled smugly. 'And if you carry on I will refuse to do any more publicity for your bar.'

Paige stuck her tongue out and Sophie smiled.

'Hi, guys, what have I missed?'

Sophie jumped up quickly and hugged Polly.

'Hi, Polly, what are you drinking, oh this gorgeous one here is Belle, by the way,' Mya said, as only she would.

'Hi, Belle, I think we've met before, but don't worry, the barmaid before you was rubbish, so you'll be fine.' Polly smiled warmly as she tugged off her beret and unwrapped her thick knit wool scarf, spring clearly not quite in its element yet, as her red hair settled down her back.

'So I've heard,' Belle said with a wide grin, retying her blonde hair up in a bun before continuing with the drink preparation. 'What can I get you?'

'Erm, rhubarb gin and tonic, please,' Polly said.

'See,' said Sophie to Paige's eye-roll.

'So come on what have I missed?' Polly pulled out the bar stool nearest Mya, but not before gently and reverently moving Mya's new limited edition designer handbag up to the next bar stool.

'Sophie has news, and Mya has to work late,' Paige explained, whilst Mya leaned over and kissed Polly on her cheek. Polly grinned at Mya before turning to face Sophie, her eyebrows raised in question.

'Polly, I have checked with the other girls and they agree. I would like you to be my maid of honour.'

'Really? Why?' Polly asked.

'Jesus, can't one of my so-called friends be happy that I'm getting married?' Sophie said, her hands slamming on the bar.

'I am excited but why me, why have one at all? We could all just be bridesmaids.'

Sophie stalled out, shit, she hadn't thought of a reason other than setting Polly up with Bailey.

'Because you were the one that came up with the idea that Marcus transform the garden. If you hadn't, Sophie and Marcus would never have got together and the proposal wouldn't even exist, let alone the wedding,' explained Paige with zero hesitation, as if she was prepared for Polly to ask that exact question.

'Oh. Well, in that case. Yes!' Polly jumped off the bar stool and pulled Sophie into her arms. 'Thank you so much, I'd be delighted.'

Sophie mouthed the words 'Thank you' and Paige nodded.

'That's more like it, that's the enthusiasm I want from all of you from now on, OK?' Sophie said.

'Yes, boss,' Paige and Mya said at once before bursting into giggles.

'Here you are.' Belle placed the drinks on the bar.

'Thanks, Belle.' Once all the drinks were passed around and paid for, Mya, raised her glass indicating that the others should follow.

'I would like to declare a toast. To Sophie, we've seen each other through the good times and the bad, and we'll see you to the aisle and down it, and every step thereafter.'

'To Sophie,' everyone cheered.

'As long as I'm not in a hideous bridesmaid dress,' Mya quickly added.

'About the wedding. I, erm, have a question,' Polly said. 'I don't want you to make a big deal of it, but I know that there is a lot of planning involved and I wanted to give you a heads-up. So, erm, can I bring my boyfriend?'

'Boyfriend? When did this happen?' Paige asked eyebrow raised.

'A week last Thursday,' Polly said, wanting to smile but still unsure of her friends' reaction.

'Wait, did you have a Tinder date and NOT come here?' Paige asked in disbelief.

'Calm down, Paige, I know the rules, OK. Yes, it was a Tinder date, and yes I came here. It was Belle's second night I think.'

'Belle!' Paige shouted and Polly was stunned at the barked order.

'Are the drinks OK?' Belle looked worried as she made her way towards them.

'The drinks are fine, but why didn't you tell me that Polly came here and had a date with a bloke?'

'Was I supposed too? Also, I didn't know who she was then, it was only my second night.' Belle was looking at them all, her eyes wide.

'Calm down, Paige, you don't need to interrogate your staff. Clare was there and she knew all about the dating set up. I was safe and it was fine.' Polly sat back, confused at the response.

'I know all about the first date rules now, but I don't have to tell you about them all, do I?' Belle asked.

Paige's bar, Barbarella, was an exceptional bar. Word had gotten out that it was a safe space, women and men were welcome here on first dates, the bar staff all knew to keep an eye on their first date patrons, and were on hand to provide a safe get out if needed. Not to mention it was in a cool offshoot of Manchester City Centre.

Paige grunted, making no effort to hide her disdain, but then she never did. Much like Mya, the pair of them had little to no filter.

Sophie patted Belle's arm. 'No, you don't. Paige is just upset that she missed some gossip. It's a rare day when Paige doesn't know absolutely everything, that's all, ignore her.'

Belle walked off looking confused, and no doubt questioning her life choices.

After another minute or two of silence, Mya shook her head. 'OK, so you met him Thursday?'

'Last Thursday.'

'OK, last Thursday, but how do you know that he is boyfriend material? Isn't that a bit sudden?' Mya asked.

'I've seen him six times in two weeks. We even pulled a sicky together on one day. Although there is a small catch.'

'What?' Paige asked as they all leaned in.

'Well, it was a tragic first date. It just kept going wrong, so wrong that it broke the ice and we were just laughing away. We gave it another go and it was like we had been seeing each other for ages. Anyway, I had seen him quite a few times and it was too late—'

'You mean you'd already slept with him?' Mya interrupted.

'Yes, anyway as I was saying, it was too late by the time I found out that we work for the same company. We're in different departments, I mean it's a huge company, so it's not completely surprising that I haven't seen him there. Anyway it turns out that he only started working for the company a couple of months ago, and it's completely coincidental that we found each other on Tinder.'

Silence again. Polly watched the cogs turning for each of her friends as they processed what she had told them. She adored her best friends; Paige and her all-knowing wisdom, Mya with her constant flirting, and Sophie with her fastidious list making ways. And Polly could understand their shock; it had been very sudden and very unexpected. She'd had a number of occasional dates and hook-ups, dick pics and ghosting, but she had slowed down the app thing until recently and, even then, it had been a very long time since she had actually labelled anyone her boyfriend. This silence was too long, however. Why weren't her friends happy for her? After another minute passed, of frankly awkward silence, Polly was starting to get angry. 'Not quite the reaction I was hoping for from my friends when I told them I had a boyfriend.'

'Sorry,' Mya said with a grimace.

'Of course we're happy for you, Pol,' Sophie said half-heartedly. 'We just didn't see that coming.'

'When do we meet him?' Paige said, without any hint of a smile or apology.

'Soon enough I would've thought. I'll bring him back to

the bar again soon, OK?' Polly could hear the tone in her voice, but what the hell?

'Make sure you do. What's his name anyway?' Paige asked, clearly still no warmer to the idea.

'Darren Selby.' She might have been mistaken but she thought she heard a groan from one of them before, in weird synchronisation, all three heads dropped down and they started typing furiously on their phones. Polly crossed her arms. She'd rather have introduced him in person rather than by proxy with his social media. She wouldn't have mentioned it at all yet but for the wedding planning.

Sophie was first to look up with a Facebook profile. 'Is this him?'

Polly reached over to look at the screen.

'Yeah, that's him. He looks better than his picture though.' Polly tried to look at his profile picture through unbiased eyes. He was good-looking, not like WOW with women dropping to their knees around him, but handsome enough and confident. Not that he was cocky or anything, Polly tried to right her thoughts as her mind went ten to the dozen.

'Is this him?' Paige next with his Instagram.

'Yes, that's him. That picture was when he did a skydive with his mate in Australia.' Yep, he was adventurous too.

'Is this him?' Mya had found a gaming profile for him, on some online gaming thing.

'Er, yes I think so, but I don't know anything about that.'

'Hmmm.' Mya was studying the details, as were Sophie and Paige on their respective phones. Polly sat quietly and sipped her drink waiting for her friends to finish their cyber investigations, trying not to fume, and failing desperately. She could totally see it from their point of view, they were trying to be protective, but one of them could at least pretend to be happy for her. Was that too much to ask?

As she waited she looked around. She felt so comfortable here, the different lights scattered across the bar providing a warm glow over the patrons. It was absolutely Paige's bar, it had her essence throughout. Warm, inviting, protective, dark in parts.

Belle walked back over. 'It's gone quiet over here, is everything all right?'

'Yes, they're just checking out Darren's online presence so that they can judge him harshly before they've even met him.' Her voice didn't sound quite as funny and carefree as she had been aiming for, it was instead dripping with snark.

'Oh well, if it helps, when he came to the bar he was nice and chatty. He was telling Clare that he was on a first date with the most beautiful girl he had ever seen.'

'Awww.' Polly grinned, Sophie and Mya pretended to gag, and Paige muttered something that sounded like 'trying too hard', but it was difficult for Polly to make it out. Belle slunk away, clearly unsure of the protocol. Polly wished that she could just disappear too. Oh, wait she could. Finishing her drink she carefully put her glass back on the bar, and grabbed her scarf and hat out of her handbag.

'Thanks, ladies, but I have to go and see my dad. Sophie, I'm delighted to be your maid of honour, text me to set something up to go through what you need from me, yeah?'

Jumping off the bar stool, Polly made sure to go round and kiss and hug each of them in turn so that they wouldn't realise how upset she was, truthfully she didn't have the energy to deal with them. Headphones in she pushed open the door and braced herself for the cold weather outside.

Chapter Two

Shaking, Bailey tried desperately to get his body under control, gripping the phone to his ear so hard his knuckles threatened to break through his skin. 'Fuck... Shit... So what happens next?' His eyes raced around his open plan apartment as he tried to take in what he was hearing, unconsciously strolling towards the balcony doors until his hand could lie flat on the cold glass.

'They're going to do some tests and we should know more next week. Listen, darling, I really wanted to tell you in person but I know how busy you are with your work, and really, at this point, there's nothing to worry about. Will you come round for dinner next week and we can go through it together?'

'Mum, what are you talking about. I'm not waiting a week to see you when you have news like this. I'll come round now.' Bailey began pacing, his hand now dragging through his hair.

'No, darling, you don't need to do that. Billy and I are going to the pub for the Monday night quiz. Luke and Richard have invited us out and you know they can't do the music round without me. But feel free to call around tomorrow if you can, but you don't need to, OK? So, no worrying. We'll figure out what happens when we get the results.'

'Oh, Mum.' All the energy fell from his body until he slumped to the floor, his back resting on the cold glass of the balcony door.

'Come on, Bailey. I love you. It's going to be all right.'

'You don't know that though, do you?' He heard her sigh.

'I know that I raised three amazingly wonderful and too beautiful for their own damn good kids. Regardless of what happens, everything will work out OK.'

Bailey could tell from the tone of her voice that she was going to get annoyed with him soon. Even though his head was in bits he at least understood that stress on top of everything else was going to do her no good at all.

'OK, Mum, I'll see you tomorrow. But just let me know if I can do anything, yeah? I can be round in twenty minutes.'

'Not without breaking the law you can't. I'll see you tomorrow, darling. I love you.'

'Love you too, Mum. See you tomorrow.' Bailey held the phone to his ear even after he heard the beeps that indicated she'd hung up. Reluctantly, he pulled the phone away. His phone had never felt so heavy and his hands weren't cooperating like they should do. Finally managing to lock his phone he put it on the floor beside him, his head hanging between his knees, his dark hair falling about his face, offering limited shelter.

'Shit.' The tears fell, despite telling his mum he wasn't going to worry, he was worrying like a pro. What about the tests? It didn't sound good. A freaking lump, of all things. His heart felt heavy and his head was banging. He closed his eyes and felt the tears cling to his eyelashes. Not his mum.

'Fuck.'

What more was there to say? Suddenly restless, Bailey wiped his face, tied his hair back and jumped to his feet. Grabbing his car keys, he marched out of his apartment towards the lift. The doors opened and the endless mirrored cage continued to throw his reflection back to him. He closed his eyes, not wanting to see the pain showing there. Once in his car, he tried the deep breathing again but that wasn't working. Turning the ignition he set off, not entirely sure where he was going to go.

Polly stretched her hands and made sure that she was comfortable on the piano stool. This moment, just before she played, where the crowd were in silent expectation was almost her favourite part. She was about to take off and fly across the keys, her voice about to flow. It was the ultimate freedom and when she was in the midst of it, that was her favourite part. She couldn't hear the audience, she had little to no knowledge they were even there and, truthfully, she didn't do it for them, but she knew they were listening. If she thought about them too much, the vines that crawled around her belly would rise and she wouldn't be able to do anything. The bit she hated most was immediately afterwards. When people cheered, yelled or booed. After nearly three years at the Speakeasy, she still hadn't figured out how she was supposed to respond. She felt vulnerable and exposed when she performed, but it was worth the high. Which was why Polly only sang at this club, and only once a week, and only because she had been coming here and listening to everyone at Open Mic night for months before she dared join in. She needed to play, she HAD to play, and so here she was, the bright spotlight warming her back, making the keys of the piano that little bit warmer.

Closing her eyes and with a small smile for herself, Polly began. It was one of her own compositions and it was getting its inaugural play. She hadn't even heard it on piano herself yet, the keyboard in the front room of her tiny terraced house a weak equivalent. She played the guitar too on occasion, but the power of the piano was what she needed tonight, and so she played, her hands flying just like her soul.

The loud applause and cheers from the crowd brought her back to the room and she took a small moment to relish the feeling of playing before the awkwardness took over. The Open Mic night regulars were always so supportive, it was one of the reasons she played here and nowhere else. Polly looked around, the lights facing her making it difficult to see everyone in the room. Still not knowing what to do with the audience's feedback, she quickly gave a little nod and rushed off stage.

'Isn't she magnificent everyone, one of our favourites here at the Speakeasy please give it up again for Miss Polly.' More clapping as Polly made her way off stage and sat down at her little table, smiling awkward thanks at the regulars who patted her back, waved or saluted. The compere Mike continued, 'We're going to have a little break now whilst we sort out our next few performers. See you back in fifteen minutes.'

Polly sat still feeling her body resettle after the high of playing, just trying to hold onto that feeling for just a little longer. As her blood started to fizz a little less, she wished that she could do it more often, but knew that, frankly, she didn't have the guts. Nor did she have the time to scope out some other place as friendly and accepting as this. She had what she needed to get by and, well it would do, it'd have to.

'That was really beautiful, Pol. You are amazing up there.'

Polly jumped, nearly taking her bottled water with her. Looking up in disbelief despite knowing exactly whose voice that belonged to, she saw his beautiful pale blue eyes first, they shone brightly in the darkness.

'Bailey, what are you doing here?' Polly squeaked.

'I knew it was Open Mic night so I took a chance that you would be here and I was right.' Bailey was leaning on the chair next to her, and for one small second, not even that, she swore she could feel his body heat next to her.

'But why?' Polly asked with a small frown.

'Can't a friend be supportive? Hang on, I need a drink, do you want anything?'

'No, I'm fine, thanks.'

'OK.' With that Bailey took off again and Polly couldn't quite figure out if her heart was fluttering because of her performance on stage, adrenalin, or something else altogether. She was also unclear about how she felt about Bailey coming to see her perform. It was private. Well, except for this crowd of a couple of dozen, but she didn't really know them, or at least she didn't know them outside of the Speakeasy cocoon. The only reason Bailey knew about her performing was because when her dad had had a second heart attack, Bailey had tracked her down using Find My Friends. That was nearly nine months ago and he had kept her secret without wavering once. It was still weird though, after performing in secret for nearly three years, to have someone she knew come and listen. It was terrifying, surreal, but also a small part of her welcomed it, all in one go.

Polly looked around the Speakeasy; this bar was her second home. Well, apart from Paige's bar Barberella, although that was probably too many bars to be considered homes from home. Where Barberella was lit up with a variety of different light fixtures, the eclectic mix reflecting the patron, the Speakeasy was darker, with discreet corners, and hushed conversations – apparently it used to be a bank many, many years ago. The decor was how you would imagine a gentlemen's club, with leather chairs, leather booths and dark wood walls. She wouldn't be surprised to find bookcases full of distinguished works and the *Financial Times* available at every table. This place had secrets, and her secrets felt safe and lost amongst everyone else's.

Bailey sat back down in front of her taking a sip of his Coke. Polly took the opportunity to look at him. He was gorgeous, there was no doubt about it. His eyes were the colour of the sea somewhere like St Lucia, and he had the audacity to have thick dark eyelashes surrounding them. It didn't help that his skin tone was a gorgeous brown, his clipped beard auburn in parts. His dark hair was loosely tied back, some of it falling over the side of his face as if he had been pulling at it. The start of his tattoo was just visible on the edge of the collar of his jumper, and as he pushed up his sleeves, she couldn't help but glance for a second at his thick forearms. The thing about Bailey was that he knew how gorgeous he was too. It was a lethal combination. One that had Polly forcibly reminding herself that she had a boyfriend and that the kiss she had once shared with Bailey was nothing to reminisce over, at least not any more, not after the first few months. It had been nothing more than a 'get out of a bad date free card', that she had used and discarded with no chance of a repeat. Despite all of this, there was something in his eyes, his smile wasn't quite reaching them maybe, or his tone was off, hard to tell exactly, but something wasn't right.

'What's the matter, Bailey?' Polly searched his face, realising then how close they'd become as friends over the last few months.

'Nothing. Why?' Bailey leaned back in his chair, manspreading to the fullest.

'OK, then what made you come here?' Polly asked still staring directly at him, looking for any hints.

'I told you I thought you'd be performing tonight and I just needed to go for a drive and clear my head and here I am.'

'Of ALL the places that you could've driven to you came here, on what happens to be Open Mic night, and what happened to be the right time to hear me sing?'

Bailey tried and failed to look innocent. 'I'm just lucky, I guess.' He winked, and she most certainly didn't swoon, well not a full swoon. Not really.

'Don't be trying any of that on with me. Not unless you want to tell me the real reason you're here.'

Bailey grinned, and Polly was most definitely not devastated by it, not one little bit, not any more. She leaned forward though, sure now that there was something wrong, and her heart ached for her friend. She'd known Bailey for years, he was her brother's best mate and business partner after all, as such she also knew that he wasn't one to really open up. Everything was usually carefree and chill in Bailey's world.

'Why are you so suspicious? I just came here to support you.'

Polly glared and waited. As the silence between them passed, she was just about to say something when Bailey dropped his eyes and sighed. 'OK, fine. I had some bad news and wanted to go somewhere I could forget about it for a while, that was all.' Bailey shrugged and half-heartedly smiled, and Polly's stomach tightened at his vulnerability.

'What was it? What's the news?' She wasn't about to let this go.

'I just said I came here to forget about it.' Bailey took a sip of his drink.

'Tell me first then you can forget about it.'

Bailey dropped his head in defeat. That was too easy, and Polly knew that he had come knowing that she would drag it out of him. Putting her hand on his forearm, and deliberately ignoring the size of his arm, and the heat of his body, she tilted further forward, sensing that it was probably something serious, and maybe something private.

'You don't have to tell me if you don't want to. Just know that you can if you want, you can tell me anything.'

It wasn't that it was awkward between them, far from it, they'd been hanging out more and more lately and they were closer as friends than they ever had been, but she remembered that his best mate was her brother and that maybe it wasn't her place to be dragging information from him after all.

'It's my mum. She's found a lump, they don't know if it's cancer, they're doing tests.'

Polly gripped his arm tighter, unaware that she was doing so. It took a minute for the information to properly sink in. It was serious, it was private, but he'd told her anyway. Now she had to think of something helpful and maybe insightful, something that a good friend would say in a situation such as this.

'Fuck.' Was that the best she could do?

'Yeah,' Bailey replied.

'Shit.' Seriously? Come on, Polly, she thought, you can do better than this.

'That's what I said.' Bailey took another drink.

'Oh, Bailey, that sucks. I'm so sorry. So when will she find out?' Polly moved her free hand until it gently covered his.

'Next week. Next Monday.'

'Have you told Marcus?'

'No, I only found out myself an hour ago. I don't want to bother him, he's planning his wedding, he's just made me partner. I don't want him to think he's made a bad decision. I'm sorry, Pol, I shouldn't have told you. Now I've put you in an awkward position.' Bailey's eyes shone impossibly brighter, making it only too easy to read the anguish burning in them.

'Bailey, have you never hidden things from your brother and sister?'

'Well, yeah, all the time. Especially when I did something naughty and they got the blame.' Bailey smiled, the cheeky twinkle slowly returning to his eyes.

'So don't worry. Just because Marcus is my brother doesn't mean I will run and tell. But, I do think that you should. He's not going to think less of you, God you've been friends for years.'

'I know, I know. I will when I know more. This might all be for nothing.'

Polly watched as Bailey forced a shrug.

'Can I give you a hug though?' Polly finally let go of his arm.

'Is that all you're offering?'

Polly smiled. Bailey was back to his usual self, trying to flirt away the awkwardness.

'Very funny, do you want this hug or not?'

'Always,' Bailey said, his grin dropping as he looked at her with complete sincerity.

Polly jumped up and got behind Bailey putting her arms around his neck, leaning over his thick shoulders. She definitely didn't smell his hair because that would've been creepy, not to mention she had a boyfriend. Letting go she moved to sit back down at the table.

'OK, well you obviously know how to find me, so if you want to talk to me about it at any time, you can, alright?' She knew that he was uncomfortable and she wanted to make him feel better. 'But for now let's get your mind off it. Do you remember the rules, before the next act starts?' She looked up at Bailey who had stopped drinking and had a serious look to him.

'Thanks, Pol.'

Polly shrugged and smiled. 'OK, so to recap the rules, we take this more seriously than my gran takes bingo. There's no talking when other acts are performing, as that's just rude. If you need to pee you go between sets. You always applaud and cheer, oh and when Lesley gets up to sing "Memory" from *Cats* you have to meow.'

'Are you serious?'

'Yep I'm serious. You absolutely cannot go pee whilst someone is performing.' The pair of them were laughing as the compere banged the top of his mic.

'OK, well we're ready to carry on with the show tonight.'

The crowd whooped and cheered. It really was like some crazy family get together.

'So without further ado, next on the stage we have Lesley and she's singing "Memory". You know what to do.' At once the crowd meowed as loud as possible, no one louder than Polly and Bailey.

Chapter Three

Bailey ran through the reasons again. He should tell Marcus what was going on because he was his best mate and this is the sort of thing you share with your best mate. But, said best mate is winning at life at the moment: he's planning a wedding and their business is taking off at a rate neither had predicted thanks to Marcus's new social media lifestyle. Bailey had only just been made partner, he was only just being taken seriously. He was still proving himself. Proving himself so much that he was working every possible daylight hour. That wasn't too bad, he enjoyed it and it meant he didn't have to go to the gym as often, and it had the added benefit of keeping him away from mithering Polly all day every day, which, let's be honest, if he could be doing that, he would. Now, with his mum's news, the work kept him from worrying, well, more accurately it kept him from doing something with the worry, like breaking into the hospital to see her records and find out for himself exactly what was going on.

He had gone to his mum's yesterday as promised, and she looked the same, which was completely reassuring and scary as hell at the same time. It made him have thoughts like; had she been ill for a while, had this poison in her body been eating away at her for ages, or was there really nothing to worry about like she wanted him to believe? Keeping things in perspective was hard, and he would hazard a guess, would only keep getting harder.

Pushing open the door, Bailey was immediately greeted with the quiet hubbub of a Wednesday night at Barbarella, his favourite bar in the world, not just because his mate Paige owned it. It was always so chill even on a Saturday night when it was sardine full. Marcus was stood at the bar in their

19

usual spot, chatting to Paige and the new barmaid that had replaced Marcus's fiancée, Sophie. He made sure to crank up his cheeky charm so it was up to its usual standard even if it was forced, it was his easiest and most frequent mask to wear. Rushing forward he grabbed Marcus from behind whilst he wasn't looking.

'How you doing, dude? I haven't seen you properly outside of work in ages!' Marcus said as he detangled himself and gave Bailey a quick look over. Bailey punched his arm and made sure that his face was pulled into full cheeky grin mode.

'That's because my boss works me too hard.'

'I think you mean partner, no boss's here, dude,' Marcus scoffed as Bailey sat next to him at the bar. The business partnership was still new and, given that Marcus had inherited the gardening business from his dad, Bailey could admit it wasn't easy to shake off their previous working relationship of boss and labourer.

'Hi, Paige.' His instinct was to avoid eye contact with her, but she'd see through that straight away, so he risked a glance up.

'How are you doing, Bailey?' Paige asked as she cleared the top of the bar.

'Yep, all good. What about you?' Bailey asked.

'Hmmm.' Paige turned to Belle. 'This is Bailey and if you want to keep your job don't sleep with him.'

Bailey watched as Belle laughed, clearly unsure if Paige was joking or not. Bailey felt his insides sour at the reminder that this was what people thought of when they saw him. That he was a cheap thrill, nothing to take too seriously. Even so, his mask remained on, with little to no effort.

'Hi, Belle, and how are you this evening?' Bailey reached forward and took her hand, giving it a little kiss as he bowed.

'Oh, I get the warning now. Nice to meet you, Bailey. What are you having to drink?'

'Beer, please. And one for my mate here.' Belle moved to get the drinks at the same time Paige did.

'So seriously, pal, how have you been?' Marcus asked.

Bailey coughed, it was now or never, and he still hadn't made up his mind, it was just easier for him to pretend everything was normal, opening his mouth to speak, Paige leaned over with a shot.

'You driving tonight?' Paige asked as Belle placed their beers on the bar and took the money from Bailey.

'No, ma'am.'

'Right, have this on me, you look like you need it.'

Bailey grumbled 'thanks' before necking the Sambuca in one go.

Paige was one of his favourite people in the world, she called it just like he did, the pair of them were bullshit free, but Paige saw everything and also had the added sense to know when to leave things be, and with the delivery of the shot she went over to the other side of the bar to talk to some of the other regulars.

'So, no Sophie tonight?' He'd lost his nerve, the moment passed.

'No, not tonight. I wanted to catch up with you one on one.'

'Oh and not because you wanted to escape all the wedding prep for an hour or so?' Bailey joked.

'Not really no, because funnily enough, that was one of the reasons I wanted to talk to you tonight. I have to ask you something.' Marcus turned on the bar stool, one leg on the floor.

'Yeah? You need help buying rings?' Bailey sipped at his pint, eyebrow raised.

'Well, as you know we want to get married as quickly as possible. We've managed to book the awesome venue we wanted as they'd had a cancellation so they can fit us in on April fourth, just three months away. There's lots to do and even more for you to do.'

'You know me, pal, whatever help you need I'm there.' He would go to the ends of the earth for Marcus.

'Yeah, but there's even more work for the best man.' Marcus grinned.

'Me?'

'Of course you, who the hell else would it be?'

Bailey jumped up and dragged his best mate of over a decade into a huge hug, the pair of them jumping up and down like giddy schoolgirls.

Pulling apart Bailey took a drink. 'I've already written my speech.'

'*What?*'

'Come on, who else were you going to ask? Besides, who else has the embarrassing stories of you that I have? This is going to be awesome.' Bailey slapped Marcus's back as he groaned.

'Well, one of your first tasks is to organise a sten.' Marcus sat back down and Bailey followed suit.

'A sten?' Bailey asked.

'Yeah, Polly's the maid of honour so you'll need to organise it together.'

'Wait, is a sten a joint stag and hen do? OK, I get it now. Right. I can do that.' And if his grin got a little bit wider, it was because he loved a good knees up and nothing at all to do with how much time he would have to spend with Polly. They'd need a lot of time to organise something awesome in a short timescale. It could take days, weeks even.

'We're also going to be looking at guest lists pretty quickly so you're going to need to let us know soon if you're bringing a plus one.'

Bailey paused his drink halfway to his mouth. 'A plus one?'

'Yeah you know, a date, a woman, a man, as long as it's not a goat I don't really care. But we're going to need to know. As best man, you'll have to sit at the top table, and as Polly will be bringing her boyfriend, we'll need to figure out how to balance the table.'

'A *what*? Polly has a what?'

'Erm, boyfriend. At least that's what Sophie told me. I think they've only been seeing each other for a couple of weeks but I take it that it's moving fairly quickly.'

'Oh, right, OK.' All signs of a poker face were slipping off Bailey's face faster than he could control.

'You alright, mate? You haven't changed your mind, have you?'

'Sorry, God no, of course not. I'm just shattered. I'm super excited, pal. I'll be the best, best man ever.' Grabbing his drink, he chugged it so that he wouldn't have to look Marcus in the eye.

'I know why you're shattered.' Oh God, Bailey really hoped he didn't, not considering that for the most part his sleep had been disturbed by naughty thoughts towards Marcus's sister.

'It's because you're working too hard. You have nothing to prove, you know? We're partners and I trust you. You can't spend every waking hour working, it'll see you off and besides which I miss you. I know I've been a bit pre-occupied but not enough to know you're going to end up breaking something.'

Bailey just shrugged. 'It's all under control, don't worry about me, worry about what I'm going to tell everyone in my best man speech.'

Forcing a huge grin and a laugh he slapped Marcus's back again before finishing his drink. Behind the grin he was torn between asking a million questions about Polly, disappearing back to his apartment, and reaching over the bar to get more alcohol. The absolutely heart-breaking thing about it all was that this was exactly the sort of thing that if he was going to share with anyone it would be with Polly, but it was exactly this scenario that he couldn't. Instead, he forced that thought way to the back and instead bombarded Marcus with any crap questions about the wedding and work he could think of.

Belle came over and took their drink orders a couple more times and the next thing he knew, Marcus was hugging him and set off back to his place, and, honestly, Bailey wasn't a hundred per cent sure he could recall everything they had talked about. All he knew for certain was that he had kept the focus off himself, he had deflected like a pro, which meant Marcus couldn't ask anything Bailey didn't want to think about.

'You OK there, Bailey? Can I get you a drink?' Belle appeared again just as she was needed. She was good.

'I'll get his drink, as long as he introduces himself to me. Hi, I'm Katie.'

Bailey looked over at Katie. A couple of years ago and Katie would've been his favourite sort of distraction. He went to shake his head.

'I insist. He'll have the same again, and I'll have a Prosecco, please.'

'Erm, great. I'll go get them.' Paige's protégé looked a little unsure but went off to get the drinks. Bailey looked at Katie, who looked like she was after a distraction of her own.

'Katie, I'm not sure that I'm what you're after but—'

'I don't even know your name yet.'

He couldn't help but smile a little. 'I'm Bailey.'

'It's lovely to meet you, Bailey,' Katie said, moving impossibly closer, and Bailey felt nothing at all as he free fell into his old, but well-used and comfortable patterns.

'What the fuck? Who's that sucking Bailey's face off?' Paige demanded.

'I think she said she was called Katie. Wait, why are you so mad? You only warned me not to sleep with him, I didn't realise it was my job to keep him celibate. Am I going to get fired for this?' Belle asked.

Paige looked over at Belle and grunted.

'My mojo is all off and I don't like it,' Paige huffed as she

24

loaded glasses into the dishwasher, with slightly more oomph than was necessarily required.

'Am I fired?' Belle asked, wincing at the sound of the glasses being shoved unceremoniously into the dishwasher.

'Not yet.'

'Are there any other people I'm supposed to keep celibate or just that one, and why is that by the way?' Belle asked.

'It's nothing you need to worry about.'

'It is if it's going to cost me my job. I like it here.'

Paige paused and studied Belle. She was telling the truth and she spoke her mind, her eyes not breaking away from Paige's defiant stare, and she certainly wasn't the quiet, unassuming woman she had been two weeks ago. Maybe Paige's intuition was just off this week, maybe she was right about Belle after all.

'You've got a lot to learn,' was all she said, before striding off to collect empties.

Belle shrugged and walked away. 'Still not the weirdest boss I've ever had.'

Chapter Four

Her hands were clenched tight, as was her stomach, when the feeling of vines spawning, crawling and grabbing began. She'd never been this nervous introducing a boyfriend to her friends before, admittedly it had been a while since she had, well, it had been years actually. She was probably just anxious due to their less than positive reaction when she first mentioned him. They'd had nearly a week to get their heads around the idea now, so hopefully, her friends would be a little better behaved today. Right?

Tugging her fine maroon knit scarf from around her neck, Polly looked around to make sure none of her friends were there yet, she couldn't even spot Paige, who was presumably in her flat upstairs. Good, she had a minute to gather her thoughts. She'd have come with Darren but he had to go see his family first or something, usual Sunday lunch thing apparently. She straightened on the chair hoping to battle her nervous vines with composure. Polly couldn't help but compare Sophie and Marcus's journey. It had been a lot easier for them, as they had both already been in their group, obviously. Not only that but everyone had been able to watch their relationship develop both in-person and online. It had been no surprise when they actually started seeing each other. But bringing in an outsider? It had been a while since that had happened, and Polly couldn't help but get the feeling that her friends were for some reason predisposed to find fault with Darren. She really hoped he wasn't going to be late. With the odds against him, he really needed to make a good first impression. Polly forced a smile as Paige made her way over to the table where Polly sat.

'Why do you look like you've lost a winning lottery ticket?' Paige asked.

Knowing better than to lie to Paige, Polly looked at her

hands. 'For some reason I'm nervous, I think it's because I want you all to like him.'

'Hmmm, and I guess we were all a little shocked by the idea in the first instance so probably didn't behave all that well last time. Sorry, doll.' Paige scrunched her nose in a grimace, causing her nose ring to move slightly.

'It's OK. It *was* shocking.' Polly smiled. 'I guess you do have to kiss a few frogs, huh?'

Polly felt her shoulders relax slightly, grateful for Paige's apology.

'So how does the work thing impact on it?' Paige asked.

'It doesn't, not really. We're in different departments, I'm in HR and he's an accounts manager. I work with a few of his managers, and some of his admin team but that's about it, and even that's only occasionally. I checked the policies again, even though I didn't need to as I advise people on them every day, and there's nothing about inter-office relationships, except when in the same department.'

'Hmmm.'

Polly looked up, something in Paige's tone suggesting she wasn't convinced.

'In fact, it's really good because when we go home, we get to bitch about the senior managers together.' Polly could hear that maybe she sounded a little defensive, it had been one of her hard and fast rules previously that she would never date anyone at work, but this was different.

'Who's bitching? Hi, loves.' Mya went around kissing them both before sitting down opposite Polly.

'Love your coat, Mya. Where's Sophie? She is coming, right?' Polly asked.

'Thank you. It's Gucci. But what on earth's the matter with you, you're practically biting your nails, Pol? And, yes, Sophie is just at the bar. Just be grateful you didn't see the goodbyes between her and Marcus. It's enough to make you want to vomit.' Mya fake gagged.

Paige grinned, whilst Polly smiled sweetly. 'They're in love, it's cute.'

'Yeah sure, you'll see what I mean at some point and then you'll reconsider. Anyway, who's bitching?'

'Polly and her boyfriend,' Paige said dryly.

'Darren?' Mya asked.

'Yeah, Darren. It's not changed since the last time I told you,' Polly supplied.

'Who about? Not any of us, I hope?' Mya laughed and Polly paled.

'God no, of course not, he wouldn't do that. It was about people at work.'

'Polly calm down, darling, I was only joking.'

Polly watched as Mya shot a look at Paige, her eyebrows raised.

'She's just a little nervous about us all meeting him,' Paige explained.

'Well, he should be the one that's nervous, not you.'

'Why? You're not going to be mean, are you?' Polly asked, gripping her drink a little tighter.

'Mean, me?' Mya grinned. Polly was not calmed.

'Mya's never mean. Critical, maybe. Mouthy on occasion, but never mean,' Paige sniggered.

'Hi, everyone. So where is he?' Sophie dropped down the drinks for Mya and herself and sat down at the table next to Paige, which left a space at the head of the table for Darren when he arrived.

Polly wondered if Darren would be nervous. He hadn't claimed to be, in fact, he seemed quite sure that he would win them over pretty quickly. Polly wasn't convinced. Going off the mood her mates were in, it would take some winning them round. And how would Darren come across? She really hoped that he wasn't too confident, but then again she didn't want him to be too nervous either. The vines tightened and increased in number, her stomach muscles tense.

'So, Sophie, how are the wedding plans coming alo—' Polly started to ask hoping to shift focus.

'Shush,' Mya and Paige said, both speaking at the same time.

'You guys are awful. I was just going to say fine. I wasn't going to go into it. But since you've reacted so favourably, I have had some thoughts about bridesmaid dresses.' Without further ado, Sophie had her phone out, her Pinterest page loaded and showing everyone picture after picture of bridesmaid dresses. Paige and Mya were shooting Polly daggers whilst saying, 'oh', 'ah' and 'lovely', in that order, taking it in turns seemingly without Sophie noticing.

'Oh God, are you looking at dresses you'd rather not be seen dead in?' said a voice, followed by hearty laughter, and a sudden complete silence from everyone else around the table.

Polly tried not to groan, as first impressions go this was going to be an uphill struggle now. Polly coughed and smiled up at Darren as he leant over to kiss her cheek, seemingly unaware of the murderous looks from the rest of the table. Oh well, at least Mya and Paige were no longer taking the piss out of Sophie, silver linings and all that. Shit.

'Everyone,' Polly said, standing up and putting her arm around Darren's waist, 'this is Darren. Darren this is Paige, Sophie and Mya.'

Polly thought it best not to mention the bridesmaid dresses and, thankfully, Darren seemed to be unaware. Polly looked him up and down trying to gauge what her friends would see. He was tall, lean, clean-shaven, and his dirty blond hair styled into a quiff. He'd obviously made an effort, he always did and Polly smiled warmly at him.

Darren smiled and waved at everyone in turn. 'Hi. Can I get anyone a drink?'

Paige stared at him, not indicating a response at all. His face dropped a little before he quickly looked away towards Mya.

'I never say no to a drink. I'll have a double whisky, please. Make sure it's Talisker.' Mya smiled, but there was nothing authentic about it.

Darren nodded, glancing quickly at the full glass already in front of Mya before getting to Sophie.

Sophie went to shake her head when there was a little kick under the table. 'Oh, I'll have a white wine, please. In fact, you'd better make it a bottle. You don't mind, do you?'

Polly groaned under her breath, shooting daggers at each of her friends before Darren turned his gaze onto her. Polly quickly smiled. 'I'll come with you.'

As Darren moved away from the table towards the bar, Polly shot her friends yet another dirty look as they tried and failed to stifle their grins.

'So how was the family lunch?' Polly asked as she dropped her arm from his waist.

'The what? Oh, yeah it was good, thanks,' Darren said just as Belle approached to take his drinks order. He didn't flinch at the price, but he did seem to make a show of handing over his black credit card. Polly shrugged, her friends had taken the piss, but ultimately she knew he could afford it, if what he was saying about his commissions was anything to go by. It wouldn't have put him out to pay for their drinks and it might even make the girls warm to him. Might, but Polly conceded, it might not.

Belle smiled as she finished getting the drinks order together. 'Hi, Pol, you OK?'

'I'm good thanks, Belle. You? This is Darren, by the way, my boyfriend.'

Darren smiled at Belle as he slid his arm around Polly's shoulders.

'Hi, Darren, nice to meet you. I'm assuming we'll probably see you around these parts a bit more often if you're with Polly?'

'I would've thought so. It's OK in here, isn't it? I didn't

get a chance to scope out much last time, but I've heard a lot about this place online.'

Nodding over at the table where the girls were all chatting animatedly, Belle winked. 'You should tell Paige, it's her bar.'

'Thanks for the tip.' Darren grinned as he grabbed the drinks and they made their way back into the lair.

To be fair to Darren, he didn't falter, his stride was as confident as always with his little swagger. Polly smiled warmly as she sat down, deliberately angling her chair more towards Darren to act as a barrier against her friends. To be fair to them though they did say thank you when they got their drinks.

'So, Darren how are you?'

Polly looked over at Paige when she asked this question, which sounded more like the warm-up act to an interrogation.

'I'm good, thanks, Paige. I was just saying to Belle how much I love this bar, I didn't get a chance to check it out so much last time, I was too blown away by Polly. I didn't realise that you owned it.'

Polly's smile got a little bit wider, she felt proud of him that he remembered everyone's names so quickly, and that he was so complimentary, even if it had been Belle's idea.

Paige smiled quickly before resuming the icy stare, as she mumbled, 'Thanks.'

'Hi, Pol, haven't seen you in ages. Where've you been hiding?'

Polly looked up. Oh, this could get a little awkward. 'Hi, Dan, yeah, long time no see. How are you?'

'Yeah, I'm good. See you around, yeah?' She felt his eyes linger a little on her lips as if remembering the one time they'd hooked up.

'See you.' Polly looked back at the table.

'Who was that?' Darren asked, taking his vape out of his pocket and sucking on it. Polly moved just slightly out of the way of the smoke as Darren exhaled. The answer was going to be a friend, but she didn't get there in time.

'Oh, it's just someone she used to date,' Mya said quickly and very sweetly.

Polly swore to get her own back at Mya the first chance she got.

'Yeah, it was a while ago now though, like last year.' Polly couldn't believe her luck; of course, she would run into Dan today, right now. Of course. It was bound to happen, Polly realised, when her friends insisted that all first dates happen at this bar. It wasn't her fault if her dates continued to patronise it after they finished dating.

'So, Darren, tell us about yourself. What do you do for a living?' Sophie asked, already knowing the answer but giving Polly a break. Polly smiled at her in gratitude.

'Well, as you no doubt know, I'm one of Polly's bosses. It's a really good company to work for, isn't it, Pol? I've not been there long but I've already managed to secure several new accounts worth hundreds of thousands.' Darren smiled obviously proud of his hard work, but Polly was a little put out about the whole boss thing.

'I think that client accounts are probably far more interesting than HR,' Polly said, knowing that she had complained about her work to her friends until she could complain no longer, and they were done listening to her.

'Hundreds of thousands, huh?' Whilst most people would probably be impressed, Mya seemed bored if anything. 'What's the highest account you've ever brought in?'

'Nearly a million but that was with another company. In fact, I think that's why I was headhunted, to be honest.'

Mya tried to smile, but it looked more condescending as if she was used to regularly handling more money than that. Polly shrugged. She still had absolutely no idea what Mya did for a living and she also had no idea Darren had been headhunted, but then she wasn't specifically in the recruitment section.

Paige still hadn't said much at that point, maybe because

she was too busy giving him 'the stare'. Except for every now and again her brow would curl and she'd look confused.

'Hi, Pol!' Simon winked before heading towards the gents. Polly smiled and waved back. What the hell was this with the ghost of dates past?

'Just a mate,' Polly said with a groan. Mya sniggered.

Darren pulled out his vape again, and Polly tried to hide her wince.

Sophie sighed, as she waved away the thick blanket of smoke temporarily covering them. 'Look, Darren, you should be honoured. Polly hasn't introduced us to anyone new in her life in an incredibly long time. You obviously mean something to her.'

Polly grinned at Darren. How cute, he was embarrassed. Leaning over she dropped a kiss on his cheek and patted his leg, trying to reassure him. But they were interrupted when his phone rang. Darren answered it in what must have been a world record, the ringtone having barely begun.

'Hi. Yeah? Really? Today? Fine. OK.' He cut the call. 'I'm really sorry, Polly, but work needs me to go in. Apparently, there's an issue with one of the contracts and it needs finalising before tomorrow. I'm really sorry. Maybe I'll see you later if I can get this finished, yeah?'

'Sure.' Polly's stomach relaxed a bit, not because she felt easier about Darren going, it really wasn't that bad, not for a first introduction. Yes it hadn't been brilliant and this quick exit probably wasn't going to win him any favours but... standing up she kissed him goodbye, and if it was awkward, it was because all of her friends were watching them closely.

'Bye everyone, it was really lovely to meet you and hope to see you again soon. Sorry to have to dash off. I'll leave some money behind the bar so that you can have some more drinks on me by way of an apology.' With that, Darren ran over to Belle.

Polly watched as they chatted and Darren handed over

some cash, saying something that made Belle smile, before waving again and taking off.

'So that's Darren.' Polly forced a smile glad it was over, but not welcoming the next bit, the critique.

Paige jumped up. 'I just need to ask Belle something. I'll be right back.'

Paige leaned on the bar, and sighed. 'My mojo is definitely off.'

'OK, boss.' Belle just smiled, having finally figured out how to placate her new boss's insights, and carried on cleaning up around her.

'What did you think of him?' Paige asked, looking up.

'Who, Darren?' Belle asked.

'Yes, who else?'

Belle looked up. 'Am I supposed to be vetting the customers now? How on earth are you making money if you are cherry-picking customers?'

'Enough of that, I don't need business advice. Tell me your gut instinct about him.'

'Fine. I think that he is loaded, and generous. I think that he is relatively good looking. Seemed polite enough.' Belle continued wiping down, hoping that was the end of it. It wasn't.

'You're being too evasive. What else, there's something else, isn't there?'

Paige leaned closer on the bar and inspected Belle.

'No.'

Paige just stared.

'I don't think it's fair to judge people too quickly.'

Paige continued to stare.

Belle huffed. 'At some point, you really need to tell me ALL the rules around here.'

Paige continued to stare her down.

'Fine, I thought he was more style than substance and I got

34

the impression that it may have crossed his mind to flirt with me a little had there not been an audience. There, are you happy now?'

'How often are your gut feelings about someone correct?' Paige asked, eyebrow raised as she leant her elbow on the bar to lean in closer.

'I don't know. As I said, I don't like to judge people within five minutes of meeting them. It's not fair,' Belle replied quickly, avoiding eye contact.

'Well, I've never been wrong. But I'm a bit wonky this week. I must be back on track though because I think the same. You can stay... for now.'

Belle shook her head as her boss made her way back towards her friends. She sighed, and rinsed out the cloth. She liked Polly and she really hoped her instinct was wrong. Although, like Paige, she suspected her first impression hadn't been wrong either.

Chapter Five

'I can't believe you're leaving me. I just… I mean… Will you still send me the free biscuits, because, frankly, I'm going to miss them more than you.' Mya grinned and ducked as Sophie threw aforementioned biscuit straight at her head.

Polly dunked her biscuit in her brew and looked around at what used to be Sophie and Mya's house and would now just be Mya's. There were boxes everywhere. It was going to take the three of them all day to move Sophie out.

'Are you going to be OK here by yourself?' Polly felt compelled to ask, even though she thought of Mya as one of the strongest people she knew, well certainly one of the most confident.

Mya rolled her eyes. 'Will I miss her drama, her endless make-up tutorials, the false eyelashes that always look like weird bugs in the bathroom in the middle of the night, the endless asking for advice, the pizzas, the catch-ups, the company? Yeah, I probably will, but, to be honest, I think I might have a few work gigs coming up soon so I might not be around to miss her that much. You like it on your own though, don't you, Pol?' Mya pointed out.

'Yeah, and if ever I don't I just nip round to one of yours.' Besides, thought Polly, if she lived with someone else she would have to explain not only where she went every Monday night, but also the actual playing of instruments, the writing of music, and of course the singing. She was much better on her own, left to her own devices.

'What's keeping the boys?' Sophie whined as she dashed between the boxes and her phone checking things off.

Polly turned to look at Sophie. 'What?'

'Oh, didn't I tell you? Marcus and Bailey are coming to help too.'

'If I had known that I wouldn't have wasted a day's leave to help you out. How long do you think it will take?' Polly asked.

'Shouldn't take all day if we're all doing it together. I think Paige is going to rock up too soon she just had to do a Costco run first. Why? Do you and Darren have a date tonight or something?' Sophie raised a quizzical eyebrow at her.

'No, I just wondered.' More tea drinking, more averting her eyes. It was because it was Monday and the new piece she had been working on was getting its first, and probably only play tonight.

'Speak of the devils,' Mya said as they listened to Marcus and Bailey reach the front door and let themselves in.

Polly watched as Marcus practically bounced into the house and straight to Sophie. 'I'm so excited,' he said before gathering her into a very nearly NSFF (not suitable for friends) clasp. Ewww. Polly looked away, not deliberately seeking out Bailey, just looking away and happening to catch his eye.

'Morning.' Bailey waved at everyone and sat down in the space next to Polly.

'Hi, you doing alright?' Polly whispered at him, not wanting to draw attention to the real reason she was asking. She didn't want Bailey to have to talk about his mum if he didn't want to.

Bailey leaned towards Polly and whispered, 'Yeah, I just want to get this done with so I can go and see my mum and find out what the results are.'

Polly held his hand for a second and smiled before going back to the last bit of her drink, her hand tingling unnecessarily.

Bailey didn't look alright, but that was understandable. She knew that she wouldn't look great either if she was in his position. In fact, it made her think of how Bailey had been there for her when her dad had his heart attack last year. Her heart ached both at the memory of worrying about her dad, but also with just how wonderful Bailey had been, and just wished that she was able to return the favour somehow. Her heart tightened as she imagined what Bailey must be going through.

'OK, so how are we doing this?' Mya asked, clapping her hands together.

'I've brought the van, and Sophie and I cleaned our new place up last week—' Marcus started.

'Marcus, Marcus, Marcus. Bless your little cotton socks.' Mya gently shook her head at Marcus before turning around and addressing the actual boss. 'Sophie?'

'Thank you, Mya. I've actually pulled together a list for everyone. It shows what's being moved and in what order, what everyone's roles are and how the day should map out.' Everyone either laughed or groaned at Sophie's fearless organisation. Polly glanced down at the list she had been given. It seemed that they were loading the van with the big items like the bed in the first run.

'Bailey, Marcus, Polly and I will load the bed into the van, presuming we can get it through the doors. Mya, would you mind bringing some of the boxes downstairs?'

'It would be my pleasure and that way I can check to make sure you aren't stealing, because, honestly, I didn't realise you even had this much stuff and I am very suspicious.'

'Come on then, Polly, let's get into bed, I mean let's go and get the bed.' Bailey winked, his eyes shining again. Polly vowed to herself that she would try and keep his mind off his mum for a little while at least and keep that shine in his eyes for as long as possible.

'We've all heard the rumours concerning your performance in bed. Will you be OK moving one? I'm not sure, I mean your arms are very spindly.'

Bailey grinned and flexed his arms in answer, causing the already tight sleeves of his T-shirt to want to split open under the pressure. Polly's mouth watered just a little, as she studied how non-spindly his arms actually were. Frankly, he was built like Thor, dangerously muscled, and defined, and worst of all he knew it. Polly laughed as he moved to flex in another pose. Laughing they both looked up to see everyone staring at them watching the interaction take place. Polly blushed, unsure as to why she felt caught out. She cast a glance at Bailey, he grinned, obviously, he was just being his usual cheeky self, everyone should be used to that.

Polly stood up. 'OK then, let's do this.'

After a lot of fumbles, and grunts and shouts of 'pivot!' they finally got the mattress down the stairs and into the van. Then they went back upstairs to get the parts of the bed frame that had already been partially disassembled, and, in true Sophie style, the instructions, photographs and a little sandwich bag of screws that were sellotaped to the headboard. With the remaining space in the van Mya began loading as many boxes that would fit.

Polly looked at the Tetrised van and had to wonder if they had managed to get everything in on the first try. Today would be over really quickly if that was the case, which was both good news and bad news as far as Polly was concerned. Bad because she enjoyed spending time with her friends, of course, and not for any other reason to do with Bailey. But it would be good to get a little more practice in before tonight if she had the opportunity.

'OK, so Marcus and I will head over to the new place in the van. Mya, Polly and Bailey it might be better if you load two cars and bring them over, or you can all get in one for the first trip. It's up to you.'

'Let's just take the one car, for now. I want to check out your new pad. We might be able to get the rest of it in one more van load,' Mya said.

Sophie shrugged before looking up at Marcus and smiling widely. 'Shall we go to our new home then?'

'Yes, please.' Marcus pulled Sophie in for a kiss, amidst the sounds of people pretending to vomit.

'Get a room!' shouted Bailey.

'Don't worry, we got a house,' Marcus called back as he let go of Sophie to get in the van. Once Sophie got in she wound down the window. 'See you soon!'

With that, the three of them watched as they drove away. 'So, whose car and who's driving?' Mya asked.

'I don't mind driving. I'm blocking you in any way,' Bailey said.

The drive to the new house didn't take long, and as Polly was sat in the back she was lost in thought, rehearsing her new song in her head and occasionally listening to Mya and Bailey. On arrival they got out of the car and all but ran to check out the new place.

Polly looked around at Sophie and Marcus's new house. It was gorgeous. It wasn't huge but it was theirs, grown-up mortgage and all.

Walking out through the conservatory into the back garden she looked around and couldn't help but grin. Hearing footsteps approaching she looked behind her at Bailey as he came to stand next to her, and, for a second, even though she always tried her hardest to ignore it, the slight tingle and excitement of Bailey's presence washed over her.

'Sophie really wants to get her money's worth out of you and Marcus.' Polly grinned as they looked around at what could at best be called a shit heap.

'She's taking the piss with this, isn't she?' Bailey's eyes looked like they were going to fall out of his head. 'Hey, Soph, what's *this*?'

Sophie emerged from the patio doors. 'I knew you'd like it.'

'I'm not doing your garden for free again, you can jog on,' Bailey called, as Polly tried to contain her laughter.

Sophie put her hands on her hips and glared, which made

Polly want to laugh even harder. She knew that Bailey was joking but it would seem that Sophie did not.

'I know,' Polly said, trying to catch her breath again. 'Why don't you both go to Marcus and see which one of you can convince him?'

Sophie grinned and Bailey sighed, in mock defeat.

'Fine, we'll do your garden again.'

Sophie blew him a kiss and ran off to find Marcus.

Finally letting out a laugh, Polly turned and swatted Bailey on his arm. 'You were always going to do the garden.'

'Shhh, don't go telling everyone I'm a good guy, I have a bad-boy reputation to keep up, don't you know?' Bailey winked and Polly tried desperately hard to be unaffected.

'Don't worry everyone knows that you're a very bad boy.' Polly lowered her eyes briefly before looking up at him again through her eyelashes. Shit, was she flirting? Oh God, that definitely felt like flirting. Double shit, she had a boyfriend. Smiling in what she hoped was a non-flirty, strictly platonic way, she linked her arm in his and walked back into the house, where, she presumed, they would be safer around other people.

'OK so now that you've all had a look around I'll stick the kettle on. Will someone grab the box marked "Brew Stuff"? It should be in the footwell of the van.'

Mya disappeared to complete the task.

'OK so I've tweaked the list slightly, I think what we'll do is Marcus and I will go back with the van and load up again. If you guys could start unpacking and if someone could put together the bed, then that will clear loads of space in the bedroom for the rest of my stuff.'

'What about Marcus's stuff?' Polly asked.

'Yeah, we need to do a quick recce to yours too, but Marcus doesn't have furniture so that's no big deal.'

'Well, why don't Mya and I go to Marcus's and pick up his stuff, while Bailey and Polly stay here and start unpacking?'

Paige said as everyone looked up in surprise as she wandered in holding the 'Brew Stuff' box, with Mya on her tail.

'Hi, Paige, thank you so much for coming to help,' Sophie said, taking the box and grabbing Paige into a hug.

Paige just shrugged, her eyes clearly saying, 'It's what we do for friends, it's no big deal.' Taking the 'Brew Stuff' box back Paige made her way into the kitchen and began taking orders. Once everyone was stood with their brews, Polly looked around, feeling uneasy. She didn't think it was a good idea to spend alone time with Bailey. Well, she did and she wanted to, but that's exactly why it was a bad idea.

'Why don't I go with Mya to get your stuff, Marcus? I know your flat better and it just makes sense.'

'Don't worry Sophie's already worked her magic on it, my stuff's all just by the door. It should all fit fine in Paige's car.'

'Oh right, OK.' Polly glanced quickly at Bailey and saw the smallest scowl before it disappeared without a trace.

'OK then drink up and then we can get a wiggle on,' Sophie called out, detailing almost exactly what Polly was worried about.

'Why didn't they just get a new bed?' Bailey groaned.

'Pass me the Allen key. I think that it is a relatively new one, to be honest.' Polly grunted as she tightened the screw.

'Where the hell does this bit go?' Bailey asked.

'Here, look she took photos.' Polly and Bailey grinned at each other.

Bailey studied the picture then put it down. 'If I ever plan to take over the world I want her on my side.'

'I already called dibs,' Polly said not looking up from her task.

Bailey gasped. 'Wait, are you saying that we would be fighting each other?'

'If I've got Sophie on my team I'm winning regardless of who I am fighting.' Picking the Allen key up that Polly had just put down, Bailey grinned. He loved it when Polly was confident, and he loved their effortless back and forth, and purposely chose not to think about why Polly had tried to NOT spend time with him.

'So, shit, why won't this tighten any more? Anyway, are you out tonight?' Bailey asked.

'You know I am,' Polly said.

'What are you singing tonight?'

'Erm.' Polly still refused to look up.

Bailey stopped what he was doing and waited for Polly as she stood at the other end of the bed frame. Her cheeks were pink and she looked uncomfortable. 'Polly, you might as well tell me as I'm going to hear it anyway.'

Bailey bent down to carry on with the task so that he could try and cover the look that would surely show on his face, the look that said he was beyond thrilled that she could share this intimate part of her life with him and no one else. Except, suddenly he thought maybe she wasn't just sharing it with him. His stomach twisting he asked the question he wasn't sure he wanted to know the answer to. 'Or is your boyfriend going?' He had to forcibly shove the words past his tight throat, and it sounded like it too.

'Oh yeah Darren, erm no. He doesn't know. No one knows except you and you only know by accident. So it needs to stay that way.'

He looked up relieved that he was still the only caretaker of her precious secret, but the room no longer felt as fun and airy as it did before they spoke about 'the boyfriend'. He wanted to go back but the humour had been sucked right out of him, in no way was any of this funny. Bending back down to put the next slat into the bed, he hated that the atmosphere between them was now toxic, but he couldn't for the life of him find a way out of it.

'So it's a good job we're making the bed,' Polly said, her eyes twinkling.

'Huh, why?' Bailey asked.

'Because I bought this.' Polly moved around the room to get her bag and inside she pulled out confetti, glitter, sparkles and streamers.

'What are you planning, Miss Polly?' Bailey's eyebrows raised.

'We're going to make the bed in its entirety as a lovely surprise with the duvet, new covers and everything and then, when they get into bed at the end of the day, there is our housewarming surprise.'

'I had no idea that you were that evil. I am shocked.' Bailey felt himself grin.

'Not evil, but you know I am his little sister, I've got a reputation as a pain in the arse to keep up, you know?'

Bailey chuckled. 'How do you know I won't tell?'

'Oh, Bailey, because you keep my secrets already and because you're just mad you didn't think of it first.'

Polly's eyes shone as brightly as they did when she was spotlit on stage. If he was honest he felt the warmth from her eyes all the way into his chest.

His grin changed and he smirked. 'I already know what I'm doing. I've bought some travel alarm clocks all set to different times that I will be hiding around the house, so now you have to keep my secrets too.'

'I swear to keep your secrets teammate.' Polly held out her little finger, and Bailey laughed as he leaned over the bed and pinky promised.

'So.' Bailey was still smiling, amazed at how Polly had engineered the atmosphere back to light-hearted so effortlessly. Bending down their heads nearly bumping, they put the last bits of the bed together. 'How's work?'

'Fine.' Polly looked up. 'No, it's still rubbish. I should leave but the pay is good, and it's a steady job with little to no risk, and I can pretty much do the job with my eyes closed. It's just the atmosphere; it's like being in a playground. There's gossip everywhere, most of it made up, and it's just annoying. It also makes my job as employee relations even more difficult because the managers keep coming to me with their rumours asking what they should do about it.'

'Why do you stay?' Bailey asked, shaking his head.

'Like I said it's good money and if I get the next promotion it's even more money. I've got the qualifications so I need to use them.'

Bailey just shrugged. He guessed he was lucky as he couldn't imagine being stuck behind a desk all day every day. He studied Polly again and knew that she didn't like it any more than he would. He knew the only thing she wanted to be stuck behind was a piano.

'OK, all done. Grab that side of the mattress will you?' Polly asked.

'Your wish, my command.' Standing on either side of the mattress they tiptoed around the room until they could put the mattress on top of the bed.

'Stage one done,' Polly said.

'We should try it out.'

Before Polly could say anything else Bailey had nudged her so that she landed on the bed. Bouncing slightly, her red hair flying about from the high ponytail she was sporting, she screamed. 'Bailey! What if we hadn't done it right? I could've broken it!'

'You're right, teammate.' And with that Bailey jumped on the bed next to her, the pair of them laughing hysterically as they bounced. Until there was an ominous creaking sound.

'Shit, let's get off before we actually do break it.' Bailey jumped off the bed, held out his hand and pulled Polly up too, albeit with slightly more vigour than he had intended, and they were suddenly pressed chest to chest. His breathing was already fast but looking into her eyes he could feel his pulse race. He still had her hand in his, and he relished the feel of her warm soft skin against him.

'Right, OK let's get this bed made. I think there was a labelled box downstairs. I'll be right back.' Polly took off a little quickly.

Bailey cursed himself before muttering, 'She has a boyfriend, dumbass.' He couldn't help but think another second like that and he would've tried to kiss her. He couldn't be sure, but for a moment it felt like she wanted him too. Groaning again, he slapped his own head, of course, she didn't, she has a boyfriend. His phone pinged and he immediately got it out of his back pocket in case it was his mum.

It was Katie. Hi gorgeous, you fancy getting a drink later? X

Bailey felt guilty as he contemplated his response, and instead of replying, he put his phone away, just as Polly walked back in the room. 'Was that your mum? Has she got any news?'

'No, it was someone else. Right, let's get this bed made, and then trashed.'

They got the sheets, the duvet and pillows and when they had finished making it, he had to admit, it looked really inviting.

'You know what we should do?' Bailey said, deliberately making his voice suggestive.

'What?' asked Polly cautiously.

'We should get into the bed before it's trashed and take a selfie to send to them later.'

'Oh my God, that's genius.' With that agreement, Bailey quickly took off his shoes and gently got into the bed and watched as Polly did the same on the other side.

'Oh man, this is one awesome bed.' Polly stretched out at the same time she pulled the duvet up to her chin. Bailey grinned at her. He knew he shouldn't but he couldn't help but think of them in their own place, in their own bed. His heart warmed at the thought. Until Polly started wriggling around.

'What's the matter with you?' Bailey asked.

Polly sighed. 'I'm on the wrong side and I don't like it. Hang on.' Without warning, Bailey was suddenly transported into a place where his fantasies were quickly coming true. Polly had her hands on his shoulders and was swinging her leg over until she was on top of him. He had a moment of feeling her body heat on his chest before she swung the other leg back over.

'Sorry about that. There we go, that's better.'

Bailey blinked several times until he could gather the use of his body to move over to the side Polly had vacated. She was right this was better, but now he thought of a hundred ways it could be better still.

'OK, it's selfie time.' Polly stretched her arm up but couldn't quite get high enough to get the picture right.

'Hang on, I'll take it with mine.' Bailey used his longer arms to try and aim the camera at them but as luck would have it they were too far apart, and before he could suggest it, she moved closer, the next thing he knew she had curled up next to him and moved his arm until it was behind her around her back, her head resting on his shoulder. Taking the picture a few times with them sticking their tongues out, laughing and pulling faces, he reluctantly pulled his arm down, but not before Polly twisted slightly, her body still leaning into his, close enough that he could smell the shampoo that she used, feel the heat of her against his side, feel her hair as it tickled his arm.

She grabbed his phone and looked at the picture. 'Perfect.' Polly grinned mischief making her shine. Turning round to look at him, their bodies warm under the duvet and surrounded by each other, Bailey was not able to move. He couldn't, he wouldn't, he didn't want to ruin this tiny fragment in time that he doubted he would ever forget. Studying her eyes he was desperate for some kind of sign that she was interested, something that would tell him it wasn't one-sided. But, more importantly, he was looking for a sign that he was worthy. Her brown eyes looked nearer gold, and Polly wasn't looking away either. In fact, she was moving nearer, their faces getting closer, her breath on his cheek.

'Helloooo. Bailey? Polly?' Mya must have said something quietly to Paige as the pair of them burst out laughing. Polly jumped up fast enough to injure herself. So fast that he could almost believe the last few minutes had been another one of his intense dreams. He got out of bed and put his shoes back on.

'We're up here. We've nearly finished the bed. We'll be down in a minute.'

Bailey watched stunned as Polly flawlessly carried on as if everything was normal, that she hadn't been leaning forward to kiss him. Bailey shook his head, trying to re-group.

'Here get going.' Pulling the duvet completely off they covered the bed sheet with glitter and streamers and confetti and everything, the pair of them laughing quietly the worse they made it.

'Right. That's probably enough.'

Polly snorted. 'It was enough three bags of confetti ago.'

Chapter Six

Polly looked down at the salad she had prepared herself for lunch. Sitting by herself in the work cafeteria, near the wall and next to the oversized prints of close up food, her stomach burned and she couldn't face eating a thing. She still couldn't quite believe that she had almost gone in to kiss Bailey. If there was one thing that Polly couldn't abide it was cheating. The fact that they didn't actually kiss was the only saving grace. True enough Bailey had come to see her perform that night, and they had a laugh watching the rest of the performers together, but she had felt awkward, so awkward that she couldn't bring herself to perform the new song she had been working on, but stuck with some of her older pieces instead. Bailey, however, had been his usual carefree self, well for the most part. But it was obvious to Polly he was struggling with everything that was going on.

Normally Polly would have sat with her colleagues for lunch, but she knew that she didn't have the energy to be part of the usual conversations, the usual inane gossip and the shop talk. She just needed some time to get her head straight. Picking at the salad with one hand she looked at her phone with the other, as always she'd been searching for other live mic nights. She had little to no intention of going to any others but a new one had just opened up on a Wednesday night, and Polly would give anything to be able to perform more than one night a week, but she just wasn't sure if she could.

'Sorry, all the other tables are taken. Do you mind if we sit here?'

Polly looked up and quickly surmised it was just two random members of staff that worked in a different section. They weren't her friends, they wouldn't need to talk.

'Yeah, of course.' It was a large table, Polly only sat at it because it was the last one that was free. She listened for a minute as they started talking. Her phone pinged.

Sophie: You've broken my hoover!

Polly: hahaha x 😂

Sophie: You totally got us, by the way. We were both exhausted from all the unpacking and we couldn't wait to get into bed. It took nearly an hour to get rid of it all. Not impressed. You and Bailey will pay.

Polly tried not to laugh too loud. She took a screenshot and sent it to Bailey, knowing it would cheer him up. There was no more news about his mum, other than they wanted to run more tests. Neither of them had said it at the gig but more tests were not likely to be a good thing.

Sophie: You did look cute in that picture though 😗 x

Polly: Haha yeah it was a fun day have you settled in ok now? x

Sophie: Nice change of subject, yes apart from the fact there seemed to be a number of small clocks all set with various alarms, but I think we found most of them, eventually. You coming out on Thursday? X

Polly burst out laughing, before quickly muttering an apology to the table sharers.

Polly: Yeah see you then if not before xx

Sophie: xx

Sophie: still haven't forgiven you though, or Bailey!

Going back to her salad, she wondered what the picture of her and Bailey looked like. She kind of wished that they had taken it on her phone so that she could look at it again. No wait, that wouldn't be a good idea. Polly's phone pinged again.

Bailey: Hahahahahaha worth it. How's your day at work going Miss Polly? X

Polly: Totally worth it. Same old same old. You? x

Bailey: Mrs Rollinson is still trying to get me in the sack but I am keeping her at arm's length for now, just in case I get a better offer x

Polly: Hmm I'm not sure that anyone can beat Mrs Rollinson x

Bailey: Oh I don't know I can think of one or two people x

Oh God did he mean her? Her blood started tickling her veins as she contemplated the implications. Was he crossing the line, was this the start of him making a move. Before she could reply back he sent another message:

Bailey: Like Mrs Rosenthal, for example, she's a hottie for an octogenarian 😉 x

Polly: 😄 LOL. Well she would certainly be experienced x

Bailey: Yeah she might even be able to teach me a thing or two. Enjoy your salad see you later x

Polly's heart sank just a little, enough to make her feel guilty for having thoughts like that about Bailey. For having a reaction like that to Bailey, if she was honest. For one brief moment, her whole body had flushed with excitement. Sighing she put her phone down. But also, how the hell did he know she'd be eating a salad? Was she THAT predictable or did he just know her too well? With yet another sigh, she pondered her own predictability. She had set up her own little routine; preparing her lunch the night before work, every Monday she went to the Speakeasy, and one night a week she went to her parents for tea, and at least one or two nights at Darren's. It wasn't that she wanted more excitement, more like she felt she could be more exciting, she had it in her, she just wasn't.

'So anyway, turns out that there is this new girl and she's working her way through the office, if you know what I mean?'

Oh God groaned Polly, this was exactly the sort of nonsense she was sick of dealing with. Firstly, so what if a new girl was hooking up? If it didn't impact on her work what difference should it make? Secondly, it was more likely that there was no new girl and someone was just making stuff up to pass the time. It never used to be this bad here, or maybe it had and, for some reason, it was grating on her now more than ever. She suspected that was the reason why she wanted to find another night she could perform, she needed the freedom.

'You know that guy who works on the fourth? Well, apparently he got sacked for misuse of information. He had got a hold of someone's private mobile number and started sending sexts.'

'No way.'

'Hmm.'

Polly rolled her eyes. At least this story was partially true. She knew that because she had been the one to assist with the investigation. Although it was a lot more boring than that. The guy, who works in IT, was asked to look up someone's info by a manager and passed it on without checking if that manager was allowed that information. Yawn.

'The only other one I've heard of is that there's an office romance. Like a big proper one.' Polly's ears perked up at this one. She was sure they weren't going to reference her and Darren because they had been clear that their 'get-togethers' were not discussed and they never happened at work. 'Yeah, apparently some new manager was nearly caught in the ladies toilets with one of the PAs.'

Hmm, that was news to Polly. But unless they were actually caught doing something, or somebody put in a formal complaint then it wouldn't make its way to her desk. So to speak. Looking for a distraction so that she wouldn't get worked up over the rumour mill, she picked up her phone.

Polly: Hi babe, how's your day going?

Darren: Hi gorgeous, I am killing it today! Boom. Do you want to come round to mine later?

Polly: Yeah ok, shall I get some wine in?

Darren: Nice one, see you later x

Looking at her phone she saw that she still had fifteen minutes left. There was no way she was going back to her desk sooner than was needed. Opening up the Facebook page she searched for 'Speakeasy', grinning as she read the reviews and comments for last night's Open Mic night. Everyone was so lovely there, it really was like a second, very secret family. Polly covered her beaming smile with her free hand as she read the rest of the comments. For a second, she wished that she could share it with someone. Taking a screenshot she hovered over Bailey's name before putting her phone back down on the table instead. Just as she did, she felt it vibrate, picking it back up she got to her messages.

Bailey: Saw this! Told you, you were awesome xx

He'd sent her a screenshot of the exact thing she had just been looking at. She started to smile, but the slightly icky feeling had returned. A double-edged sword feeling; of keeping secrets, with the wrong person, but also being incredibly excited to be sharing secrets with the wrong person. Putting the phone down again, she played with her watch strap, opening and closing the clasp. Maybe she needed to tell Darren about the Speakeasy, that way they could have these conversations and then she wouldn't feel as guilty and maybe wouldn't have these errant thoughts about Bailey. Who was she kidding? It had been a secret for too long now, the thought of telling anyone made her shiver. No, she couldn't tell Darren. Besides, that would then kick Bailey out altogether. She groaned a little too loudly. The two girls next to her quickly packed up their stuff and left the canteen. Oh great, now there'll be gossip about 'the girl from HR having a breakdown'. Well, at least they'd be right this time.

Chapter Seven

Katie: OK then gorgeous see you later xx

Bailey smiled at his phone, Katie was actually fun to hang out with. She also wasn't worried about being serious, and he could keep his mind off the fact that Polly was seeing someone else. If Bailey did feel bad, and he did often, Katie was very quick to remind him that she was up for a promotion at her work, what with her working in a hotel chain, and if she got through the next round she'd be moving away. But, if he was honest with himself, he still felt a bit ragged, like he was being unfaithful. Although his fling with Katie reeked of falling into old habits, the one thing that he had never done, at least knowingly, was to be unfaithful. With that thought in his mind, he wasn't sure how much longer he could meet up with Katie, but at the same time, it wasn't as if Polly was sat alone each night knitting, was it? He could reason it out with himself as much as he liked but really in his gut, he wasn't happy. Then again, as his mum would say, 'a change is as good as a rest', and whilst Katie didn't have the same effect on him as Polly, maybe this way he could start getting Polly out of his head a little bit. It might actually help him to move on, finally. It had been a long two, nearly three years whilst he pined for Polly. Or maybe that was just a good excuse.

Setting his head right, reminding himself that he wasn't doing anything wrong and that it might all work out for the best, he stepped into Barbarella for the semi-regular Thursday night wedding planning drinks with the gang. Sophie and Marcus were sat at a large booth in the corner, and as he approached he realised that they were making out.

'You guys are actually getting worse. Are you going to be able to keep it PG at the wedding?' Marcus stopped kissing

Sophie long enough to stick his finger up at Bailey. 'I'm going to the bar, do either of you want anything?'

'No, we're good thanks, dude.'

With that Bailey walked over to the bar and smiled when he saw that Clare was working tonight.

'Hi, beautiful, how you doing?' Bailey asked, his warm smile genuine.

'I'm good thanks, handsome. What can I get you?'

'San Miguel, please,' Bailey replied.

'No problem.' Clare got the glass from under the bar and began pouring his drink.

'So did you get in touch with that chiropractor I recommended?' Bailey asked.

'Oh, Bailey, Calvin is a GOD. He is amazing and worth every penny. Thank you for sorting it.'

'That's OK he's an old buddy from school. But I knew he was good as he sorted my back out for me in no time.' Bailey shrugged.

'Did you do any acupuncture?'

Bailey raised an eyebrow. 'A bit, yeah. It's weird, isn't it?'

'Yeah but so good.' Clare's eyes rolled heavenwards and she grinned.

Bailey looked back at the booth to see Sophie and Marcus still huddled together. Groaning he turned back to Clare. 'Where's Paige?'

'She's in the back. Do you need her?'

'Yes, I can't go sit over there with them two without backup.'

Clare nodded over at them. 'Don't worry you won't need to, Polly's just arrived.'

Bailey spun his head around and was immediately grateful to find that she was on her own, yet his heart plummeted. It hadn't occurred to him that she would bring her boyfriend, but thinking about it, she would bring him at some point, she'd have to. Bailey was just glad it wasn't tonight.

'Ewwwww. Pack it in you two or we're sitting somewhere else.' He watched as she chastised her brother and best mate before she made her way over to him at the bar. He tried to not smell her hair as she gave him a hug but it was impossible when she was so close. He wrapped his arms around her for a brief second and felt his shoulders relax. Calvin would kick his ass if he wasn't careful, carrying stress around his neck like that, then again between Polly and his mum he had a lot going on to be stressed about.

'What can I get you, Miss Pol?' Bailey asked.

'Erm. Ohh I was going to say gin but I want a San Miguel now, please. Hi, Clare, you OK?'

'Fine thanks, Polly. You?' Clare said as she placed Bailey's drink on the counter.

'All good.'

As Clare went to get another pint he looked over at Polly trying not to stare for too long. As always she looked beautiful, she was wearing her hair in a plait and it fell down her back as she unwound her scarf. He tried and failed to not think about undoing the plait, preferably whilst they were both naked. His eyes continued to travel of their own accord and saw that she was wearing her maroon cord skirt, wool tights and knee-high boots combo that always made him think a bit too much about her legs. He took all of this in, in less than a second and then studied her face. She looked a little tired; her eyes weren't quite as bright as usual. He hoped it was her work that was making her look like that, and not that she was up all night with her boyfriend. He felt a quick sharp stab of something unpleasant in his stomach.

Polly leaned in. 'How you doing, Bailey? How's your mum?'

Bailey sighed. 'She's OK. Well, she's fine really, it's the rest of us that seem to be taking it all worse than she is. I spoke to Duncan and Seb and they know as much as I do. We're all going for dinner tomorrow night. So really as far as Mum and Billy are concerned it's business as usual.'

Polly waited to reply as Clare reappeared with her drink.

'How are Duncan and Seb taking it?' Polly asked.

Bailey smiled, it always made him chuckle when Polly referred to his younger sister by the family nickname.

'Same as me. I guess that's the positive, as a family we've been through enough that we know it's best just to be honest with each other. Well, for the most part, I mean Seb and I usually have to drag stuff out of Duncan but, yeah, it's hard, but we're all just taking Mum's behaviour as the lead. She's OK for now, so, we are too.'

'If you need anything at any time you know you can call me, right?'

Bailey looked down at where Polly's hand held his, he absolutely definitely could not get choked up.

'Thanks, Miss P. But aren't you a little busy yourself at the moment?' Bailey asked, his headache starting to return.

'It's only songwriting, Bailey. I can do that anytime.' Polly took a long drink.

'Erm, I meant with the boyfriend.'

Polly coughed. 'Oh yeah.' She was holding her drink tightly. 'Well, yeah, but Darren's cool. He would understand.'

Bailey felt his body heat up, a hot burning pain in his stomach.

'Not that I've told him what's going on, and I wouldn't, you know that, right? It's just that he's pretty laid-back, that's all.'

Bailey shrugged as he tried to put out the fire that was his internal temper.

'Hey, guys. You both OK?'

Saved by Paige once again, thought Bailey, because there was no doubt it had been about to get really awkward between him and Polly if she hadn't shown up when she had.

'Good thanks, Paige. You?' Bailey winked.

'All the better for seeing you two. They were making me feel sick,' Paige said, nodding towards the booth as she poured herself a drink.

Paige came round their side of the bar and the three of them walked over to join the So-cus, as they had all taken to calling Sophie and Marcus behind their back.

'No Mya tonight?' Polly asked, sitting in the booth next to Sophie.

'No, she's working. Again.' Sophie sighed. 'But she did say that she would Skype me later so that I can fill her in.'

'I'm sure she's thrilled,' Paige muttered as she sat down at the end of the booth next to Marcus. Faced with no other choice Bailey sat himself down next to Polly trying to squeeze on the end of the booth so as to not get too close. It wasn't comfortable, he was essentially perched on one bum cheek.

'OK so with only a couple of months until the big day, I have a list of things that need sorting out.' Bailey laughed into his drink as Sophie pulled out the tome that could only be her wedding planner and her iPad. Picking up a piece of paper she placed it in the middle of the table. 'I have a load of things that we need to discuss, dates that need to be booked and jobs that need to be assigned. Has everyone got a drink?'

'Yes, boss,' everyone including Marcus muttered.

'OK, first on the list. Wedding and bridesmaids dresses, and grooms suits.' Sophie unlocked her iPad. Bailey shuffled in his seat trying to get comfy, he looked up to see Polly giving him a weird look.

'These are the colour schemes that we've decided on,' Sophie continued as she pointed out a soft pink and gold palette.

'Oh that's lovely,' said Polly, whilst Paige just shrugged.

'I know what style of dress I think I would like but obviously I can't show you that now. There's a boutique in town that has designer dresses in stock, so I need a date from you, Polly, and you, Paige, when we can go with my mum to try on both the bride's dress and the bridesmaids' dresses. I've spoken with my sisters, and whilst I would love for them to be bridesmaids, they are more than happy that it should just be Polly, Paige and Mya. And frankly, it was going to be such hard work to match the aesthetic of five bridesmaids against three groomsmen. I'm assuming you've spoken to Euan and Smithy?'

'Yup, all confirmed.' Marcus nodded.

'Great,' Sophie continued. 'For the bridesmaids' dresses, I was thinking of something like this.' She pressed on something else, and Bailey leaned over. Polly and himself both looked over at Paige who again just shrugged and smiled. Bailey tried not to snort at the idea of seeing Paige in something that flowy, and that colour. Paige only ever wore jeans. Jeans with holes in. She had a variety of T-shirts, usually of bands, and then the rest of her was covered in badass jewellery. He doubted she owned any shoes that weren't Converse or DMs. He was surprised to see how calmly she was taking it.

'OK, so can you do the twenty-fourth?' Sophie asked.

Polly and Paige both grabbed their phones and started flicking through. Bailey looked over at Marcus who winked at him and grinned. That was one happy dude. He just radiated it. He wasn't rolling his eyes or making any wise arse comments, he was just there, supporting his soon to be Mrs and whatever plans they needed to make. They really were an awesome team. Something tugged hard at Bailey's heart.

Bailey sipped his drink as dates were discussed, and then just as quickly Sophie's piercing stare was aimed at him.

'Right, Marcus and Bailey, this is the place that you need to go to hire your suits. You can pick from any of these. I'll get the ties and pocket squares so don't worry about those. Can you arrange a date with your dad? Then just let me know and I'll tell my dad. Obviously, it needs to be sooner rather than later, but you have more time on this than we do. With regards to Euan and Smithy, just get their measurements as best you can and we'll sort it out. '

'Will do, Soph. Let me get the details.' Marcus pulled out his phone and took a screenshot off the iPad. It was at this point Bailey started zoning out again. He was still listening but none of it was for him. The sarcastic comments were minimal, and Sophie, despite being supremely organised, was gracious enough about everyone's time and energy, so that as much as this group of friends bitched and moaned, it was going to be a special day and Bailey knew that they were all feeling proud to be a part of it. He wondered what his own wedding would be like, or if he would ever be fortunate enough to have one. Unless it was with Polly he wasn't able to visualise it. He'd be tempted to Vegas it.

His backside was cramping up from trying to stay away from Polly, he had no choice but to slide into the booth properly and in doing so knew that his thigh was going to be against hers. She turned and smiled and then carried on discussing what needed to be done about colour theme accessories. For the first time in a long time, he wished he was sat somewhere else. Physical contact with Polly, however small as now, with the heat from her body so close to his, was becoming painful.

'OK, then, that just leaves the other major thing that has to happen sooner rather than later. The sten.'

Bailey looked up. 'Happy to help, boss. Do you have any idea what you'd like?'

Sophie and Marcus looked at each other and both said, 'A surprise.'

Sophie continued as she fished out the relevant paperwork. 'We've talked about it and we trust you and Polly entirely. Frankly, we have too much going on at the moment to think about it so we are handing it over to you both. This is the weekend we've booked out for it, this is the list of people we want to invite, this is the budget we've set and this…' Sophie rummaged around in her planner.

Bailey turned to Polly an eyebrow raised, Polly shrugged, and Bailey marvelled at how often they communicated without saying a word.

'Where the hell… oh, here they are. As you know I've been talking about the wedding on the ol' social media. Well, this company specialise in stag, hens and stens. They're having an expo type thing next Sunday at the Conference Centre in town. I have two tickets. Have fun.'

Chapter Eight

'Sweetheart, can you stop looking so glum and pass me the roasts, please?'

Bailey looked over at his mum, trying desperately to look like he was alright, but frankly his energy for faking it was flagging. The results had come back and they were not OK, and he was struggling. He reached over and passed the food as required, adding a small smile, it was the best he could do.

'What's the matter with you anyway?' Serena asked.

Bailey looked up and raised his eyebrows. 'Erm, gee, Seb, what do you think is up?' The room fell silent until all they could hear was the elephant in the room trumpeting loudly over the Yorkshire puddings.

'Well, you're not the one with cancer so why are you acting like you are?' Seb retorted.

Duncan exhaled. 'Jesus, Seb.'

'Well, you're not, are you?'

'OK, kids, let's calm down. As the person with cancer at this table, I get to say who can and can't talk about it and seeing as how you all have it on your mind let's talk about it, and then we can hopefully move on.'

Bailey looked over at Duncan who shrugged and didn't need to say out loud that Seb was just being Seb.

'Right, so I have my mastectomy booked in for next week, I'm finally going to get the boobs I've always wanted. From there we will find out what treatment I will need. Best case it will be chemotherapy, worse case if it's spread into my lymph nodes then we're probably looking at radiotherapy. Once treatment starts I know it's not going to be pretty, but I've already chosen some wigs that I like so I'm not too worried about that. In fact, I'm not really worried about any of it. I'm really lucky that I don't have to work, and I don't have to worry about money.' With that Denise patted Billy's knee and smiled. 'I have an amazing husband and some wonderful friends. I'm sorry if it's confusing for you all that I'm not more upset about it, but the specialist seems to think that everything should be OK. My prognosis is positive. The next few months will be rubbish, I'm sure, but then it will be over and we go from there. There's nothing more to it. Do any of you have any questions?'

Denise began eating the roast dinner that Billy had made. Bailey couldn't tell if she was faking or not, but she seemed to have made her peace with it. Bailey looked at his plate, his appetite not what it used to be. Ever since Billy joined their family ten years ago, he'd made a legendary roast dinner, in fact, it was one of Bailey's favourite meals after spicy chicken wings and extra spicy sauce. The hotter the better. Even so, his stomach churned and he knew it was unlikely he was going to be able to eat much of his food. He would go so far as to say he was sulking. He felt like a teenager again.

'How many courses of treatment do you have to do?' Duncan asked.

'Won't know for sure until after the mastectomy.'

'I want new boobs too.' Seb sulked.

'Of course you do.' Duncan rolled his eyes. Seb glared in response.

There was a moment or two of silence, as everyone around the table digested both the information and the food.

'What are your wigs like?' Seb asked.

'Here have a look I've saved pictures of them.' Denise opened her phone and passed it over to Serena.

'Oh my God, I love the purple one, that's so cool.'

Bailey leaned over and had a look. It was pretty wild, it would suit his mum down to a tee. She really was the only person he could think of that would take something as serious as cancer and turn it into something fun. Well, something that nearly resembled fun at any rate. He was just having a really hard time getting his bearings with it all. Looking around the table he couldn't understand why he was the only one upset by the whole thing? Surely cancer meant that everyone should be upset, shouldn't they be consoling their mother?

'Bailey, sweetheart, you're still really quiet. What can I do?'

Bailey looked at his mum, she really didn't look any different. It was still terrifying to him, he hated the fact that he couldn't see the cancer. It made it impossible to gauge what was going on, how it might be spreading in her whilst they sat and talked about wigs and ate a roast dinner.

'Mum, you don't have to do anything. I should be asking you that,' Bailey said as he re-tied up his hair.

'Well, don't take this the wrong way but I'm worried about you,' Denise said, placing her cutlery to one side.

Bailey halted. 'Me? Why?'

'I worry you're lonely.' The look on his mum's face tore through him until it sat quite comfortably within the boiling churning in his gut.

Serena and Duncan both snorted. 'Him? He's been holding the title of Mr Man Whore for the last six years!'

'Serena,' Denise quietly scolded.

'Well, I'm not wrong. Trying to find a woman that Bailey hasn't had is the only reason that Duncan is still with Elizabeth.' Seb grinned. The way she said Elizabeth made it clear, if it wasn't already, that Serena did not think much of Duncan's girlfriend of three years.

'Don't bring me into this.' Duncan carried on working his way through the meal. All eyes returned to Bailey. The result of which made him go from a sulk to pissed in record time. This house really must have stored all his excess teenage hormones, because he could feel himself regressing. If he sat here much longer he would be trying to hide Seb's toys again.

'Look, I'm not lonely. I have loads of mates, I'm even seeing someone at the moment so you don't have to worry about me.'

The atmosphere in the room plunged and Bailey was sure he'd be able to see his own breath. His feelings were clearly not well disguised by his tone at all. The icy air lowered until all he could feel was the cold stares of disbelief from everyone else in the room.

'Wait, why are you only worried about him? What's wrong with me and Seb? She's hardly Mrs Maturity?'

Seb stuck her tongue out at Duncan and Bailey was grateful for the moment's reprieve. As the older brother Duncan had always, and, by the look of things, always would act as peacekeeper when it was needed. It didn't always work but Bailey appreciated the effort.

'I know that you are all hard-working, loving people. Duncan, you've been with Elizabeth for a while now, and, Seb, I know you've only just recently broken up with Sean but you two were together for nearly a year.'

Bailey's prickly attitude melted a little as he smiled softly at his younger sister. He hadn't known she had split up with Sean.

'It's OK. He's a tosser. I'm better without.'

Duncan winked at her, and Bailey threw an arm around her, pulling her in for a quick hug, knowing that she wasn't as fine as she claimed.

'It's more about you being happy on your own and, well, you've never had a long-term relationship—'

'See even Mum thinks you're a player.' Seb chuckled.

'Billy, help me out here.' Denise sighed, picking her cutlery back up.

'Bailey, I think that we've all seen a change in you over the last year or so, you're working harder than ever and we, that is all of us, couldn't be more proud. But your mum and I would like to know that you could have a long-term relationship if you wanted one. But ultimately, and this applies to all of you brats, we just want you to be happy.'

Bailey looked at his mum and could see that she was

genuinely worried about him. He considered for a moment telling her the truth but he wasn't entirely convinced he knew what that was. He could tell them that he was sort of seeing Katie. That was a truth, but it wasn't going anywhere and it was far from serious. He could tell her that he was in love and doing his best to forget it, but that would probably only make her worry more. Shaking off his funk as best he could, Bailey summoned up the very last of his energy to use his best weapons; charm, humour and diversion.

'Mum, you aren't thinking of setting me up with anyone, are you? I don't think it would work so well, you as my pimp.' Charm done, humour done, next step. 'Seb, I've just remembered, Sophie wants to ask you if you will help out doing some of the designs and printing for the wedding. She's going to message you about it, if that is alright?'

Serena squealed and jumped up. 'Oh my God, Bailey, you're the best. Will she mention me on her vlog? She'd have to. I'd get so much coverage.'

Diversion nailed.

'What would you be doing?' Billy asked.

'I could do the seating plan, and maybe the invites, I'm guessing? I can't wait to find out. Oh, I've got some gorgeous new fonts I can't wait to show her. They will be beautiful.'

The conversation naturally flowed into wedding talk, with Seb bullying her brother about getting married to Elizabeth one day. Bailey watched, grinning at the appropriate moments and inputting where he needed to in order to keep the focus off himself. He glanced up at his mum and saw the soft smile she gave him. She knew what he was doing, just like she always did. But now he had more to worry about, not just his mum and the cancer treatment, but also how she was worried about him, being lonely of all things. He wished he could alleviate that stress so that she didn't have that extra burden, but what could he do? The only thing that came to mind was to carry on and show her how happy he was in his life just as it was. But was he really happy? He was worried that Marcus would regret making him a partner, he was worried that this thing with Katie was dragging him back into old patterns, and he was worried that Polly was in love with Darren. So, in other words, he just needed to lie. Bailey had no choice but to move his food around the plate and make it look like he was eating it, but really his stomach was on fire and everything he ate tasted like ash, and the ache in his head was beating so loudly he was surprised no one could hear it.

Chapter Nine

'I saw Sophie's mum yesterday. We're getting so excited. We've started talking hats. That woman is going to go hard on the hat front; I won't be able to afford to compete. Not unless your father wants to treat me?' Brenda was not so subtly shouting at that point.

'Huh?' George grumbled, not glancing up from his iPad where he was undoubtedly reading one of his gardening magazines.

'I need a new hat.' Brenda rolled her eyes.

'OK, sure.' George just smiled and shrugged.

'He has no idea what's he's just signed up to,' Brenda whispered.

Polly glanced over at her dad and saw his quick smile. He knew exactly what he had signed up to financially, but it was clear from his face he was happy making his wife happy, especially when she thought she'd got one over on him and that made her even happier. It was easy to see, Polly conceded, why Marcus had fallen for Sophie as he had. The easy back and forth, the wanting to know how each other worked so that in time, they would know each other almost better than they knew themselves. With an internal sigh, Polly cut off her thoughts at that point, not wanting to find out what would happen if she applied that filter to herself and her current relationship.

Getting her own iPad out, Polly's mum began searching online for hats. Sitting in the conservatory they were able to see through the early March drizzle to the beautifully landscaped gardens beyond. Not surprising, given that her father had had a successful gardening company that he had handed to Marcus after his first heart attack. Polly looked at her dad, the vines swirling in her stomach when she thought about how poorly he had been, and how even with the little heart attack he'd had recently, she wasn't sure if she would ever not worry again. Not wanting to dwell, Polly moved around so that she could sit with her mum and see the hats she was looking at. Ridiculously expensive hats.

'How's work going, Pol?' Brenda had put her iPad down and was now looking at Polly a little too closely for her liking.

'Yeah, same old same old.' Polly shrugged and went to look at the fairy lights running around the edge of the conservatory.

Her mum continued to stare at her, Polly glanced over and was given the classic, 'I see through your lies', Mum glare.

'It's just boring and there's lots of stuff going on at the moment that I'd rather not have to deal with. The promotion post has been put on hold whilst the company gets to grips with the finances or something. It's just got a really bad vibe at the moment, that's all, but I'm sure that it will pass.'

'You don't sound happy. You've worked so hard to get the qualifications for your job, is there no way of making it better?'

'Not really, Mum, not at the moment.' Polly half-smiled wracking her brains for something to change the subject. She didn't like talking about work at the best of times.

'Can't you find something else?' Brenda asked.

Polly shrugged. Yeah, she probably could, after all, she had the experience and the qualifications, but the idea of restarting her HR career path in a new company made her neck itch. Really in the grand scheme of things, she didn't want to be in HR at all, but she wasn't sure she could tell them that. At least now, although it was shit, it was shit she was familiar with, better the devil you know type thing.

'You'll figure something out, love, you always do. At least I know that with a job like HR you're never going to worry for an income. You don't know how lucky you are having that stability, that regularity.'

And there it was. She remembered the year that her dad had an injury and couldn't work. She'd remembered getting her little pink backpack together with her favourite toys. They'd packed up ready to leave the house, but they'd gotten a last-minute reprieve from an insurance policy. But the effect of that year had never really left her mum, nor had it left Polly for that matter. It was no wonder Polly had chosen to shelve her passion for music, in order to go for stability. On the occasional bad day, she could say that she felt a little bit broken, but then Monday night would come around again and she'd be able to perform and she would be glued back together, if only temporarily. But the monotony, the stability, it felt more like she had been cemented to the desk.

But she wasn't that person. She absolutely had a wild side. Every Monday night she proved that. Every first date she dared to go out on, they were all tiny adventures, where she felt free. They piled up. She could even say by daring to go out with a colleague that was a bit risky. But then again they only really went to his flat, and they only did that one or two nights a week.

'I can be wild,' Polly muttered louder than she had intended.

'Yeah?' her mum asked, eyebrow raised.

'Yeah.'

Brenda smiled softly. 'What do you think of this one?' She was looking back down at her iPad again.

'I must be a little wild.' Oh no, Polly thought, don't say anything further, rein yourself back in.

'Yeah, how come?' her mum asked, still not looking up from the iPad.

'I'm dating a guy from work.' Shit thought Polly it's out there now. No way I'm getting that one back.

'Really?' Now her mum looked up.

'Yup.' What the hell are you doing Polly!

'So is it serious? When do we get to meet him? Are you allowed to date someone from work?'

Oh boy. This is what she got for being momentarily wild. Goaded into revealing something she had no immediate plans to share. She looked at her mum and knew it was a big deal to her. Well, it made sense, she didn't tell her mum about every random date she went on. Well, she did tell her about the bad ones, they'd quite often enjoyed a glass of wine or two as Polly shared stories of dick pics and requests for worn underwear, and other people's hygiene and a million other things. Which reminded her, she should probably talk to Darren at some point to find out if they were serious enough to delete their dating apps. That could wait. Looking back at her mum, she realised, it had been a while since she admitted to actually seeing someone. Then again, it had been a while since she could state that anyway. But now, now she was going to have to answer the questions that she hadn't been wanting to think about. There was one thing she was grudgingly clear on, however, and that was WHY she didn't want to think about it. And that was because of Bailey. She was trying desperately to not let him affect her, but she knew that he did. She only had to think about him and butterflies started making their way around her body but she really didn't want Bailey to be part of the equation. He definitely wasn't factoring her into any decisions, if this rumour of a new fling was anything to go by.

Her mum was still waiting patiently for an answer, sipping her white wine as she did so.

'No, I don't think that it's really serious, it's quite new, to be honest. We met over Tinder first, and then after I'd seen him for a while I found out we worked at the same place. It's a huge company and we work in different departments, and we don't meet at work so it's not really a problem. In fact, it's nice, it means that we have something in common to talk about, you know?'

'OK.'

Something about the way her mum said that meant that

71

she had given away far more than she meant to. Her mum did not look overly convinced or enthused and this was obvious as she went back to looking at hats on the John Lewis website.

'He'll be coming to the wedding. Well, I've asked if he can be invited anyway.'

'Oh wow, so it must be sort of serious then,' George supplied. Polly jumped not having realised her dad was paying any attention whatsoever.

'So, what's he like? Tell me more.' The iPad was down again, John Lewis forgotten.

'Well, he's got an adventurous side, he's really confident, he seems to be doing well at work. He's an accounts manager and he is paid a decent salary and has commissions on top of that.'

Polly's mum paused for a minute as she digested what Polly had just told her. 'So what do the girls think of him?'

Polly swallowed. What did the girls think of him?

'They've only met him once, and I don't think they've made up their minds yet. But then again we're all riding on the wedding train at the moment as there's so much to do. Especially for me as the maid of honour and Bailey as the best man.'

'Oh, I do love Bailey. He's going to look so hot in a suit.' Brenda grinned unrepentantly.

'Mum!'

'Well, he is, darling. I'm not blind.'

Polly knew that her mum had always had a soft spot for Bailey. His charm and cheekiness had worked on her since the first time they met when he and Marcus were teenagers. Worst of all, she was right. Polly hadn't thought about it, but seeing Bailey out of his usual casual wardrobe and in a suit would be devastating.

'Anyway, we have to go to this sten conference thing on Sunday,' Polly went on, feeling a little more like she was on comfortable ground.

'What's that?'

'Well, as the timescale is so short, Sophie and Marcus have decided that they would like to have a joint hen and stag do. Bailey and I have to arrange it. The company that is doing the expo have given Sophie two free tickets. So I guess we go around, look at all the options, and get something booked in.'

'Just you and Bailey, huh?' The tone in her mum's voice was best ignored.

'Yep.'

'Hmm.'

Monosyllable stalemate. Polly decided that the best thing to do would be to move on quickly, so she picked up the iPad this time.

'Oh, that's a nice hat. Do you know what colour you'll be wearing?' Polly asked.

'Well, that's just it. Gail and I wanted to complement each other, you know, to show that the two sides of the family are on board. I can't wait I'm so excited. I just love Sophie, and Marcus has never been happier. It's all a mother could wish for.'

Polly tried not to do so, but she could take a hint. A sledgehammer with the phrase, 'I can tell you're not that happy' written on it would've been more subtle. Polly picked up her wine glass and drank, hoping her mum would focus on the other man in her life, and sure enough, her attention was brought back to Mr John Lewis.

Chapter Ten

Waiting for Polly at the coffee house at Manchester Piccadilly Station Bailey felt his mind wander as he stared into the pattern created by his latte – the barista deciding to finish it with a little heart. He almost smiled. Almost.

His mind kept flipping inconsistently between what an over eighteens only expo might involve; how his mum was, was she recovering from the mastectomy, when would they get the next lot of results, how to make his mum stop worrying about him, how in love Polly was, how much work he needed to do, how much his head ached, how much his heart stung and how exhausted he was by the whole thing, but also how much he was looking forward to spending all day with Polly.

Finally, he'd been toying with the idea of talking to Katie and introducing her to his family, but it felt wrong, on every level. For all intents and purposes, Katie was a prolonged one-night stand and they both knew it. However nice Katie was, Bailey wasn't sure that he could carry it on much longer. His gut pinched when he thought about it, and as much as he had hoped it would create space between him and Polly, it really hadn't done anything except make him feel like a shitty person. So, no, introducing Katie wasn't going to work. That kind of left him out of options. Unless he could magic up a genuine girlfriend, someone that he properly cared about, loved even. Then he would be happier and his mum would be happier. Maybe he should have a fake girlfriend, a pretend one? He could ask Mya or Paige, but frankly, he didn't want them to know what was going on. Not yet. Obviously, that left Polly and that didn't warrant any further explanation.

'Hi, gorgeous. Oh is that tea for me?'

Bailey looked up and grinned at Polly, marvelling at how

she could make him forget everything even if it was only momentarily. Right now she was his balm, but he knew that he couldn't keep letting her make him feel better, but for today, well today, he needed her to rescue him, just a little. Standing up he wrapped his arms around Polly, able to feel her warmth through all the layers she was wearing and felt relief when she snaked her arms around his waist holding him close. Grudgingly letting her go before the hug was too long it became awkward, he watched her as she took off her layers, her hair flying as her favourite green scarf was pulled from around her neck. Once sat down, she busied herself sorting out her tea, before taking a sip. Her eyes were still looking a little duller than usual. Mind made up, he was going to talk to her about her work today. He got a distinct impression that she didn't enjoy it. It seemed to Bailey that it was getting her down. That being said, any other person probably wouldn't be able to tell, because he supposed not everyone would pay her the sort of attention that he did. She looked up and grinned, and as always when her huge smile was aimed at him, he felt the magic that she held over him.

'So, are you excited for today?' Polly asked whilst sipping her drink, and sighing. 'Thanks for this by the way, I needed it.'

'Yeah, it must be what twenty minutes since your last cup of tea?' Bailey chuckled.

'Yeah, something like that. So do you have any idea what today is going to be like? I was going to look online but decided I would rather be surprised.' Polly's eyes widened in amusement, her hands cradling her cup.

'It's going to be interesting. Do you have the details about the budget and dates and everything?'

Polly reached into her satchel and pulled out a notebook. 'Yup all the details are in here. We've got quite a budget for this, thanks to Sophie's promo thing.'

'Does that mean that the sten will be online for everyone

to see? You're not going to be able to really let your hair down, in that case, no dancing on bars, taking shots off a naked man's torso.'

Polly laughed, and though it was a foolish thing to think about, he loved that sound and that he could make her do it. It made him think of other sounds he could tease out of her given half the chance.

'I didn't realise you had been on so many nights out with me.' Polly laughed softly. 'I don't know the specifics but I think that Sophie just has to take a couple of pictures from whatever it is we end up doing. So don't worry, your secrets will be safe, from the general public at least.'

Bailey winked and smiled.

Polly put down her cup. 'So, before we get going, how are you? How's your mum?'

Bailey blew out his breath, looping the loose strands of hair behind his ears. 'She's not too bad.'

'You don't sound convinced. Is she recovering OK?' Polly asked, her eyes searching his.

'Yeah seems to be. She's meeting with the consultant to go over the results of her mastectomy. Then, by all accounts, they want to start the first round of treatment as soon as possible.'

Polly gave a soft smile. 'It's natural to worry, Bailey. She's your mum.'

'I know. I think more so than anyone else in the family. No, that's not fair, everyone is worried, and wants to do their bit. It's just that my bit is a little harder, it's a bit more specific.' Bailey flexed his arms over his head before leaning back on the table.

'What do you mean?'

Bailey groaned, he hadn't planned on telling Polly, but then again who was he kidding. At the moment Polly was more like a best friend than his actual best friend. It wasn't anyone's fault, it's just the way that it was currently. Well, technically it was his fault, for not actually telling his best mate what was going on. Bailey looked down at his nearly empty drink.

'My mum's worried; she thinks that I'm lonely. More specifically she's worried that I can't have a long-term or at least a serious relationship. I hate that I am adding more worry on her plate, and I just want her to know that I'm fine. I'm not lonely. I could have a serious relationship if I wanted.'

Looking up from his latte he glanced at Polly to see how she was taking it. She had picked up her cup and was deliberately taking her time sipping her tea, giving serious thought to what he was saying.

'Can I be honest with you, Bailey?' Bailey rolled his eyes at the ridiculous question. 'I can understand where she's coming from.'

'Huh?' Bailey's back straightened.

'Please don't take this the wrong way. I absolutely think that you could do a serious relationship. I have no doubt about that. But you just haven't, have you? We're both aware of your reputation, and I have no problem with that, as I am sure your mum doesn't either. I think what it boils down to is that she just wants to know that you're happy. We've only been really close the last six months or so, but if I had to guess, I would say that you're not really as happy as you let others believe. But then again, what do I know?'

As Polly bent back down to her brew, Bailey blew out his breath. His thighs twitching with how uncomfortably close Polly was to having him completely sussed. But something in her lack of gaze, something in her posture, something gave her away too. Or maybe he just wanted a diversion, anything to stop him from looking too closely at his own motivation.

'Are you alright?' Bailey asked.

'Yes, just something my mum said sort of freaked me out, but let's sort your problems out first, then we can sort out mine.'

'But that's just it, how do I sort out the problem? I'm not in a serious relationship.'

Polly cleared her throat and shifted in her seat. 'Not even with Katie?'

She immediately resumed the intense studying of her brew. Bailey was momentarily floored. It hadn't been a secret that he had met up with Katie. Paige saw the original get together at the bar, well part of it anyway, so it definitely wasn't going to be kept a secret. He studied Polly's face for any signs that she was upset that he was seeing someone. She had an excellent poker face, or, more likely, she genuinely didn't care. After all, she had a boyfriend. And that was the mantra that he knew he had to keep repeating to himself over and over again.

Now it was Bailey's turn to shift in his seat. 'She's not really a serious thing. We're just hanging out.' For the first time in his life, Bailey felt embarrassed at some of the decisions that he had made. Well, this decision anyway. 'So no, I don't think presenting her as a girlfriend is going to be convincing, nor is it going to help when we break up again so quickly afterwards.'

'What about a pretend girlfriend? Someone that can stick around for a bit, whilst your mum goes through chemo?'

'Yeah, maybe, but who? I don't really want the world to know what's going on with her at the moment. I'm still processing it myself.'

Polly's hand gently touched the side of his face, stroking the edge of his beard and he felt his entire body's nerve endings move towards that one spot.

'Bailey, you're not lonely. You're just a little unhappy. Your mum is right to call you on it. I would bet anything that she was going to have this same conversation with you sooner or later without the cancer. You're going to get through this. You're all going to get through this. You're one of the best people I know. You've got this. Let's get through today and maybe we can come up with a plan.'

Ah shit. There was no way he wasn't completely in love with this woman in front of him. She removed her hand and whilst the heat of her touch remained, he wished more than anything he had the right to kiss her. And at that moment he knew things with Katie were done.

Taking her hand he kissed the back of it. 'Thanks, Pol.'

'No worries. So is there a plan of attack for today?'

'No not really. Let's just get in there and have fun.'

'OK, then let's have an amazing Polly and Bailey day and forget about everything else.'

Bailey was fine with that, taking his now empty mug he raised it in a toast. The pair of them grinning, excited about what might await them.

'Holy shit,' Bailey whispered, his eyes widening.

'What in the... where the hell do we even start?' Polly asked, a matching expression on her face.

Polly and Bailey both stared at the frenzy that was the giant Central Conference Centre. They'd just walked through the main entrance and immediately stood still, as people moved around them. The place was huge, almost stadium-sized. There were stalls everywhere, huge displays, neon lights, a handful of no doubt overpriced bars, and—

'Are they strippers?' Polly asked.

'Given that, apart from a few well-placed sequins, she's completely naked, I would say yes.' Bailey grinned. 'Polly you look so shocked. Have you never seen a stripper before?'

'Well, nearly, once when I was following Mya, but, yes, I think I can say I have now. She's really good on that pole. Woah. I think I just saw the eye of the storm.'

As soon as Bailey could catch his breath from laughing, he saw Polly's eyes shine brightly as they messed around with one another like usual.

'OK so let's get a feel for the layout and then hopefully get some ideas.' Bailey hadn't realised he had put his hand on Polly's back until it was too late. This was exactly the effect she had and it was his response that was going to cause problems.

Walking into the masses, various companies and agencies were encouraging people to their stall with various titbits of information.

'Hi there, gorgeous couple, are you interested in booking something a little different? We have cocktail crazy golf.'

'We have a gorgeous array of naked butlers for your hen dos.'

'Life drawing classes, we'll provide the naked models and the art teacher.'

'Fancy paint-balling?'

Polly spun around. 'Wait. What?'

'You know paint-balling on a field or warehouse in teams.'

Bailey pulled her away. 'Jesus, Polly what did you think it was?'

'Isn't it obvious? I thought it was balls being painted. I was like who the hell would want to do that, is that for stags or for hens, then I thought of those potato stamp things we did as kids in school. Don't look at me like that? This place is confusing. Everything that sounds normal is rude, everything that sounds rude is normal.'

Bailey was creased up, he couldn't breathe.

'Stop laughing at me, Bailey.' Polly hit his arm.

'Sorry, Pol, but you are the funniest person I know, I swear to God.' Pulling her into a side hug, his arm around her shoulders so that she knew he was sort of laughing with her and definitely not at her, he felt her arm slide around his waist.

'But Jesus, ball sack painting is not something I ever want to see. Having said that it has given me the best idea for a house-warming present for Sophie and Marcus. We could even do a piece together if you wanted?'

Now it was Polly's turn, laughing she wiped the tears off

her face as people muttered around them as they stood in the middle of the concourse.

'Come on, we're not going to get this sorted,' Bailey said. 'We need to… oh look you go over there and get drinks, I'll go grab a brochure and we can sort out a plan.'

Polly nodded and unwound her arm from his waist and walked towards the food hall.

Making his way back towards the entrance, Bailey approached the guy with the brochures.

'Hi, can I have a brochure please?' he asked.

'Hi there, oh wait, you have a VIP wristband, let me get you a goody bag, hang on.'

The next thing Bailey knew he had hold of two tote bags, one with random goodies and one with so many flyers and the brochure. 'Erm, thanks.' Putting them onto his shoulder he went back to look for Polly.

Chapter Eleven

'What have you got there?' Polly asked as Bailey made his way towards her.

'Me? What have you got?' Bailey was nodding towards the drinks.

'What? It's a sten expo and it's five o'clock somewhere.' She watched as he unloaded the bags before sitting down next to her at the table and taking a sip of his pint.

'You only went for a brochure. What's with the bags?' Polly asked, picking one up and looking through it.

'Oh yeah so apparently Sophie got us VIP tickets. It meant we got these bags, and I am guessing there are some other freebie type things we might get as VIPs.'

Polly frowned. 'I wonder if there's a VIP bar somewhere, bet I could have got cheaper drinks.'

Bailey grinned as he located a map from the tote of never-ending flyers, and laid it on the table. 'So here's the layout, and from the looks of it we have loads of the individual activities that could be done anywhere. There's also a load of companies that seem to organise everything from start to finish, and then there are the holiday ones as well. Thoughts?' Bailey asked.

'Erm, are we best going to someone that can organise the whole thing? It gives us more time to just mess around?' Polly suggested.

'Polly! I am shocked. I thought you were taking your maid of honour duties seriously and now you're telling me you want someone else to do all the work on your behalf?'

'Don't you?' Polly asked.

'Yeah, of course. OK, well once we've finished these drinks, we can go over and see what we can get booked. Then we can go and explore and see things you've never seen before, and see what other freebies VIP passes get us.'

'That sounds perfect.' Polly grinned, and it was natural, she was already having a fun day. Being around Bailey was so easy, at least for the most part. She didn't have to pretend or save face, he just got her and her jokes. Her heart flipped a little until she remembered Darren. That was OK though, she rationalised, because she was really only thinking about how great Bailey was as a friend. They had great banter. That was it. Just friends.

Bailey interrupted her thoughts. 'So you didn't tell me before, what was it your mum said to you?'

'Huh? Oh yeah, that. Well, it wasn't really anything. I just— Well, we were talking about work, and how I was in a steady stable job, I hinted at how much I disliked it and her reaction was to see if I could do HR somewhere else. She's right, of course, I could, but the idea of being locked into HR forever sent me over the edge. But more than that it just got me thinking that I'm maybe a bit boring.' Polly rolled her eyes.

'I don't know, I think you could be wild if you wanted to be.' Bailey winked.

Polly's eyes were glued to his. 'I am wild, I go on lots of dates, I sing my own songs in a bar every week. I'm not exactly staying home and knitting every night.'

'Yeah and now you can say that you've seen a stripper as well. You're so wild!'

Polly snorted. 'See. I knew I was.'

She watched as Bailey laughed at her. Did he think she wasn't wild either? Why the hell did it matter? She had enough going on at the moment with the usual nonsense at work, her secret life as a singer/songwriter, her maid of honour duties and Darren. Wait, she didn't mean to quite lump him into that category but still.

'OK so is there anything that you would like to do, that's wild and that you've never done before?' Bailey asked.

'Like what?'

'I don't know like a tattoo? Piercing? Stripping?'

'Let's just change the subject.' She really didn't like the idea that Bailey might think that she was boring or plain.

'Polly, for what it's worth, I think that you are plenty wild, and I think given the right situation and the right person you *definitely* would be wild.' Bailey grinned, and Polly felt her cheeks heat. Damn this red hair and pale skin. For the most part, she had a remarkable poker face, she'd needed to have with all the times she'd avoided talking about her singing passion. But Bailey kept throwing her off balance. She absolutely wasn't thinking about how wild she would be with Bailey. She sighed, even with Darren she really wasn't that adventurous, although she knew she could be. The sex was alright, but she wouldn't call it wild. In fact they hadn't even really been doing it at all lately, wild or otherwise.

'But about the work thing.'

'What about it?' Polly sighed.

'Look I know it's probably not my place to say but, you hate your job. It's wearing you out. You need to find something else, or better still come out of this creative closet you've put yourself in and be a singer. You have immense talent. Plus I think you're just wild enough to do it.'

The tone in his voice sounded like a dare, and Polly had to slam the door on her immediate go-to-response, with Bailey she needed to be careful. She would do anything he dared, and more. He brought out the wild side in her all right.

'Ah, on that one you are wrong. I, erm, I don't perform anywhere else or for anyone else. It still freaks me out that you know. But actually, it's quite nice, to have someone to talk to about it, really nice actually.' Polly felt suddenly shy.

'Why don't you do it anywhere else?'

'I had a couple of bad experiences when I was starting out that I haven't quite been able to shift. I'm still learning about music and performing and its bloody terrifying as much as it is thrilling. Anyway I only perform where I am comfortable with the people around me, and that only happens at the Speakeasy. So for now, I must carry on with the boring HR work and pay the bills.'

'Hmmm.' Bailey looked like he wanted to say more and frankly she felt like she had shared too much of herself already. She knew where he was coming from and if the roles were reversed she'd be saying the same thing, but frankly, nothing could change. So she just needed to plod on.

Bailey opened his mouth clearly about to carry on. 'I just think—'

Poly interrupted, 'I should be your girlfriend.'

Bailey spluttered and spilt some of his drink, before carefully placing it back on the table. 'I mean I should be your fake girlfriend. I already know what's going on, I like hanging out with you. I can hang out as much or as little as you need me to whilst your mum goes through her treatment. Long enough that she knows that you're happy and in a "serious relationship".'

Polly took a breath, aware that that was quite a ramble. She'd been toying with the idea of suggesting it since he first presented the problem, but she wasn't sure she'd be very good at pretending. But it got Bailey off her back about work, it helped him, it helped his mum. Really there wasn't a good reason why not.

'Pol,' Bailey looked down, 'I'm not sure it's a good idea.'

'Why not?'

'There's a few reasons, the main one being Darren, your boyfriend?'

Polly swallowed. It wasn't that she hadn't thought about him, she had, he just didn't factor very high. In this instance.

'Well, as I see it, I'm helping a friend out. No problem there. I am helping someone be in a better place so that they can kick cancer's butt. That's altruistic. I'm almost a saint. Finally, Darren doesn't actually need to know. But listen, if it's going to make you feel weird or awkward then forget it, it's not a problem, just a suggestion.' With that, she shrugged and began playing with the spare coaster. It had just tumbled out of her, but she stood by it. It felt like the right thing to offer, it was entirely up to Bailey now if he wanted her to play along or not.

Bailey leaned in close enough that she could smell his amazing aftershave and something else that was pure Bailey. It made her stomach tighten, and her heart flutter as it took her straight back to Sophie and Marcus's bed, when she had been lying next to him their bodies pressed together. Polly felt herself being drawn towards him as she leaned in too. He took her hand, and gently stroked the back of it with the other. Polly momentarily lost her train of thought as she stared into his eyes. The eyes were where Bailey kept his power, she concluded. When he was being cheeky they twinkled, when he was being funny they crinkled, and when he was intensely focused on something or someone it was like a powerful laser.

'I'm not sure that you're fully aware of what it is you would be signing up to.' He spoke softly and Polly was lost.

Polly's lips were suddenly dry. Quickly licking the bottom lip she watched as Bailey's eyes briefly followed. Her breath now ever so slightly harder to catch.

'Like what?' Why had her voice gone all weird?

'Well when we're with my family, we would have to be really close, there'd be lots of hand-holding, gentle caresses and presumably lots of kissing.' Bailey had inched closer, his features now blurry as she stared into his blue eyes.

'Yeah. I kind of figured that would be called for,' Polly whispered.

Bailey leaned in closer still holding her hand, and Polly was gone. They were so close she could feel his breath and she could see how this close, his blue eyes held specs of turquoise. His scent had completely surrounded her, and she felt locked into his magnetic force. He could ask anything of her at this moment and she would do it, her only worry was that he would ask for nothing at all. She studied his eyes, trying to find her bearings, but losing herself as she fell further into the blue. He had a slow smile that crept slowly, sinfully up to his eyes, making her feel hot in all the right places, before a look of, Polly wasn't sure what, discomfort maybe or pain, flashed across his eyes. Abruptly Bailey sat back.

'I'm not sure it would work.'

'Why? We've even fake kissed to get me out of that bad date so it's not something new.' For some unknown reason, she felt a flickering of panic. The laser look returned to Bailey's eyes, and Polly had no choice but to lick her lips again at the memory of that kiss. Shit. Maybe this was a terrible idea. What if she fell even further? No. She would walk the line for Bailey.

'If the roles were reversed don't you think you'd offer to do the same thing for me?' Polly asked.

'It would be too easy for me to get carried away with you Polly.' She wasn't really sure what he meant by that, but he looked concerned.

'I'll keep you in check. But I would have one condition. In fact, I have a condition regardless of whether you say yes or no.'

Bailey raised an eyebrow.

'You need to tell Marcus. Not just that we would be pretending to be going out together, but also why.'

Bailey dropped his gaze and Polly's hand. She looked at her hand and marvelled at how much it still tingled after his touch, but how empty it felt now. Polly took the moment out of his direct gaze, to straighten her spine and try to regain some control over the parts of her body that had gone haywire under Bailey's intensity. Even with this tiniest moment of reprieve, Polly's head was buzzing with how much she wanted to do this for him, and how much she prayed he would say yes.

'OK, I'll think about it.' Bailey jumped up. 'You ready to get a sten booked?'

'Yes.' Polly nodded and stood up. 'Let's do it.'

'Polly?'

She twisted back around as Bailey held onto her hand again. 'Yeah?'

'Thank you. You're a good friend.'

She wasn't sure, but he looked sad about that for some reason. His eyes momentarily dull. As soon as he was stood, she grabbed him in a hug pressing tightly. 'I've got your back, Bailey, whatever you decide to do.' She did, she really did, even if he said no, she'd just help him come up with something else instead.

Chapter Twelve

Polly looked over at Bailey as he drove them to his mum's house. Since agreeing to be pretend boyfriend and girlfriend only the day before, Bailey insisted that there was no time like the present and got them booked in for dinner. It was only a quick one, a trial almost, because Polly was due at the club later for Open Mic night, but it didn't stop her heart from racing, her mind from running away with thoughts about potentially kissing Bailey again this evening. If she brushed her teeth twice before she left her house, well then, that was her just being a good friend, wasn't it? If the job of being a pretend girlfriend was worth doing, it was worth doing well, and that's why she'd also used mouthwash.

'Oh God, I never asked, what have you told Katie about all of this?' Polly was chewing her lip, grateful that Bailey couldn't see her face as he focused on the road ahead.

'I haven't and I don't need to. We've stopped seeing each other.'

Polly was stunned. He must have done that immediately after the expo. He hadn't exactly had any other time to do it.

'Oh no, how come?' Polly congratulated herself on her tone, it was almost lazy.

'Oh, it's nothing bad, we weren't a major thing anyway.' Bailey's voice faded out, his concentration on the road ahead.

Polly was torn between pedalling for more info and trying to not think too much into it, in the end, all she could think of to say was, 'OK, cool.'

Polly swallowed and tried to hold back a smile. She certainly didn't want to think about why that little bit of information made her happy. It's not like she had any say in who he could and couldn't sleep with.

Deliberately changing the subject, Polly said, 'I still can't believe all the awesome things we've booked for the sten. It's going to be amazing.'

'We really did a good job. I always knew we'd make a great team.' Bailey gently hit her arm for a second as Polly grinned.

'Tonight we get to be more than just a team,' Polly said, casting a quick glance Bailey's way.

Bailey shot her a quick look, his hand clutching his chest, his mouth falling open in fake and somewhat overly dramatic shock. 'Are you coming on to me, Miss Polly?'

Polly sputtered. 'I meant as a pretend couple, as well you know.'

Bailey raised an eyebrow and grinned.

'Are you sure you're alright about this?' He gently took hold of her hand, the tingles, oh lord the tingles… she needed to pace herself. Bailey grinned holding her hand tightly. 'I figured I should get practising.'

Polly held on tighter, entwining her fingers around his as it lay on his thigh. She couldn't help but look at it. He would let go occasionally to change gears, and hold it again, her hand remaining on his thigh in between.

'Yeah, totally. You?' Polly asked, realising she hadn't answered, her eyes still glued to their hands.

'Absolutely. Oh, we've been seeing each other for a month by the way.' Bailey looked at her for a small second before turning back around.

'OK, any other backstory I should know about?' Polly asked, aware that the heat from her hand was travelling up her arm and into her torso.

'No, that should be it. Everything else we can just pinch from real life.'

'Alright.'

'But as you had a condition for doing this, I have one for you too. No secret singer-songwriting stuff. More people need to know so if it comes up tonight you should tell my family what you do,' Bailey said simply as her eyes widened.

'Why?'

'Don't worry and don't sound so panicked. I just figure it would do you good to get used to telling people.' Bailey shrugged.

'Do you think?'

'Yes, and it will go no further than them. Trust me.'

He squeezed her hand again. Polly looked down. His hand was so big against hers and their differing skin tones, light brown and white. His skin was slightly rough, presumably because he was a labourer. All of that was nothing compared to the hot electricity that was flowing from both where the hands joined but also, and rather more powerfully, where her hand rested on his thigh. Shit, she was in trouble already. As for telling his family about her singing, well she'd just hope it wouldn't come up.

'Polly, it's so lovely to see you again.'

Polly wasn't sure what she had expected from Bailey's mum but it felt lovely to be swept up in a gentle hug as soon as she walked through the door. Lovely and slightly horrible, as she felt guilty at the fact that they were not lying so much as pretending. No, they were lying. For a good cause, but lying all the same. 'It's lovely to see you too.'

'OK, Mum put her down. Wait...' Polly watched as Bailey craned his neck and tilted his face. 'Have you invited everyone?'

'Oh, Bailey, family don't need an invite. It's just a lovely coincidence that all my children are here on the day you're finally introducing Polly as your gorgeous girlfriend to us, although, obviously, she doesn't need much of an introduction.'

Polly glanced at Bailey, and threw him a glance that said, 'Oh crap'.

'Come on and meet everyone, Polly.' Bailey's mum led the way down the hallway at the same time Bailey put his arm around her shoulders and leaned in.

'It's OK. It's better this way, don't worry,' he said quietly.

'I am worried, Bailey, I don't want to mess this up for you.' Polly fell into Bailey's arms as he abruptly spun her around, hair flying until they were facing each other as his hands gently held her face.

'Don't worry, Pol, you're doing a lovely thing, for a lovely reason. Let's just have fun, yeah?'

Polly gulped. 'OK.' Feeling the nerves in her belly, she couldn't help but wonder what the next two hours had in store when her thought process was rudely interrupted, in the most glorious way possible. Bailey was kissing her, his lips gentle but warm, as were his hands on her face. Polly gasped as her body suddenly caught up with the programme, and promptly took over, all thoughts forgotten. She wasn't sure who had started it but now that their tongues were involved, it was every man for himself. Her hands grabbed onto his hips and held on tight as she was devoured. The smell of Bailey, his dark aftershave was all around her, adding to the tingles moving throughout her body, and Polly had visions of them together, his smell on her everywhere. His hands moved into her hair and tightened so that he was able to angle the kiss perfectly, and Polly surrendered completely.

'Ewwww. Can you two not keep your hands off each other for a second? Mum, they were making out in the hallway. They might need a minute to collect themselves.' Seb snorted as she turned around and walked back from wherever she had emerged from.

Although they had stopped kissing when they were interrupted, Bailey still held her face as he gave his sister's back a dirty look, and she realised she still had a death grip on the belt hoops at his hip. Bailey turned his face back around until they were looking at each other again, inches apart.

'See? No need for awkwardness now, no need to worry about what you say or don't say. They know that we have kissed, and we got our first fake kiss over with. Better?'

'S-second,' was all Polly managed to stutter.

Bailey smiled slowly and confidently. 'Oh yes, second fake kiss. Are you OK?'

Weirdly it had made her feel better. Well, it had made her feel a whole host of things, mainly hot delicious things, but also better. She was no longer worried about the show that they were going to put on, as they'd already got to the main part. Polly smiled and raised up on her tiptoes to gently place a kiss on his lips.

'All better. Let's go.'

With that, Bailey took her hand and led them into the house, Polly's heart hammering in her chest the entire time, but no longer with nerves.

They had just finished taking on pork tacos, nachos, ribs and everything else at the table, when Bailey leaned back in his chair, for the first time in a long time, stuffed. He had somehow managed to resist taking Polly's hand and whisk her away somewhere private where they could finish what they had started in the hallway. Plus, he'd also managed to not stare at her too much. In other words, he was nailing it.

The lemon cheesecake was doing the rounds now and Bailey took the opportunity to look up and saw his mum smile at them both. Bailey could tell it was genuine and it made him realise that although maybe a little bit deceitful, it was absolutely worth it if his mum was happy and worry-free. The problem would be keeping things PG with Polly because once again kissing Polly had completely knocked him sideways. He had kissed her to put her at ease, the same was true for himself. He had been worrying about it. He didn't want it to be awkward and staged. He'd also assumed, well hoped, that the effect their first fake kiss had had, was a one-off, a fluke. He was delighted that she also seemed to remember that kiss. He'd held that memory close for a long time and it thrilled him beyond measure that Polly certainly hadn't forgotten it either.

Now that they had the second fake kiss done, he knew he'd been right to worry. It wasn't like the first kiss at all. It was far, far worse. He had lost himself in Polly completely and he had been seconds away from pinning her against the wall and going to town. She made him reckless, she made him forget absolutely everything else that was going on around them. His neck prickled as he forced himself to remember that this was pretend, that she had a boyfriend. Like he could really forget that? Whilst that might have left a bitter taste in his mouth, Polly certainly hadn't and he knew he wanted more. Not just more, he wanted all of her.

In the meantime, he put his arm around the back of her chair and was gently stroking her back. He watched as Polly straightened and she looked at him slightly quizzically. Sure, no one could actually see what he was doing, so he didn't necessarily have to do it. It just felt right.

'So tell me all about this sten that you two are organising. Is that how you got together?' Denise asked.

Polly looked back at Bailey and smiled overly sweetly. 'Why don't you tell the story of how we got together, babe?'

He watched as her eyes clued him in on the fact that she was toying with him. Well, two could play at that game.

'Are you sure, darling? I know how much you love telling the story to all our friends,' Bailey said, his tone covered in mock sweetness.

'I'm sure, babe. I want to hear you tell it.' The gorgeous red-haired devil was batting her eyelashes at him.

'OK.' Bailey waited until everyone at the table was listening. 'We got drunk and shagged.'

'Bailey! I cannot believe you just said that.' Polly felt her cheeks redden, and her neck itch.

'Bailey, look how much you've embarrassed Polly. I raised you better than that! I'm sorry, Polly. I thought I had raised a gent but clearly I was wrong.'

'I'm joking, I'm joking. Actually, it's not really an entertaining get together story. As you know, we've known each other for years, but recently we had to spend more time together. I'd fancied her for ages anyway. We started hanging out more and more and one thing led to another. I don't think I ever officially asked her out, but here we are.'

Grinning he looked at Polly knowing that every word he had spoken was true, but could see the confusion in her eyes as she tried to figure out if it was real or not. Bailey hadn't wanted to directly lie to his family, well, no more than he already was doing, and figured that would be the best way to explain it. He also wanted Polly to suspect that he had more than 'fake' feelings for her without actually having to say it.

'I'm sure it was romantic in its own way.' Denise rolled her eyes. 'Anyway, tell me about the sten expo.'

'Yeah, Pol, tell them all about how you pole danced.' Bailey laughed as Polly slapped his chest before placing her hand on his thigh discreetly digging her nails in. He just smiled wider, it was fun winding her up. And if it meant that she had to grip his thigh, it was not likely to make him stop, was it?

'Polly, do you really pole dance? I briefly dated a stripper once—'

'That's probably a story for another time,' Billy interrupted Seb. Bailey knew that was a good idea, his family had a notorious lack of filter at the best of times.

'I do not pole dance. Thank you, Bailey, for that. I just tried it briefly at the expo. But we have booked burlesque lessons for part of the day. But only the girls are doing that bit. We've got a busy weekend organised, haven't we?'

Bailey nodded, he was looking forward to it for the most part.

'What else have you got planned? The last one I went to we did clay pigeon shooting, nerf war, and whisky tasting,' Duncan said.

'Yeah, and what are you going to have at yours when you marry your darling Elizabeth?' Seb asked sweetly.

'Seb stop winding your brother up,' Denise said, in what was clearly her mum voice.

Bailey looked at Polly and raised his eyebrows in a this is what it's usually like kind of way.

Polly smiled gently. 'Yeah well, on the Friday night we're just going out for a meal to get to know one another. There's a few people that are outside of the usual group, and we want to make sure that everyone feels included. Then the activities start Saturday morning, the girls doing one thing the boys another, before we all meet up again at a swanky nightclub for more food and dancing. Then we recover enough to get back home on the Sunday. We've only got a few weeks to pull the last few things together but everything is booked and that's the main thing, including the farmhouse we're staying in. It should be good.'

'Polly, Sophie is so lucky to have such a thoughtful friend as her maid of honour.' Denise smiled.

Polly mumbled thanks, her eyes focused on the table.

'She's not only thoughtful she's an incredibly talented singer-songwriter, aren't you?'

Polly slowly brought her head back round to Bailey and glared at him, WTF plastered across her face as clear as day. Bailey watched as the blush on Polly's skin that had just about cleared came back with a vengeance, and he wanted nothing more than to kiss every last inch of it.

'It's alright, Polly, nobody here is going to say anything. It's a secret you see. No one knows apart from us.'

'Wow. Of course, we won't tell a soul. Do you perform? Where do you do your composing? What instruments do you play? Where do you find the time working full time?' Denise's eyes lit up and Bailey knew that this would be a good thing for both of them to bond over and that pang of guilt rose again when he remembered that this wasn't actually real, it was simply becoming too easy to forget that last bit.

'Well.' Polly coughed to try and clear the lump that had immediately placed itself in her throat, she straightened in her chair and turned round to face his mum. 'I perform one night a week at an Open Mic night in town, in fact, I'm due over there in a little while. I write at home. I learnt to play the piano when I was a kid, and then whilst I was at university I learnt basic drums before I dropped out to work full time and get my HR qualifications, and then I also learnt guitar. Oh and I learnt recorder at school, but who didn't? I love the ukulele as well, but that's self-taught.'

Bailey grinned, his heart swelling to hear her talk about her talents.

'We would love to come and see you perform at some point, if that would be OK?'

Polly was chewing on her lip again, and itching her neck. 'Oh well, erm, I'm not sure.'

'Not to worry, Polly, I get it. It's a private thing, but if you ever change your mind just say the word and we will be there.' He watched as his mum reached over and patted Polly's hand.

'Mum used to be in a choir,' Bailey pointed out.

'I was the lead on a number of occasions, if you don't mind, and I still give it a go every now and again, I can't help myself. I can't stay away for long.'

Polly's eyes lit up. 'What's your range?'

'I sing two-octave soprano.'

'Wow.' Polly's awe was obvious, and he watched as she began working something out in her head, her lower lip bitten. 'Well, I guess you would be more than welcome to come anytime. I feel the same, I have to do it, I can't keep away.'

Denise slowly got up from her chair until she was stood by Polly's seat. Bailey wasn't sure but he thought he could see tears in her eyes before she quickly gathered up Polly into a hug and whispered something in her ear. Polly's arms reached around and hugged in return. Bailey was a goner. Clearing his throat with the realisation that his family loved Polly too, at that moment Bailey swore to himself that the second Polly ditched her boyfriend, he would try his hardest to make their fake relationship real.

Chapter Thirteen

Digging the absolute shit out of Mrs Rosenthal's garden to create the perfect edging, Bailey was able to utilise all of his frustrations into his work. He caught himself thinking again about how lucky he was to not only do a job that he enjoyed but how he could tailor it to fit his mood. The idea of feeling this frustrated, this angry, whilst sat at a desk was enough to make him shudder. He wouldn't say that the digging was helping his mood, but it certainly wasn't making him feel any worse. His plan for most days was to work himself to exhaustion so that by the time he got to bed, he would pass out. It wasn't working though. So much for plans, huh? He was getting some sleep, enough to function, and almost always enough to have insanely hot dreams about Polly, but not usually more than four hours a night. The problem with it was two-fold; one it served to remind him that dreaming does not equal reality, and second, it almost always left him feeling guilty that when he woke up from the amazing dreams, he was happy for a minute or two until he remembered everything that was going on.

Whilst he was chuffed to bits that Marcus had made him a partner, he was conscious that his reputation had left him in the position where he felt he needed to prove himself. It was fair to say that up until about two years ago he hadn't really taken anything seriously, and whilst that had been a whole lot of fun at the time, it had soon become the self-imposed concrete bricks that meant he found himself going nowhere fast. Whilst he had brushed himself off and had gotten a new attitude relatively quickly, in no small thanks to Polly, he knew that his reputation would not be as easy to shake. He would hate it if his best mate of forever would regret making him a partner, but at this moment in time the ache in his muscles, particularly in his back and his arms, calmed him a little.

'I knew that I would find you here.'

Bailey jumped at the interruption. 'Hi, bud. What are you doing here? Have you come to check up on me?'

'We need to talk,' Marcus said solemnly.

'What's wrong?' Bailey asked not looking up, not stopping his task.

'I should be asking you that. Don't think I haven't noticed you working yourself to death. You're working with me on the Hazeldine project and then any spare daylight hours you're doing maintenance? Come on, dude. What's going on?'

Bailey shrugged and carried on edging the last bit of Mrs Rosenthal's garden.

Marcus's hand on his arm stopped him again. 'What's going on?'

'I'm nearly finished, hang on.'

Clearly getting the message, Bailey watched in his peripheral vision as Marcus began clearing away the excess lawn that had been removed. Bailey grunted thanks, and before he knew it, he was knocking on the door to tell Mrs Rosenthal that her late husband's pride and joy was as perfect as always. Taking the equipment and putting it into the back of his pickup truck, it was too soon before they were all done, and Bailey was no clearer as to where to begin.

'Have you got time to come to mine? Play some FIFA?' Bailey asked.

'You're my best mate, of course I have time. I'll meet you there in twenty, yeah? I'll pick up some food.'

'OK, cheers, pal.'

Even to Bailey's own ears he could tell that he didn't sound right. That wasn't hard, he had never felt more removed from his usual funny carefree self. He was too tired to pretend and that was saying something. The fake date with Polly the other night had been amazing and they would be doing it again in a week or so, but in the harsh light of day, it had left his mind reeling.

Getting into his car he pondered all the things that he could tell Marcus and wondered if he had the guts to say any of it. He couldn't figure out what was stopping him. As he got to his apartment, he was no clearer about what he would say or how. He'd just gotten showered and dressed when the intercom buzzed and before he knew it Marcus was at the door. Well, technically the huge pizza box was at the door being held up by Marcus.

'Here take this,' Marcus grunted.

'How many are we feeding?'

'Shut up and take it.'

Bailey did as instructed and put the larger than life pizza on the coffee table, before going back to the kitchen to get his hot sauce.

Marcus pulled a face. 'What's the point of having any toppings at all if you're going to cover it in that stuff? You're worse than Polly.'

Bailey stopped shaking the bottle, the slow drip of the hot sauce now landing on the box. 'Huh?'

'Polly, she's the same. Has to be covered in hot sauce. I don't get it.'

Bailey lowered his head conveniently hidden by the lid of the pizza, having no idea what expression would be on his face.

Once they were settled with drinks and pizza, and of course hot sauce for Bailey, Marcus raised his eyebrows. 'So?'

Bailey chewed his pizza. Taking his time, trying to see if he could get some last-minute inspiration, but unable to come up with anything.

Clearly unhappy about the silence Marcus started. 'Are you mad because I'm not seeing you as often? I mean, I feel bad about that but I'm with Sophie and— Ow! What the hell was that for?' Marcus rubbed his arm where Bailey had punched it.

'Shut up. I am beyond happy for you and Sophie, don't be a dick. It's my mum, she has breast cancer.'

Well, that came out a lot easier than he thought. But why stop there, best let it all out in one go. 'I'm worried that you'll regret making me a partner, I'm worried about my mum, my mum is worried that I am unable to have a serious relationship with anyone, and I'm pretend dating Polly.'

There, now it was all done. A quick glance at Marcus revealed that he was stunned, his mouth wide open. Deciding to let Marcus have some time to process what he had just thrown at him, Bailey continued to eat his pizza in near silence, watching the TV that was on low in the background. A minute or so later and Marcus still hadn't said anything, at which point Bailey threw his crust into Marcus's wide-open mouth.

'Goal,' Bailey cheered.

Marcus spluttered and coughed up the crust.

'Ow. Why the hell did you punch me?' Bailey was rubbing his arm now.

'You dick. Why didn't you tell me any of this sooner?' Marcus growled.

'It's all happened pretty suddenly, to be honest. Ow. What was that one for?' Bailey rubbed his arm again.

'I'm still pissed. I might need to kick your ass.' Marcus was speaking quietly.

'OK, FIFA or Battlecry?'

'We need to eat, talk and then I need to kick your ass on FIFA.'

They ate pizza with the only noise coming from the TV that neither of them was watching.

'So where's your mum up to? What's happening?' Marcus asked in between bites of pizza.

'She's had her mastectomy and the good news is that it

hasn't spread to her lymph nodes so it's just chemotherapy, and they want to start pretty quickly, so it's likely to begin at the end of the week.' Bailey put his pizza down unable to eat any more, but grateful that he had at least been able to eat some.

'How are you about it all? How's the rest of the family?' Marcus asked.

'My head is up my arse, mate, but my mum is handling it all fine. She's amazing, she really is. Except for this whole relationship thing, but pretending to have a relationship with Polly has settled that as well so now she can just focus on getting through her treatment. The doctors are happy that she will. We've just got to get through it. The rest of the family are like me, just trying to support Mum and Billy as best we can.'

'How did the dating Polly thing come about?'

Bailey looked over at Marcus, studying his face, trying to figure out if there was a 'big brother' tone about him. 'Don't worry, dude, it's nothing major. She's just coming to my mum's for dinner a couple of times, that's all.' Bailey continued to watch Marcus.

'So Polly knows everything?'

'Yes, and technically the fake relationship thing was her idea. Ow. Stop punching me. What was that one for?' Bailey moved further down the sofa out of hitting range, his arm starting to go numb.

'For replacing me with Polly. You can't just swap out your best mate for their sister you know?' Now it was Bailey's turn to sit with his mouth open. Of all the things he thought Marcus would be upset by, this wasn't one that had occurred to him.

'You're my best mate, and you always will be. You just had a lot on your plate with the wedding stuff and I don't know... I just didn't want to bring you down. You're right though, I should've told you.'

'OK, let me work through the rest of the list.' Marcus rubbed the scar on his eyebrow.

'What's this crap comment about business partners? Do you think I was born yesterday, or maybe that I had only just met you? I know who you are. I knew what I was taking on when I asked you to be my business partner. I asked my hardworking, loyal mate, who deserved it. So quit with all the extra work, OK? You're going to knacker yourself out and then where will I be? Also, you're making me look bad, so just pack it in. We'll figure out a plan month by month, job by job. OK?'

'Jeeez, Mum, OK. Have you finished telling me off yet?' Bailey was starting to feel a little lighter, a little less like he was trying to carry the world in his head, granted it wasn't full to the brim with brains, but there wasn't that much space.

'No, I don't think so. How does Polly feel about you?' Marcus asked.

Bailey didn't know where to look, again. 'What do you mean?'

'Is she going to get hurt pretending to be your fake girlfriend?'

Bailey thought about that for a moment. He wished he could take the word fake out of there, and see how Marcus would really feel about him and Polly together. Then again, what difference would it make, Polly had a boyfriend and presumably no interest in him anyway.

'She has a boyfriend, so I think she's cool. I would never intentionally hurt Pol, you know that right?'

'Yeah, of course, I know that. I just don't want her to get hurt accidentally.'

Bailey almost guffawed. At this rate the only one getting hurt was him, and he was big enough, he could take it, but that was the one thing he didn't think he could share with Marcus. Besides, any hurt would be worth it for the duration of their fake relationship. And if he happened to be round at his mum's more frequently, so that they could pretend couple more often, then so be it. Although he was probably a bit more into kissing and holding hands than he had been in any of his other relationships.

'Your sister is one of the best people I know. I will never be able to repay her for what she is doing for me and my family.' Moving the pizza around in the box, unable to eat anything else, he avoided looking into Marcus's face.

'Right, hurry up and finish that slice. I desperately need to kick your ass on FIFA and if that doesn't work, we need to play Far Cry so I can shoot you a couple of times instead,' Marcus said, cleaning his hands on some kitchen roll.

'Sure thing, pal. Whatever you need and look, I'm sorry.' Bailey looked up.

'Just tell me, OK? Anytime, whatever it is, just tell me,' Marcus stated.

Bailey nodded. 'Will do. Right, time for you to try and kick my ass, even though we both know that's not going to happen.'

Whilst it hadn't solved everything, and whilst he hadn't come clean about his true feelings towards Polly, Bailey really did feel better. Maybe even better enough for a decent night's sleep. Maybe not, but he could hope.

Chapter Fourteen

'I'm so happy that we could all do this together, it wouldn't have been the same without you, Mya.'

Polly smiled. Sophie was right. As much as Mya and Paige might bitch and moan about the wedding stuff, she could tell that they were happy to be here, and not just because they were sipping on complimentary Bellinis.

'Well, I'm glad that my latest business venture didn't work as planned and I was able to get home sooner. I can't wait to see your dress.'

'What venture was that Mya?' Polly asked, always eager to try and figure out just what it was Mya did for a living. Everyone else seemed to accept Mya's vague occupation, but it drove Polly mad not knowing. But then again Polly could admit, to herself at least, that she was just nosey that way.

'Wouldn't you like to know, Pol. Anyway, how's the boyfriend? Will we be seeing him again soon?'

'Nice deflection,' Paige mumbled as Mya tossed her beautiful shiny dark hair over her shoulder and winked.

'Yeah, how's it going, Pol?' Sophie asked as she turned to look at Polly.

Polly opened her mouth and then hesitated, realising that she was about to update everyone on Bailey and not Darren. Her heart fell into her stomach as she acknowledged that she would really need to do something about that soon, she just wasn't sure what she wanted to do, why she wanted to do it, and how she would do it. By 'it', of course, she meant to question whether or not they should be in a relationship. For now, with everything she had going on, it was easier to carry on as normal and keep the status quo. She was still seeing Darren twice a week, he was pretty relaxed about the whole thing, only occasionally grumpy that he couldn't see her more often. Or, more specifically, when he wanted to. Polly suddenly realised that everyone was staring at her.

'He's good and, yes, you'll see him soon enough and, if not, you'll see him at the sten in two weeks. Anyway, Paige, I want to know how you feel about trying on a bridesmaid's dress? I don't think I've ever seen you in a proper dress.'

Paige did a little grunt and a half-smile, 'It's going to be good. I like change.'

Polly looked at Paige giving her the once over. Her half-shaved head, and piercings all up and in one ear, the one in her nose, her Doc Martens, her startling green eyes that saw everything. Polly was having a hard time visualising her in a bridesmaid dress. Today was going to be fun.

'Right, ladies, are we ready to start?'

The wedding boutique owner had simple dark trousers and a cream blouse, but somehow on her, there was nothing simple about them. They were perfectly tailored, and her red shoes precisely matched her red lipstick. Polly looked down at herself, she was pretty happy with her own style, admittedly she preferred the autumnal season for the woollen tights with denim shorts or skirts, and she loved scarves, but as it wasn't quite spring enough yet she could get away with it for a little while longer. But at that moment Polly envied Louisa the wedding dress consultant. Louisa was pure class. Mya had a very similar style, but perhaps a little more revealing. Sophie, on the other hand, was as happy in a hoody as she was in a ball gown, and, Polly was sure, absolutely beautiful in a wedding dress.

Looking around as she perched on the central sofa, Polly took in the wedding dresses that were lined up around every wall. The space was beautifully lit and the runway in front of them led off to separate dressing rooms, two on each side, and one large one at the back that led straight onto the catwalk, each with thick navy velvet curtains for privacy. There were no particular dresses standing out anywhere and she had no idea what sort of dress Sophie had chosen, and there was no indication of what she had finally chosen for her bridesmaids either.

'I'm sorry, we can't start yet as we're just waiting on a couple more people. They should be here soon.' Sophie smiled. 'Let's give them two more minutes and then I'll call them. In the meantime can we do some photos and videos for my social media? I'll make sure that you're tagged in them all and that your website is listed in the comments.'

'Of course, that would be wonderful.' Louisa beamed, clearly understanding the impact Sophie's social influencing could have on her business. Louisa must have such a happy job, putting people in wedding dresses all day long, thought Polly. Except maybe if they get returned new, that part must be a little depressing. Louisa only looked a couple of years older than herself, but the impression she gave was of someone driven and accomplished. It must have been hard work getting all of this set up at a relatively young age. She could see why Sophie liked her so much, in that respect they were two peas in a pod.

'Who else are we waiting for? Presumably not Marcus?' Mya asked.

'God, no. He's not seeing the dress. Which reminds me, Mya, can I store the dress at yours once it's ready?'

'Aren't you worried I'm going to sit around in it eating Doritos watching *Peaky Blinders*?'

Sophie looked alarmed. 'I am now. Paige, can it stay at your place?'

'Aren't you worried that I'm going to sit around in it eating Doritos watching *Peaky Blinders*?'

Polly and Sophie both nearly snorted, Bellinis nearly coming out of their noses. Even Louisa gave a little chuckle, clearly having already sussed Paige's style.

'Somehow, I don't think that's going to be a problem. But will it be safe from your cat? I don't want him trying to climb up it,' Sophie said.

'Yeah, you're right. It's safe with me, and I'll keep it away from Mr Higgins, besides I'm more a *Walking Dead* girl.'

'Thanks, Paige.' Sophie rolled her eyes.

'But who else are we waiting for?' Polly asked once again, eager to know everything.

'Well you know one of them very well, and the other one, I know very well.' Just then the little bell on the door went, and Sophie and Louisa both disappeared, but it wasn't too long until multiple voices could be heard.

'Sophie, I'm just so delighted that you invited me to be a part of this, it means so much I can't tell you.'

'Mum? I didn't know you were coming.' Polly stood up and gave her mum a hug.

'I know, sweetheart. I wanted to surprise you. Hi, girls.'

'Hi, Brenda.' Mya and Paige went over and gave her a hug, just as more people made their way into the shop.

'Ladies, I'm so excited. I can't wait to see my baby girl try on her wedding dress. And when these two heard I was coming there was no stopping them.'

Gail, Sophie's mum, went around hugging everyone as Sophie's sisters, Hollie and Jenny, made their way in. Hugs were given to everyone, then more Bellinis were handed out, more chairs were magic'd up until finally they were all sat facing the runway. Everyone giddy as they sipped their drinks and took in all the beautiful dresses around them.

'OK, then, Sophie, if you're ready, let's go. Did you bring the undergarments?' Louisa asked above the noise.

'I certainly did. Let's do this.'

'Yay.' Everyone screamed and raised their Bellinis, getting more and more excited as they watched Sophie and Louisa move towards the largest dressing room.

'So I understand that there are a couple of dresses she wants to try on, but that she's seen the one she thinks she'll love, is that right?' Gail asked, looking at Polly.

'Yeah, I think so. I'm not sure what she's settled on, she wanted us all to be surprised.'

'Polly!' Sophie's voice shouted behind the curtains. 'You need to come in here, you need to learn how they go on because you'll be responsible for making sure I'm poured into the dress properly on the day.'

'I'm glad it's you, I think I would be too nervous.' Gail patted Polly's arm as she stood up and made her way to the dressing room.

Pulling open the curtain Polly saw Sophie in the most beautiful lingerie she had ever seen. It was a strapless basque in white that had the most intricate lacework in the bodice, the fit absolutely perfect. The simple white silk French boxers, so elegant, made the complexity of the basque stand out even more.

'You look so beautiful and as long as I keep forgetting that it's for my brother's benefit, you look stunning.'

'Thanks, Pol. There's more to it. But we don't need the full get up for today.'

'Sure.' Polly playfully grimaced.

'OK, so what you're going to need to do is to pool the dress carefully on the floor, there's quite a bit of it,' Louisa said. 'Sophie, if you would carefully step into it for me, thank you. Now this one has a discreet zip on the side, but the other dress she's picked has got a row of buttons, which I will need to show you how to fasten using a crochet needle. OK, Sophie, you stay still whilst we gather this dress up and around you, OK?'

'OK.' Sophie was a little breathy and Polly grinned at her.

'Sophie, if you wouldn't mind putting your arm through here, and again put your arm through here. Polly the zip runs through here and then is closed off there. It's so discreet. I can immediately see that this will need altering a little, but not too much. What shoes are you wearing?'

'I don't have them yet, but I do know that they have a

four-inch heel. So I bought some stand-ins with me. Pol, would you mind they're in the bag just there.'

Polly turned around and delved into the bag pulling out a pair of sparkly silver shoes. 'Are these the same ones from the vlog awards?'

'Yes, they are. I've got my eye on a pair of Louboutin's that I think are amazing, but I'm going to have to see if the budget can stretch.'

'Hmmm. If not, I think that these would work. Besides these are the shoes you were wearing when you told Marcus, and the world, that you loved him for the first time.' Polly looked up once she had placed the shoes on Sophie's feet, stunned as Sophie's face began to crumple.

'Pol. That is so lovely.' Sophie sniffed. 'I don't see how I could wear any other shoes. It has to be these ones.'

'I didn't mean to make you cry, Soph, sorry.'

A watery smile greeted her.

Polly looked at Louisa who sort of shrugged and smiled as if this was perfectly normal behaviour. Polly took a step back so that she could see the dress in all its glory. Before she knew it she was wiping away a tear of her own as Louisa smiled again.

'Polly, why don't you go and sit back out there and tell everyone we will be out in a minute. We're just going to add the finishing touches.'

Polly nodded and then grabbed Sophie in a hug. 'You're so beautiful.' And then practically ran out of the dressing room before she full-on wailed. Sitting back on the sofa at the head of the mini runway, everyone was nudging her and asking what she thought.

'She'll be out in a minute and I am not saying anything.' She didn't say a word, what she did do was reach over to the side table and pass tissues to Gail.

'OK, everyone ready?' Louisa asked from behind the curtain.

'No pictures, guys, I mean it. This HAS to stay secret, OK?' Sophie could be heard through the curtain.

'OK, just come out already!' Mya screamed.

There was a loud whisper as the velvet curtain opened and they all watched eagerly as Sophie leaned down to pick up the end of her dress and walk down the mini runway until she got to the section that had mirrors on either side. Polly marvelled at Louisa and the store design, the lighting was perfect. It made Sophie look like she was glowing, not just from the dress, but from the inside. But the dress. Oh God, the dress.

Sophie looked up and bashfully smiled. 'What do you think?'

There was a moment of quiet reverence before the distinct sound of sniffling could be heard. Polly looked around and was surprised to see that it wasn't the mums crying but Paige and Mya. It was understandable though, the dress was a beautiful combination of ageless elegance and a vintage lace finish. The lace material covered her and continued down her sides and towards the back. There was white material behind the lace at the bust, and the white material continued downwards until it reached the floor before spilling into a train a metre long. It made Sophie look like some sort of Victorian Grecian Goddess. She looked taller and the way the lace pulled in around the bust and towards the low back made her waist look tiny.

'My darling girl. You look beautiful.' Brenda sniffed.

'We thought we would try the shorter veil on this one. But you don't want the veil to go over your face anyway, do you?' Louisa asked as she was righting the train to make sure that it looked perfect. It already did.

'No, I don't want to miss a single second. I want to see it all.'

Well, that was it, now the mums were crying and those that weren't certainly had tears in their eyes. Polly watched as Sophie looked at herself in the surrounding mirrors, a warm glow settling in her heart. Her best friend looked so happy that it was flowing out of her until everybody in the room felt it seep into their pores.

'I just love the lace.'

'That train is phenomenal.'

'You look amazing.'

'How are you going to pee?' asked Paige.

'Well, that's where my bridesmaids come in. It's going to be a team effort.'

Hollie and Jenny snorted at each other, obviously grateful that they weren't bridesmaids, but, to their credit, Polly noticed that Mya and Paige didn't bat an eye. Toilet duty would be no different from the various other times they'd had to look after each other over the years, usually after a couple too many drinks, shots, cocktails and chicken nuggets.

After a few more minutes, a few more twirls, it was time for Sophie to try on dress number two.

'Come on, Pol.'

Polly dutifully followed Sophie, Louisa taking a minute just to show her how the train should be held. Once in the dressing room, Louisa explained again, but this time about how to get her out of the dress successfully. Once the dress was hung up, the second dress was revealed.

'Oh, I need the hook. Polly, see if you can get Sophie in this, it's very similar to the last one.' When Louisa disappeared, Polly leaned forward and gave Sophie a hug.

'You look so beautiful and so happy. It makes me melt.'

Polly heard Sophie sniffle. 'Don't. You're going to make me cry again.'

'I thought we should get all of the soppy out of the way now so that we don't do this on the day and ruin your make-up,' Polly suggested.

Sophie laughed. 'Ruin my make-up, my God could you imagine what that would do to my reputation?'

Polly giggled as she gently pooled the dress on the floor. The colour for this one was slightly different, more towards ivory and slightly warmer in tone.

'Polly?' Sophie whispered.

'Yeah?' Polly wasn't looking at Sophie, too focused on gathering the material of the dress so that as Sophie stood in the middle she could pick up the right bit.

'Marcus told me about the relationship with Bailey. How's that going?'

Polly sighed. She knew that this was coming at some point, she just thought that they would be too busy today and therefore hadn't mentally prepared.

'Look, I don't want everyone knowing about it, OK, for Bailey's sake. I don't want anyone knowing about his mum until he wants to tell them.'

'Of course not, that's why I'm whispering to you about it now. But, is it OK? Are you alright?' Sophie asked, stopping Polly for a moment by holding her wrists.

'Of course, what's not to be OK about? I'm just helping a friend out. I'd do the same for any of you. Well, more likely Paige, seeing as none of you would probably need a girl, but you get the point.'

'Hmmm. But this is Bailey. I remember what you were like after the first time you fake kissed. That took some getting over.'

'No, it didn't.' It did.

'It did, Pol. You took yourself off all the dating apps. Said that it didn't feel fair.'

God, why does Sophie have to remember everything? 'Look it's different this time. I have a boyfriend, in case you forgot. This isn't something that I will need to get over, this is just helping a friend.'

'How does Darren feel about this?'

Shit, why had she brought him up? Now, this was going to sound worse. 'He doesn't know. He isn't going to know. He doesn't need to know.'

'Hmm.' Wisely Sophie held her counsel on that one, but the lack of words didn't stop Polly from understanding the look on Sophie's face. The look that was clearly implying a real relationship probably wouldn't have secrets like this.

'So what does this fake relationship involve?' Sophie asked.

'What do you mean?' Polly said as Sophie finally let go of her wrists so that she could hold the straps for Sophie to put her arms through.

'Holding hands, kissing, making out?'

'Yes, yes and, no, of course not.' Although as Polly said this she knew that she had gone red. How could she not when she thought about how carried away they got in the hallway of his mum's house no less. They had been seconds away from roaming hands and clothing removal.

'You've gone red,' Sophie pointed out, the mirror in the dressing room, making it unnecessary.

'So would you if you were holding up the weight of this dress. It's hard work this.' Polly tried deflection but knew it wasn't going to work.

'Whatever but—'

'Here we are, I have my hook. Polly, it looks like you've done a great job. Let me show you how to do the first button and then you can try and do the rest.'

Polly had never been so grateful to see someone in her entire life.

'Sure.' Polly was more than happy to be given a task that would halt the conversation. She didn't need anyone from the outside looking in. It made sense for her and Bailey and, frankly, that was all that mattered. But the Darren thing was definitely getting uncomfortable. Sophie was right, even if she didn't say it. She needed to figure out if she and Darren were serious, and if they were, then maybe they shouldn't actually have secrets. Her heart dropped at the thought that Darren might ask her to stop helping her friend. Surely he would see that what she was doing was for the greater good? Right?

'Perfect. You had no problem with that, you're obviously very dextrous.' Polly just smiled, yep she needed to be to play the piano as she did. Oh God, another secret. Polly felt herself slump an inch lower. Her brain too heavy in her head.

'All done. Polly, do you want to go and take your seat again?' Louisa asked.

'Sure.' Polly almost ran out of there. She would just need to make sure that she wasn't alone with Sophie again, and how hard could that be, right? It's not as if a bride needed to spend any time with her maid of honour. Oh God.

'Is this one not as nice?' whispered Mya.

Polly stalled, she actually hadn't been paying all that much attention to the dress. 'No, it's beautiful. Why?' It was bound to be beautiful, surely.

'Your face looked all tight then for a second.'

'Oh no, just a headache, that's all.'

'Everyone ready?' Louisa called again from behind the curtain as she swept it up and out of the way. This dress had a fitted bodice with thin delicate straps and lots of detailing that went all the way around the bodice. At the back following all of the buttons, lace detailed with silver stitching and small crystals. It all added to the bodice without being too much. There was a small band of material in the middle before all of the pleated tulles fell from the waist, in layers and layers, looking like a perfect fairy-tale princess.

Polly looked around, there didn't seem to be as many tears this time, they had all become acclimatised to the beauty.

'Oh, the detailing.'

'That skirt just flows beautifully.'

'It's timeless.'

'Does it have pockets?' shrieked Mya.

Sophie felt around until her hands were hidden. 'Holy shit, yes it does. But I genuinely don't know which one I prefer. What do you all think?'

'Hmm.'

'Errr.'

Louisa coughed politely. 'Why don't you wear that one for a little while and see if the detailing in the bodice is going to irritate your arms. We could get the bridesmaids dresses and then see which dress goes best with them, if you prefer? Just no Bellinis, OK?'

'That would be brilliant thank you so much, Louisa. OK, girls, up you get.'

With that Polly, Paige and Mya stood up and walked towards Louisa, as Sophie gathered up her skirts and sat down, the mums and sisters marvelling and fawning.

Polly looked at Paige. 'You ready?'

'As I'll ever be,' Paige all but grunted.

'OK, girls, you have each been assigned a room and in it you will find your bridesmaid dress. The size should be close, but alterations are expected. Don't worry about underwear or shoes at this point. Mya, do you want to give me your Bellini?'

'Whoops, sorry.'

'Paige, you're in this room, Polly this one and Mya that one. I'll come in and out but shout if you need any help.'

Polly wandered into her room, thinking that if ever she wanted to get married, she would absolutely be coming to see Louisa. Then all thoughts stopped as she saw her dress. It was in the most beautiful golden colour. It was strapless and floor-length and the fitting was around the bust, before it flowed down, the corset back bringing it in at the waist slightly. After taking her now completely drab clothes off including her bra, she pooled the dress down on the floor and stepped into it. Holding the dress to her body, Polly marvelled with the red of her hair and the warm gold of the dress, she looked amazing. Polly giggled, seeing Paige in this dress was going to be hilarious. Paige would hate it.

'Knock knock can I come in?' Louisa's gentle voice from behind the curtain.

'Please do.'

'I had a feeling you would be ready first. OK let's get this corset done and we can see how it fits.'

Polly watched in the mirror as Louisa fitted the corset effortlessly.

'OK, so it needs taking in around the waist a little to give it a bit more shape. How are we on the boobs? Oh, that's perfect. What do you think?'

'I think that you are amazing. You have a gift. I have never looked this awesome before ever. Thank you.'

'It wasn't all me. Sophie had the basic ideas, I just knew the styles. I was right with this one though. It's fab. Do you want to go out now or wait until everyone else is ready?'

'I'll wait if that's alright?' Polly said her eyes glued to the mirror in front of her.

'Of course.'

Polly caught a little knowing smile of Louisa's reflected in the mirror before she quickly disappeared closing her back in.

Polly just stood and stared at herself. She was tall anyway, not Paige tall but at five-foot nine, she knew that sometimes she could look a bit gangly. But not in this.

Turning slightly she noticed that the dress had a slit in the skirt. It was subtle until it wasn't. If she stood perfectly still you couldn't tell, you might get a hint of it when she was walking, but the fact that Polly knew it was there was like a super sexy secret. She couldn't stop looking at herself, she looked like a goddess, as if she held some sort of secret power. She felt the gorgeousness of the dress feed into her soul. She stood taller, her shoulders straightened. She must have been staring at herself in wonder for a good few minutes because the next thing she knew Louisa was speaking. 'OK, girls. We're all ready for you now.'

Polly stepped out and couldn't wait to see Paige's face.

'Holy crap.'

'What the—?'

'Is this right?'

Polly stopped looking at her co-bridesmaids and looked over at Sophie who was grinning widely from ear to ear.

'Louisa you've done it again, they look amazing,' Sophie said.

Polly, Paige and Mya were silent as they checked each other out. They were all in a lustre-gold dress but that's where it ended. Mya's was glued to her curves, the thick straps coming down in a vee until they covered her breasts but left plenty of cleavage before hugging tight and finishing at her knee, but rather than just a Saturday night out dress, the material used and the cut was exemplary. Then there was Paige. The dress – and it was a dress – stopped mid-thigh. There was a top part of the dress and there was a bottom part of the dress, but the stitching that ran throughout was incredibly charleston-esque, without the flapping. It was art deco gorgeousness with capped sleeves. It was both elegant and sophisticated and also not too bridesmaidy. It was different and somehow suited Paige wonderfully.

'You girls all look too beautiful for words.' The mums were sniffling again as Hollie and Jenny beamed.

'I can't believe you managed to find three different dresses that go together in such a short space of time,' Gail said.

Louisa and Sophie just grinned at each other. 'Teamwork, I guess. Oh and Paige, if you're OK with that dress we have found the perfect shoes to go with it so just leave that to us, OK?'

'Sure,' Paige mumbled. It was clear that she was out of her comfort zone but, to her credit, she didn't make a big deal of it and she didn't look like she was struggling.

'With dresses like these, you'll find your own husbands at the wedding for sure,' Gail said.

Paige rolled her eyes and grunted before walking back to the changing room.

'Don't need one. I could date myself in this dress. I am HOT.'

Mya started sashaying around the catwalk before grabbing Sophie. Feeling like a billion dollars herself, Polly joined in too as they danced in front of the mirrors.

Chapter Fifteen

Polly sighed. Unfortunately it was loud and her colleagues were giving her strange looks again. She hadn't slept well. It wasn't really all that surprising given the state her head was in. She really needed to get some things figured out and fast. By things, she knew she meant Darren. She liked Darren, and if she hadn't started pretending to be Bailey's girlfriend she strongly suspected that they could carry on as they had been doing. It might even have developed into something more serious, although that was unlikely given how little time they actually spent together. Polly sighed again as she realised even her thoughts had become past tense. They had met up last night, had some food and chilled, but then instead of staying over, she'd gone home, again. He wasn't impressed, but she didn't want to stay. Could she keep going until this thing with Bailey was finished and then really invest in Darren? Maybe she could tell him about her music? She shuddered. Not because she didn't want Darren to know but because she still really didn't want anyone to know.

Whatever was going on though, Polly performed. She needed to and at times of confusion, depression or anything icky, Polly needed it even more. Which would explain why she'd been researching a potential new gig venue. She needed to perform her music more than anything else. It superseded how she felt about Darren, Bailey, the wedding and work. She just wasn't sure she had the balls for somewhere new. But given the current state of things, she wasn't sure if she could pass it up. What's the worst that could happen? She'd lived through it before, she'd been heckled and booed. She could always stay at the Speakeasy. She wouldn't have to do it again if it went badly.

Picking up her phone, her instinct was to text Bailey and

ask him what he thought, but instead she switched to the website of the new bar and signed up before she lost her nerve. There. She'd done it. Tonight. It was happening. Once she did it she had to put her phone down as her hands were shaking and her stomach was in knots. Taking a breath and deciding to try and focus on work instead, she looked at the policy she was currently trying to update. The rumours of flings around the office, the extra work it was causing managers and the whole of the HR department, meant that the policy needed clarifying urgently. It was boring, and work that made her squirm slightly as she knew that at this moment in time it was aimed at people like her. She was having an inter-office romance. Of sorts. Even with the updated policy it still wasn't strictly forbidden. Plus the fact that no one knew, and that they didn't see each other at work, meant that she was all right. She knew she wasn't putting herself into any trouble but it was still tedious.

'Polly, can I have a word, please?'

Polly looked up at her boss Leanne, her stomach dropping. This sounded formal. Maybe Darren had let something slip. 'Sure, of course.'

'We'll just find a free meeting room.'

Polly followed as Leanne led the way to the meeting rooms, Polly ruminating about all the possible outcomes. She could get a warning, maybe a written warning. Probably not fired. Unless it had nothing to do with Darren and she'd messed something else up, like a contract or something. Polly waited until Leanne was sat before picking the chair on the corner of the table.

'How's the Relationship Policy coming along, Polly?'

Looking up, Polly tried not to squirm again, it wasn't actually called that but they all knew that that's what it was for. 'It's fine. It should be done by the end of tomorrow.'

Leanne moved in closer before lowering her voice. 'Between me and you, Polly, the sooner we have a new policy we can launch the better. I don't know what's going on at the moment but the rumour mill is in overdrive and I can't take another call from a manager wondering what to do about their staff. It's like they're all in heat.'

'Yeah,' Polly added, not sure of what else to say.

'So hopefully this will help. Then we can focus on the usual ineptitudes, and contracts and recruitment. In fact, that's what I wanted to talk to you about. I have heard from the Senior Management Team that they are looking to expand, so there's likely to be a massive intake. They've asked me to recommend someone to lead on it. That person would need to lead on the recruitment and then the training plan. I was thinking that this would be a perfect promotion opportunity for you. But keep it to yourself, for now, they've got to finalise some budgets. I just wanted you to know that I have you in mind.'

'Thanks.' Polly smiled but it was with effort and she wasn't sure if Leanne would be able to tell or not.

'Are you OK?'

'Yes fine, just didn't sleep well.' Polly smiled a little bit larger, and a lot more forced.

'Is everything alright?'

'Yes, yes, of course. Just a bad night, you know how it is.' Polly prayed to the gods of make-up and hoped that her foundation would cover the blush that would inevitably make its way to her face if she gave the real reason for why she hadn't slept well. The reason she was in a funk, and why her head was spinning. She'd had a sex dream about Bailey. She wasn't sure who it was at the start but when she saw his strong hands holding her inner thighs wide open, her legs on his tattooed shoulders, he looked up from between her legs, winked, grinned, licked his lips and gone to town, it was absolutely Bailey. Polly crossed her legs trying to quell the feeling that was building up as she remembered the vivid details, including the feeling of his trimmed beard on her—

'OK, great. Well, I should know more about the promotion next week. It would be temporary whilst the project is completed. You'll also have to manage a couple of members of staff and work closely with some of the accounts managers. But other than that I don't know much more. But, Polly, this really would be a great opportunity.' Leanne stood up and tucked her chair in. 'I'll keep you posted.'

'OK, thanks, Leanne. I really appreciate it.'

Leanne left the room and Polly waited a moment to process what had just happened. A promotion, that was wonderful, and managing a team was the only gap in her CV preventing her from being a senior manager in the future. This really was a fantastic opportunity. Polly looked down at her hands, one of which was currently twisting the watch on her wrist. Why did she feel so hollow? Shouldn't she be excited about the career progression?

'Hi, babe, I thought I saw you in here.'

Polly shot up, banging her hip into the table. 'Darren, what are you doing here?'

'I just had to nip and talk to someone in admin about something. Then I saw you, how could I resist saying hello?'

Polly was stunned. They didn't see each other at work and on the rare occasion they did accidentally bump into each other, they always played it cool. She rubbed her hip where she had banged it until she was even more stunned to find his lips on hers.

'Darren! Not here,' Polly whispered loudly, pushing him away.

'I missed you last night. Also how cool would it be to have sex on this conference table?'

'You're joking right?' Polly glared at him, before quickly looking around making sure that no one had seen them.

Darren grinned. 'Maybe.'

'We can't do this here and you know that. I'm writing a policy about this exact thing.'

'No one can see us. Besides we aren't even doing anything we're just talking. But alright, babe, I just wanted to come and say hi. Will I see you tonight?'

'Erm no, I can't do tonight sorry.'

'What are you doing this time?'

Polly was still processing how she felt about a life sentence of HR work, and how angry she felt about Darren kissing her in the conference room, which meant that her brain was ticking incredibly slowly and she was already taking too long to come up with a reason.

'I don't get to see you that much any more you're always out with your friends or seeing your family. Come on, please?'

'No, I can't sorry. I have to help my friend out with something tonight. Maybe tomorrow? Besides we have the sten next weekend, we'll have all weekend together.'

Polly watched as Darren studied her, she didn't like the look in his eye, it made her uncomfortable and she tried not to squirm.

'OK, sure.' He took out his phone and began typing something.

'Thanks, Darren.' Polly forced a smile and watched him as he started doing something on his phone as he left the meeting room. He didn't seem as bothered as she thought he would. She wasn't complaining, it made her life a little easier and anything that made her life easier at the moment was all good.

Chapter Sixteen

'Bailey help me I think I've made a mistake.'

The phone line was bad and Bailey couldn't be sure what he was hearing, but he walked towards the balcony doors in case it would improve the signal. 'Polly, calm down. What's the matter?'

'I've come to a new venue to gig at an Open Mic night. I'm freaking out.' Her voice was strained, but now easier to hear.

'You're going to be fine, Pol. You're an amazing performer. You have absolutely nothing to worry about. Where are you playing?' Bailey asked.

'It's a bar called the Three Barrels in town. It's just down the road from the Speakeasy but it might as well be on a different planet. I don't think I can do this.'

'Polly, listen. You don't have to, you can just go home. But I know that you can do this, alright? Everything's going to be fine,' Bailey assured her, whilst pacing the length of his balcony.

'I'm sorry, Bailey I shouldn't have bothered you. You're right. I'm overreacting. I'll get going, thanks, Bailey. See you soon.'

Polly signed off very quickly and Bailey was left battling his instincts. He hadn't seen her in a few days and he desperately wanted to go and see her, reassure her, and just be a supportive face in the crowd. Except, she had rocked his world again last night, albeit only in his dreams, and he was struggling to keep it, well not platonic, but keeping it fake. Just fake. Polly was an adult and she had been fine performing without him for years. She could do this and had done this many times before, without his mug staring up at her. Except then he remembered that no one else knew and she would be all alone. He stopped pacing, toying with the idea of getting his car keys. Saved from any further discussion his phone rang again, without looking Bailey picked it straight up.

'Look, Pol, you're going to be fine, don't worry. Do you want me to come over?'

'Why what's wrong with Polly? Is she OK?' Whoops, not Polly.

'Oh, hi, Mum. Sorry I didn't look at my phone. How are you? Is everything alright? I wanted to ask how the first day of treatment went but didn't know if you would be in bed.'

'I'm a little tired, but they've told me that I won't feel really bad until day three or four, and maybe not at all until later chemo rounds. So Billy and I were at a loose end and thought that we might go for a drive. I want to do something before I'm too sick to do anything, you know? But come on, I'm worried about Polly now. What is it?'

'Well, she's decided to try and perform at an Open Mic night that she hasn't performed at before and she's freaking out. But she'll be OK.' Bailey sighed.

'Why aren't you there?'

Bailey hesitated. Truthfully he hadn't known she was going to do it. He probably would've done if he'd texted her, but he'd been trying to put a little bit of recovery space between them. It wasn't working and now he was worried he'd let her down. What a backfire.

'Well…' Bailey stalled.

'Do you think she'd mind if we went?' Denise asked.

'What?'

'Were you not listening. This would be a perfect night out. You know how much I love music, I can't drink but I can enjoy the atmosphere. Who knows I might even have a little sing for old times' sake. But if you think Polly would hate it, then obviously we won't.'

Bailey thought for a minute, his heart bursting with love as his stomach burnt with guilt. If Polly really was his girlfriend, he would love so much for his family to love her too and with what his mum was suggesting, he knew they were already well on their way.

'We can sit in the back and hide. Then we can see how she reacts to you. If she's outraged that you're there we can sneak out. I'd love it, and I'd love to see her perform and it sounds like she could do with some people cheering for her.'

'Erm.' He wasn't sure he was going to be able to stop her, and he couldn't think of anything quickly enough.

'OK, so it's settled. Text Billy the address and I'll just get changed. We'll see you there in about forty minutes.'

Bailey's phone beeped in his ear. Stunned he looked down at it. So that really just happened? Looks like he was going after all. Unable to stop himself, he grinned. His head and his heart both happy with the decision that had been made for him, he rushed to get ready. Who was he kidding he had wanted to be there all along. He was maybe just a tiny bit peeved that she hadn't told him in the first place. But who's fault was that? He hadn't texted her and there was that little thing about them not actually being girlfriend and boyfriend.

'Oh, hi. That was good timing, shall we go in? It's bloody freezing out here.'

Denise was right, the weather had certainly not realised that spring was overdue, the wind freezing and the rain always ready to drop.

Bailey leaned down and kissed his mum on the cheek and gave Billy a quick hug.

'You alright, lad?' Billy asked.

'All good, Billy. Come on then, let's go in.'

Bailey held the door open and let Billy and his mum walk through. The pub itself was quite big, but a little generic. It wasn't one that he had been too before, but he knew the layout as he figured it was part of a chain. There were a group of people at the back that were drinking heavily and talking loudly. The stage at the front was fit for purpose with a small keyboard and a microphone. It would work for Open Mic night, but then it would also work for karaoke and DJs. It lacked any character, especially when you compared it to the Speakeasy and Barbarella. If he were honest, it was a place for cheap-ish beer, probably a curry night on a Wednesday. This was a cheap meet-up pub, but not the sort of place you want to hang in all night. Billy nodded towards a small round table at the side. There were a number of empty tables to choose from. The table that Billy had chosen meant that they could see the stage but they wouldn't be in the eyeline of the performers. Bailey had been searching the bar for Polly since the second they got here but he hadn't seen her yet.

'What you drinking, Bailey?'

'Oh, just a Coke, please.'

Billy nodded and headed off to the bar that ran along the sidewall nearer the entrance.

'Can you see her?' Denise asked.

'No.' He hadn't spotted Polly but he had spotted a man with a clipboard. His limited experience of Open Mic nights would suggest that he was the one organising the event and so Bailey made his way over.

'Hi, pal, is there a Miss Polly on your list to play tonight?'

'Yeah, why?'

'Just checking, she said she was coming but I couldn't see her. Thought I might have missed her,' Bailey said.

'She's on third.'

'Cheers.' Bailey walked back over to his family, the owner or organiser or whoever the hell he was, giving him the stink eye. Bailey got the distinct impression that this bloke did not get any level of job satisfaction. Bailey looked around again when he got back to his table, his worry escalating. If this was the Speakeasy she would be at her table surrounded by allies and comrades. The guys on the table at the back were getting louder and louder, there were a small number of limited supporters, and he suspected that all of those were also performers, of which there were about five in total.

'Erm, hi, everyone. First on the line-up tonight we have Ziggy.'

Wow that was a warm intro, thought Bailey, as the clipboard with attitude got off the stage and headed back to the bar, the resulting applause far from deafening. Ziggy took to the stage and sang his heart out to his namesake. Bailey kept an eye on the crowd. Ziggy wasn't at all bad and had obviously done this a few times before, and he didn't let the lack of audience participation slow him down. What that effect would have on Polly though he wasn't sure. His worry increasing he took out his phone and sent her a quick text.

Bailey: Pol you ok? x

He waited, studying his phone to see if she was going to read it, yep there it is.

The three dots stopping and starting but without receiving a message back. Deciding enough was enough he got out of his seat and walked through the crowd towards the ladies. Poking his head in he saw that it was mercifully quiet and before anyone stopped him he walked in properly and saw Polly at the sink.

'Pol, what you doing hiding in here?'

Polly shrieked. 'Bailey what are you doing here? This is the ladies, you know.'

Bailey studied Polly, she wasn't crying but her eyes were tight and her hands were knotted, her wrist red where she had been playing with her watch. Before he had a chance to do anything else she had launched herself at him and was in his arms. He pulled her close as her arms were tight around his neck. Resting his chin gently on her head, he stroked her back. He surreptitiously smelt her hair and felt his body relax, knowing intuitively that despite his early doubts he was precisely where he needed to be. After a minute Polly pulled back. 'Sorry, Bailey, I really needed that, but how did you know?'

'You were hardly cryptic, Pol. You said you needed my help and here I am.'

'Did you see Ziggy? Did you see the audience? They're going to heckle. They don't mind a song they can sing along to but an original composition? I don't think I can do this. I want to but I just don't know.'

'Come on.' Bailey took her hand and led her out of the toilets. Once out in the pub, they watched the second performer as she battled out 'Tiny Dancer'. When she finished there was a polite smattering of applause. He looked at his mum and Billy and saw that they were the only ones that clapped earnestly.

Polly squeezed his hand, and he pulled her into a hug again, this time bending down and whispering in her ear, 'If you want to do this, I know you can. I'll cheer you on so loudly you won't care if anyone else is. If you don't, I'll drive you home and we can try another one another time. It's your call, Pol.'

Leaning up Polly kissed his cheek. Before he could turn to capture her lips with his own, Polly had already straightened. 'You're the best, Bailey. Thank you.'

'OK, guys, next we have Miss Polly.'

'Hardly a big introduction, do you think he would rather be doing absolutely anything else in the world right now?' Bailey murmured.

Polly laughed and began the short walk to the stage. Bailey waited until she was settled at the keyboard and played the first few notes before he took his seat with his mum and Billy.

'She's absolutely amazing. Has she written this song?' Billy asked.

Bailey nodded his eyes focused ahead. As he watched, Polly closed her eyes, losing herself in the music like she always did. He felt his own blood pressure lower in response.

'Do you think she might let me sing it at some point?' Denise asked as she gently swayed to the rhythm.

'You'd have to ask her,' Bailey said, unable to take his eyes away from the stage, but seething that the gang at the back still hadn't shut up.

'Does she know that you can play the piano too?' Denise asked.

'No, why? I would hardly call what I do "playing".'

'No child of mine was going to go through life without the joy of music. You should tell her you can play.'

'Hmmm.' There was no way. It would be like Bailey telling Picasso that like him he could paint, because one time he put paint on paper, absolutely not comparable.

Bailey continued to study Polly, his heart in his mouth, just hoping that she would get the reception she deserved. As she hit the last note, he didn't have time to stand up and be the loudest member of the audience, as his mum and Billy beat him to it. Smiling at them, he got up and walked over to where he was stood before, so that Polly could find him easier, clapping and cheering as he went.

Polly nodded in thanks and quickly got off the stage. He saw her search for him and when she spotted him she sped towards him, her lips turning up, in a smile just for him. She didn't hesitate as she pulled his face down to hers and kissed him. It started off as a small thank you kiss, that was borderline platonic. Then it became a PDA. Then it was borderline NSFW. He held her lower back as he pressed her closer, making sure that he could feel every inch of her against him. The fact that they were back in the quiet corner near the toilets their only saving grace, but certainly not invisible and his mum was bound to see them. He hadn't realised that Polly had spotted them but that was obviously why she was kissing the bejesus out of him now. With that realisation he slowed them down until they were still close, sharing breath but no longer kissing.

'Thank you, Bailey,' Polly said breathlessly.

'Don't mention it.' Bailey winked and held her hand as he brought her over to the table his family was sat at.

'Polly you were amazing. My God that song was fantastic. Do you think you might let me sing it at some point? You have some serious talent, lady, come here.'

Bailey watched as Polly stuttered, her step faltering before she quickly gathered herself and returned Denise's hug.

'Hi, Denise, Hi, Billy. I had no idea you were here. Oh God, I'm embarrassed now.'

Bailey watched unsure if she was genuine or not. If she hadn't known they were here then the kiss…

'You have nothing to be embarrassed about, sweetheart. Neither the song nor the way you pounced on my son.'

Bailey grinned as Polly went redder and redder.

'It's OK, babe. I'm irresistible I know.' He put his arm around her and bent down to kiss and nibble her neck, taking full advantage of the fact he could pretend for the next hour or so. He was just debating with himself how far he could take it before Polly elbowed him in his ribs.

'Thank you for coming. I, erm, apart from Bailey, no one I know has ever heard me perform.'

'You cannot keep this talent a secret, Polly. You are amazing. I'm not just saying that. You really are something special.' Denise was beaming.

'Thanks, Denise. Can I get you all a drink?'

'That's OK, Pol. I'll get you one. What would you like?' Billy stood up.

'A white wine, please, Billy.'

'I'll make it a large, yeah?'

Polly nodded.

Chapter Seventeen

Taking her maid of honour duties seriously, Polly had taken the Friday off work to make sure she was the first at the farmhouse they'd rented for the sten. Mya was currently in the not-working stage of her career, whatever the hell that meant, and was currently decorating the house in the appropriate attire which consisted mostly of cocks. Cocks of various shapes and sizes in banners, balloons and paper on every available surface. Standard. Sophie and Paige were due to turn up soon. Paige was having a minor heart attack about leaving the bar and Mr Higgins to Clare, India, Belle, and the rest of the team for a full weekend. Sophie, meanwhile, was finishing off a meeting with the companies that were providing some of the sponsorship both for the sten and also for the wedding.

Sophie had been very clear that the wedding itself wasn't going to be broadcast, but she knew that her followers not only wanted, but also in some small way deserved, to be a part of her big day. So the photographer was sponsored, and she would be releasing some of the images from the wedding on the day, and some of the suppliers, like the room decorators, were sponsored so that parts of the evening do could be shared, but Sophie was adamant that that would be it. It meant that her fans would be happy, and despite several celebrity magazines approaching for exclusives, Sophie was happy to be giving the exclusives straight to her fans.

'Surely that's more than enough cocks?' Polly asked with a smirk.

'Can there ever be enough?' Mya asked as she artfully arranged the cock straws within a vase. 'Speaking of, what time are the boys rocking up, and are there going to be any hotties?'

'They're coming up in one car. Obviously there's Bailey and Marcus. Then Euan, Smithy and Calvin. I think Bailey said they would be here for about six, then it's a quick get ready before going out for a meal, or a huge takeaway. Oh, and, of course, Darren should be getting here around then too. Apparently, he had some big meetings at work so couldn't get here before then,' Polly explained.

'Is Calvin the gorgeous one?' Mya flicked her long nearly black hair over her shoulder, her trademark move.

'If you mean is he the one that they went to school with, who is tall, athletic, an ex-professional tennis player and now a chiropractor, then yes.'

'Hmmm.' Mya had a faraway look in her eyes that wasn't difficult to interpret. Poor Calvin didn't really stand a chance.

'Who are the other two?' Mya asked as she continued to move cocks about the place.

'Euan I think used to be a labourer for Dad back in the day so I guess an ex-workmate, and Smithy has been around for ages. He travels a lot, nobody really knows what he does, but apparently they hang out whenever he's around. He's mysterious, like you Mya.'

'Is that it? Is anyone else coming?' Mya asked.

Polly shook her head before looking outside as the sky darkened. 'I'm thinking takeaway tonight instead of going out. Let's all get drunk. It will be like a house party.'

'Girls! We're here!'

Polly ran to the front door, hugging Sophie and then Paige as they stepped over the threshold.

'I'm so excited. Happy sten do!' Mya screamed as they came inside.

'Wow, this place looks amazing,' Sophie said awestruck, possibly at the number of cocks adorning the farmhouse.

'Yep, your contacts at the cottage website thing have really pulled out all the stops. They've even supplied us with some nibbles, a hot tub, and a wine fridge full of Prosecco!' Polly offered.

'Oh my God, that sounds amazing. Shall we do a live video now before it gets too wild? Would that be OK? Show me around first though. I want to see everything. Then I reckon we should take over the hot tub before everyone else arrives!'

As the girls started to show Sophie and Paige the frankly gorgeous farmhouse, Polly couldn't shift the slightly unsettled feeling she had in her stomach, the vines present and curling viciously. She was a little bit nauseous, but with everything that she had going on she wasn't sure what it was particularly that left her feeling that way, but her wrist was starting to get sore from where she had been twiddling her watch all day.

'So there are four double bedrooms, and one double pull out sofa. Two huge reception rooms, the best kitchen I have ever seen, with another eating area and sofas, then an extra dining room and bi-fold doors that show you all of this.'

Mya led them through the kitchen and out through the bi-fold doors that overlooked the amazing scenery outside. The view was extraordinary, despite only being an hour from Manchester, you would be forgiven for thinking that you were in the middle of the deepest countryside. The vista in front was of a plateau of various browns and the hint of green as spring made itself known. The trees desperately trying to grow new leaves, the hills a bumpy patchwork with a hodgepodge of spring colours, and all that could be heard was the sound of the birds and assorted wildlife living their best life. Given that it had been raining just a little before, the smell of freshly watered earth was everywhere.

Almost without thought, they all stood there quietly taking it all in whilst breathing deeply. Polly would like to say that she could feel her anxiety lessen, but until this sten was underway, or maybe not even until it was over, did she think the twisting vines in her gut were likely to disappear.

'Right let's crack open the first bottle of Prosecco then, girls. Let the sten begin,' Sophie announced as she marched back into the kitchen, and with the pop of the cork, the sten weekend was officially underway.

'OK, I've ordered the takeaway. Should be here in forty minutes.'

Polly was being very responsible. Bailey hadn't seen her drink that much, certainly not compared to everyone else. She seemed, to Bailey at least, happily keeping an eye, making sure everyone was having a good time.

Marcus, Euan and Smithy were all stood chatting and Bailey was starting to feel a little soppy, all of his favourite people were together in one room and all merry, all relaxed. He walked over to his best mate and punched him on his arm. Marcus retaliated by dragging him into a hug.

'Thanks for organising a great sten, pal. You're the best.'

'It wasn't just me,' Bailey mumbled into Marcus's shoulder.

'Oh yeah. Polly get over here.'

Still holding Bailey with one arm, Bailey watched as he threw his other arm around Polly bringing her into a hug. Polly moved so that, in a tight circle now, one arm could go around her brother's waist, the other around his. They grinned at each other only inches apart. They hadn't really gone into the specific plans for the evening but ultimately it was the sten, and they had agreed that they needed to get the bride and groom pretty steaming. Not blotto but certainly the level of drunk where they were soppy-happy. Achievement unlocked.

'What's the group hug for?' Sophie asked as she walked towards them.

'I'm thanking our organisers.' Marcus smiled.

'Oh well in that case. Thanks, guys, I love you.' Sophie stepped in and threw her arms around Bailey and Polly.

Sophie and Marcus being ever so slightly tipsy hugged even tighter pressing Polly closer to his own chest until he could feel her body against his. Clenching his jaw until the hug was over he quickly glanced at Polly. She was blushing and, if he had to hazard a guess, she was maybe avoiding his eye contact.

Suddenly Polly squealed and Bailey noticed that someone had swept her up into an embrace.

Presumably Darren.

He had no idea when Darren got here, and no idea how long he had been watching, but if Bailey had to guess, he was making short work of marking his territory. Hugging and kissing Polly, but looking up occasionally to make sure that everyone was watching. It made his brain itch and his fist clench. Marcus caught his eye and raised his eyebrow. Non-verbally saying, 'Who the hell does this guy think he is?' Bailey shrugged. It helped to know that it wasn't just him and his overzealous reactions when it came to Polly. Trying to not watch but looking out of the corner of his eye he saw Polly pull away.

'Oh hey, you're here,' Polly said as Bailey tried and failed not to examine her response.

'Hi, all. Looks like you're having a great time already. I bought drinks.' Reaching down into his possibly designer duffle bag Bailey watched as Darren emerged with Dom Pérignon and what looked to be Tequila. Bailey appreciated that the bloke was trying to make an effort. That was all the courtesy Bailey had in him to extend because whether Darren knew it or not, he was preventing Polly from being able to choose him. Bailey decided to be the better man and, in order to keep the party going, he was just going to stay away from him as much as possible. Well, he would if—

'Bailey, this is Darren.'

Shit, Plan B it is then. The look in Darren's eyes was the same he'd seen in many a bar, his misbegotten youth having put him in front of a disgruntled boyfriend or two. It was the very quick up and down, the slight curl in his lips. Darren was clearly assessing how much of a threat he was. Ordinarily, Bailey would steer clear of any situation like this. It was usually his cue to move on and look for someone or something else. Not because he couldn't stand up to the scrutiny, more because he couldn't be arsed with it. It was a waste of his, and everyone else's time. However he felt compelled on this one occasion to stick it out so he may have straightened up to his full height, his chest maybe just a little more extended, and the friendliness in his eyes may have left just for a moment so that Darren could see the viable threat that was just underneath. Just for a second. He quickly glanced at Polly and saw she was looking at her feet. He took a breath. For her, he would calm it down. For her, he could play the friendly mate. For her, only for her, he forced his body to relax back into neutral, not really sure what had just got into him, and extended his hand. 'How's it going, dude. I've heard loads about you. Welcome to the group. It's going to be a great weekend.'

Darren took the hand, and squeezed. 'Thanks, bro. I'm looking forward to it.'

Bailey returned the handshake, casting another quick glance at Polly to serve as a reminder not to break Darren's fingers. Jesus, he had been having so much fun, and now he felt a possessive streak that he'd never before experienced, and his mood was quickly diving.

There was an awkward moment. Maybe two.

'Well, let's get you a drink, shall we? The food should be here soon,' Bailey said, tapping into his safety persona of charm and wit.

'Can I just grab a Coke for now?'

'Sure, come with me, we'll see what we can find.' He threw his arm over Darren's slightly smaller shoulders, and led him towards the kitchen, but not without turning back to wink at

Polly. Her face relaxed before she grinned. She'd clearly been worried about their meeting, and Bailey knew that playing nice was the best thing to do, and he could and would do that for her.

Chapter Eighteen

Oh God, that was so awkward. She'd been dreading Bailey and Darren meeting. Besides a small moment, where she nearly ducked to avoid the spray of testosterone that was thrown around the room, it had gone OK since. Darren and Bailey had actually chatted to each other a few times. It made Polly a little uncomfortable. She didn't have to look too hard to figure out why. It wasn't that she was hoping they would fall out because, let's face it, it would be a rubbish sten if they did, but their getting on made her feel sick too. Like somehow they would have some sort of secret conversation that would spill out Polly's innermost thoughts.

Confronted with both of them side by side, Polly had to concede that the main reason she felt sick was because she knew that Darren wouldn't stack up against Bailey. Facing the both of them she knew which of the two she was drawn to – and it wasn't the one it should have been, which meant only one thing. She was going to have to split up with Darren. Balls. She'd need to ask Mya for some advice, but the whole topic felt in woefully poor taste on a sten. It would have to wait until the weekend was over. It wasn't that she necessarily wanted to be with Bailey – OK who was she kidding – but for the main part she acknowledged that quite simply she didn't have the same level of feelings for Darren. Now that she knew that, she knew it wasn't fair to carry on. She looked over at him, watching as he messed with his phone and took a selfie. She turned back round to Bailey, and she knew it was over with Darren.

Taking a deep breath that reached the bottom of her lungs, she noticed that her heart was lighter at having finally come to her truth. It soon weighed heavy again, however, as she contemplated what the rest of the weekend was going to be like, the vines that had been winding their way across her stomach were now making their way up to her throat.

Taking another sip of Prosecco, she forced it down and glanced around the room, trying to take her mind off her internal reckoning. They were all sat at the huge dining table: Darren was sat next to her twiddling with his e-cigarette, Mya having told him point-blank he couldn't vape in the house. Euan was on his other side and on Polly's other side sat Sophie, with the cock centrepiece on her head like a crown, and then Marcus. Paige sat at the head, presumably so that she could watch everyone, as was her want. The other side of the prawn crackers sat Calvin, Bailey, and then Smithy at the other end. There was something weird about the way Mya was sat, yes she was giving the eyes and chatting to the incredibly athletically handsome and absolutely Mya's type Calvin, but it was more like she was staying away from Smithy. Polly looked over at Paige and could see she was watching the interactions with interest too. Looking back towards the other end of the table she caught Bailey's eye. He subtly winked at her before joining the conversation with Calvin and Smithy.

It was getting late when the last of the food had been removed and Paige pulled out Cards Against Humanity, the Mr and Mrs games already done. Polly knew things were about to get much more drunken, and dark, very dark. Deciding to keep her head she switched to soft drinks. It was several rounds later that Darren, letting his competitive side get the better of him, started to get annoyed playing a game where it's all about dark humour rather than ability. In the lead were Mya and Bailey, which surprised no one.

She watched as Darren still hadn't won a hand, and it seemed like he was starting to change, his pleasant demeanor disappearing. He was getting a little snappy, and a little cocky in conversation. She wasn't sure many other people had noticed, but this was not like the Darren Polly was used to seeing, but it felt a little bit truer, or maybe it just helped her to feel better about her decision to finish things with him. She couldn't be sure but it was certainly revealing. Paige always said if you wanted to know someone play Cards Against Humanity with them and she was right – oh and to go to an all you can eat buffet with them. If the sight and sound of someone eating ribs doesn't make you feel ill, you're apparently on a good footing for a serious relationship, according to Paige at least. She'd tried to watch Bailey eating before, but watching him lick his fingers clean had been more than enough to know that what she felt was far, far from revulsion.

Heating up at the memory of his long fingers Polly sipped her Coke, knowing it had been a wise decision to move to soft drinks. She didn't want to feel like death tomorrow, she had to keep everyone in check, and she noticed that Bailey had done the same. She looked at Darren and only then did she realise that he hadn't drunk all night.

'Oh, this is going to have to be the last one, guys. My gorgeous wife-to-be has just fallen asleep on my shoulder.' Everyone laughed as Marcus pointed out a drool spot on his shirt. Sophie opened her eyes.

'I der not.' Sophie smiled, well she tried to, but her eyes weren't managing to stay open.

'OK bedtime, my beauty. Let's go.' Marcus stood her up.

'Pol, der I tell ya 'bout break—'

'Yes, you told me that there was going to be a complimentary drop off of coffee and croissants. Don't worry it's all under control. Here take this.' Polly reached over to the non-alcohol fridge and passed a bottle of water.

'Thanks, Pol. Love you.' Sophie blew a kiss, at least that's what it seemed like she was doing, really she just slapped her own face. 'Ow.'

'Night, Soph, see you in the morning.' Polly laughed.

Sitting back down, the game finished, Mya was unsurprisingly declared the winner. Smithy said something that Polly couldn't pick up and Mya scowled briefly before announcing that she was going to bed. Paige followed. Euan and Smithy set off to their room.

'Calvin, you and I are on the sofa bed, sorry.' Bailey nodded towards the lounge.

'That's fine, although looking at the size of the sofas I'm just going to drop onto one of those,' Cal suggested as he set off towards his 'bed'.

'Works for me, saves making the bed.' Bailey shrugged.

Bailey grabbed some glasses and put them on the counter near the dishwasher. 'OK, well I'm going to the bathroom, I'll help clean up in a minute.'

Polly had been listening to the conversations around her as she began clearing away the rubbish. Hearing Darren's voice, Polly tried not to jump. 'Pol, I'll meet you in our room, yeah?'

For one brief moment she had sort of forgotten Darren. She quickly nodded and watched as he all but ran into their room. She did not welcome the prospect of sleeping in a bed with a man she was planning on dumping once the weekend was over. Sten or not she really needed to get some pointers from Mya. It had been a while since she had been the dumpee but Mya was more practiced in the kicking out routine.

Polly took her time clearing stuff away and loading the dishwasher. There wasn't that much to do really as they had been clearing up regularly throughout the night. Just as the last of the stuff went in the dishwasher, and Polly was wiping down the surfaces, Bailey emerged.

'How you doing?' Bailey asked, leaning his hip on the counter next to her.

'I think we're doing great, what do you think?' Polly asked as she straightened.

'I think we make an awesome team but then we knew that already.' Bailey grinned and before she knew what was happening she was leaning in, edging closer, her eyes on his lips, before an overly polite cough had Polly jump away.

'Just came to get some water,' was all Paige said, but the look on her face was inscrutable.

'Sure, night.' Polly quickly walked away.

Walking towards the bedroom, Polly felt sick. At least she knew sex wasn't on the table, as it were, it was far too full a house to get away with that – she hoped. Well, she wasn't anyway. There was no way she was having sex with a man she was about to dump. She realised then that they hadn't actually had sex for weeks, and in hindsight Polly realised that she had been coming up with excuses for a while.

Still, the vines coursing through her stomach and up her throat had also shot downwards tangling her feet into the floor, making it incredibly difficult for her to keep walking. Taking a deep breath preparing herself she tapped on the door before opening it. She stood for a second surveying what was happening in front of her.

'Work has called. I have to go. I'm so sorry, Pol. I'll make it up to you, I promise.'

Darren, duffle bag in hand, strode past her towards the front room, where Bailey and Calvin had been arranging their duvets on the sofas whilst chatting with Paige, all now paused watching the interaction between Polly and Darren.

'What do you mean work has called? Have you seen the time?' It was nearly two in the morning. There was no way it was work, if indeed there had been a call.

'I know, it's more that they're going to need me first thing so I need to get back now and prepare.' He kissed her cheek. 'Sorry, Pol. Have a great weekend.'

Polly stood still as the door closed. What the hell? There was no way that work had called at this time and told him he was needed. There was no way they would need him in the middle of the night, or first thing Saturday morning. Her alcohol-infused brain slowly caught up with the lifesaver she'd just been thrown, her mood quickly shifting from pissed to relieved, the vines that had been running throughout her body immediately starting to shrivel and loosen.

Suddenly, the earthy spice scent of the remnants of Bailey's aftershave was around her as he pulled her into a hug. That smell alone was enough to directly impact her reasoning. His arms wrapping around her tight, his face next to hers as he whispered in her ear.

'I'm sorry, Pol. That really sucks.'

Bailey must have assumed she was sad about him going. She wasn't. Not really. It just meant that she didn't have to be awkward with him for the weekend, she could just be herself. She was biting back a smile at the position she now found herself in, both mentally and physically. She reluctantly pulled away but not before giving in and stroking the width of his back through his T-shirt.

'Don't worry, Bailey. It's fine.'

He still had his hands covering her shoulders. His eyelashes ridiculously long at this angle as she looked up at him. 'Are you sure, Pol?'

'Absolutely. Night, guys.' With that Polly untangled herself and walked into her room, got into her pyjamas and star-fished in the bed, and sighed. She couldn't deny that she was happy that Darren wasn't there. The vines all but disappeared now, she realised with a start that Darren was the issue that had her worrying about the entire weekend. Now that wasn't going to be a problem. She knew that whatever it was that had called him away, and she strongly suspected it wasn't work, would call him away for the entire weekend. Now she was able to enjoy her weekend relatively guilt-free. But the biggest thing was the realisation that she knew what she needed to do in order to be happy. In some ways, she couldn't wait for Monday to come round so that she could get on with her life. Taking a deep breath she felt her lungs open wider than they had in ages, she almost felt like she could sing.

* * *

Calvin was already snoring as Bailey walked with Paige back towards the kitchen.

'Bailey,' whispered Paige.

'Yeah?'

He watched her face closely as she stopped. 'Can I ask you a question?'

'You don't normally ask permission,' Bailey said.

'Why aren't you with Polly?'

Bailey spluttered. 'What, why on earth—?'

'Bailey, cut the crap. You can be honest with me. Is it because of Marcus?'

Bailey's mouth was still open. He was torn with how to answer that question. He was used to brushing it off and not really taking himself seriously and used to other people not really taking him seriously either. Now he knew he had a choice, he could come clean and lay it all on the line, or he could carry on with his secret feelings, carry on with his half-life, where everything was kept just far enough away so as to not directly reach him. He could put on his mask, his persona that kept everything contained and allowed people not to worry. Or, he could acknowledge what was happening. Knowing Paige she'd already know everything in his head anyway.

'I'm sorry. I didn't mean to make you feel awkward.'

'I've been in love with her for about two years, probably longer. At first, I figured it would pass, but it didn't. Then I figured out that I had to work on myself, get my shit together. Then the timings just never worked I guess.'

There. He'd done it. It was all out there now. It was impossible to take that back. He'd uttered his truth out into the world. His heart settled comfortably in his chest, happily in place knowing that what was spoken was the undeniable truth.

'Hmmm, I see. I'll give it some thought. Night, Bailey.' Paige gave him a quick hug before walking towards her bedroom, and Bailey grabbed a drink of water before making his way back to the sofa, a small smile never leaving his face. He knew that nothing had changed on the surface but underneath he felt a shifting, like the fates had heard his desires and were now running around looking for ways to make it happen.

Chapter Nineteen

'OK, Sophie, are you ready for your next surprise?' Polly was slowly guiding her down the corridor, the rest of the girls following.

'YES!' squealed Sophie, her eyes hidden behind a blindfold as she was led unknowingly into a dance studio. They'd just got out of a limo after a ten-minute drive, which had seen Sophie screaming and shouting out of the sunroof. Before that had been the cocktail making, then a light lunch with loads of Prosecco, followed by the life drawing class, and they were all a little bit tipsy, hence the screaming out of the sunroof. It was now time for the final activity before they met with the boys and continued the drinking and eating at the nightclub. They'd gotten booths in the VIP section, and, apart from the threat of karaoke later, it was going brilliantly so far. Now that most of the planning and prep was done, and especially now that Darren was no longer around, Polly felt like she could really let her hair down. Not to mention how she felt mentally. The decisions she had made meant that she felt nearly weightless and fizzy with happiness, both experienced and potential. As long as she didn't think about the prospect of dumping Darren.

The music started, Polly recognised it as 'I am a Good Girl' from *Burlesque*. The gorgeous, slow but heavy sounds of horns and saxophone, creating a deliciously naughty, slow, and sexy seduction. The dance space was kitted out with six chairs a wall of mirrors and soft red velvet curtains everywhere else.

'Oh my God,' Sophie squealed again as Mya removed the blindfold.

'Hi, everyone, I am Cherie De Lune. Welcome to burlesque.'

And with that, the girls watched stunned as the music got louder and Cherie went into a full burlesque routine. She had on a gorgeous sequinned bodice that was full-on rhinestone on baby doll blue satin. She had ruffled panties in the same colour, gloves that went up to her elbow, which she was now slowly taking off in time with the music. Polly couldn't be sure that she wasn't in love, a quick glance at the rest of the girls and they were all in the same state of adoration that she was. Cherie was stunning, her blonde hair pinned up in a retro style similar to Dita Von Teese. Her make-up sparkly, with dark eyeliner. She had a wonderfully curved figure that was being teasingly revealed inch by torturous inch. Polly had never really thought about it before but realised that she could be turned on by women, or at least by Cherie. As the music continued, she slowly removed the bodice, dropping it first from one arm and then the other, showing her back and hiding from view the front of her, until she turned, perfectly in time with the music stopping to reveal gorgeous Cherie in nothing but French panties and nipple tassels. She grinned and everyone applauded as the music stopped.

'Thanks, ladies. Now I don't want anyone feeling self-conscious, you might not be able to dance like that on your first try. Today is just a quick taster, but by the end of the session, we will have some sort of a routine between us. Whilst you might think it's about slowly stripping off to the music, there is so much more about burlesque. The most important thing I want you to feel today is that you're doing this for you. No one else. Even if you're a professional performing in front of hundreds or thousands. Burlesque is for you, for you to feel hot and sexy and fierce. OK, which one of you is Polly?'

Polly stepped forward, hand raised.

'Did you get my instructions about wardrobe?'

'Yes. Hi. I did.' Polly felt like she was stuttering a bit, she was still a little hot, and the idea that she might even look a tenth as hot as Cherie gave her a tight, fiery sensation that travelled around her body.

'OK, you can all get changed in there. Just come out when you're ready. I'll get everything set up in here. Oh, I'm going to lock the door and close the curtain but if you need to go at any point you can do.'

'OK, thanks, Cherie,' Polly said as they all went to the back of the studio where they eventually found a gap in the curtains that once opened revealed a small space to change in.

'Oh my God.' Mya fanned herself.

'Right? I mean it's not just me, is it? She's seriously gorgeous?' Polly asked.

'No, it's not just you,' Paige said, with a grin.

Polly rolled her eyes smiling.

'Anyway. OK, Sophie, here's what you need to wear for this.' Polly opened the bag at her side and pulled out a black leotard, black tights and high heels. 'You'll need this, this and oh these.' Polly threw the nipple tassels at her.

'I'm not wearing those!' Sophie looked surprisingly scandalised, and Polly couldn't help but laugh.

'Why not? I've been wearing mine all day.' Mya lifted her T-shirt and flashed everyone.

'Oh my God.' Polly laughed, shaking her head.

'Yep. Apart from getting stuck in my T-shirt occasionally, they're not too bad. It's quite nice not wearing a bra either.'

'Polly, have you got nipple tassels for everyone?' Sophie asked.

'Afraid not. I only got some for you. I didn't count on Mya already having some of her own. Oh hang on, is that what you do for a living? Travelling the world burlesquing everywhere? Is that why you have your own nipple tassels?' Polly asked eagerly.

'You're going to be so upset when you find out I'm just an accountant,' Mya pointed out, pulling her T-shirt back down.

'*What?*' Polly's head moved so fast to look at Mya that she nearly pulled something.

'No, Pol. I'm not an accountant, nor am I a burlesquer,' Mya said, rolling her eyes.

'How do I know you're telling me the truth?'

'You don't and you never will. Ha!' Mya grinned and straightened her T-shirt.

'Grrr. OK, well, let's just get ready. Come on,' Polly said.

They all got ready in their black leotards, tights and heels or, in the case of Paige, black Converse, leggings and T-shirt, and made their way back to the hall.

The sound of the heels clipping on the wooden floor, and the squeak of the Converse was the only noise as they made their way over to a slightly more clothed Cherie. She was wearing the same as them, black leotard with tights and heels.

'OK, ladies, there are a few basic moves in burlesque that we are going to do today. The main thing is that every move is done deliberately and slowly with as much rhythm as possible. Those of you that are naturally rhythmic might have an advantage. But don't worry if you're not because there are some moves that you can add that will look like you have rhythm even if you don't. So, first things first, take a seat. Second, if you have your hair tied back, don't, and lastly underneath each chair is a pair of opera gloves, put them on.'

After ninety minutes of intensive burlesque training, Polly couldn't stop grinning from ear to ear. 'Every single girl in the world should do burlesque. I've never been so in love with myself, I feel like such a hottie right now,' Polly said.

'You were so good though, Polly. All your gorgeous red hair flying about everywhere, and you just nailed it with the music. You should find somewhere local and keep practising.' Sophie was practically skipping down the road as they made their way through the dark and thankfully dry night to get to the nightclub, their old clothes safely back at the farmhouse, where they had stopped to get ready sans boys.

'You definitely have lots of rhythm, Polly,' Paige said, with a small smile, her stare piercing.

'OK, come on then, more drinks and snacks and let's find the boys. Fingers crossed they all made it in one piece.'

Walking into the nightclub, Polly felt invincible. As great as she felt before, now she felt empowered, confident, and damn right sexy. She had on her tailored black shorts and knee-high boots, matched with her green sparkly halter top. Polly had decided as her back was bare that she would go braless. She blamed the burlesque as she felt sexy as sin and it was amazing. Sophie even had time to do her make-up for her. They'd all been drinking whilst getting ready, and it was safe to say they all strutted into the nightclub. She may have leaned in a little closer than was necessary as she whispered in the bouncer's ear that they were on the VIP list. Polly imagined that this was how Mya felt all the time.

Following the bouncer in the dark of the nightclub, the spotlights and occasional strobe bouncing off the jewels in her top, she felt Sophie grab her arm.

'Thank you so much, Polly. This is all just so amazing. I love you so much. I am so happy that we're going to be sisters,' Sophie said, her eyes already teary.

'Me too. You deserve it, Soph. Enjoy the rest of your night.' Polly clutched Sophie's arms before letting go.

'You too, Pol, you and Bailey have obviously worked really hard on this.'

As they got to the area in the VIP bit, courtesy of Sophie's contacts, the lads were all there, drinking whisky, laughing and chatting between themselves, until Marcus noticed Sophie and turned.

'Hi, ladies. Hello, wifey.'

'Oh God, Marcus, how drunk are you?' Sophie asked, wincing.

'About the same as you, wifey. Wanna dance?'

'Hang on.' Sophie grabbed and downed a glass of Prosecco

and Polly watched as they ran off to the dance floor a few meters away.

As was always the case she could feel Bailey approaching without even looking. Maybe it was the fact that she could smell his gorgeous aftershave, or maybe she just had excellent peripheral vision. He leaned forward. 'Hi, Pol. You look gorgeous. Do you want a Prosecco?'

Bailey gestured towards the table where, next to it, there were several wine coolers with bottles of Prosecco in each of them. She looked back at Bailey as her heart hammered as heavily as the bass. Feeling her newly found confidence, mixing with excitement – Bailey, burlesque and being braless was intoxicating – an amazing feeling surged through her veins. Getting closer to Bailey than was in any way necessary, pushing her breasts into his arm, she reached and took Bailey's whisky. She drank some. Swallowed and licked her lips locking eyes with him.

'That's better,' she said.

Bailey looked momentarily stunned, like he couldn't keep his eyes off her. She was his sole focus. She didn't need anyone else's confirmation of how hot she was, but just in case she did need it, she could see it in the look Bailey was giving her.

'You're going to be trouble tonight, I can tell. I'm going to stay near you, just in case.'

'OK.' With a quick burlesque style hair toss, she handed the rest of the whisky back to him before working her way through the group and the chairs, until she was sat down with everyone else. Bailey sat down next to her, the denim of his jeans not containing the heat of his skin as he pressed his thigh against hers, deliberately she hoped, sending delicious shivers throughout her body, but refusing to move away, she turned to him.

'So how was it today?' Polly asked, her voice loud to be heard over the music.

'Yeah, what did you boys get up to? Polly wouldn't tell

us.' Mya pretended to pout as she and Paige got seats next to Calvin and Euan.

'Hang on, where's Smithy?' asked Mya.

Calvin nodded towards the dance floor where they could just about see him making out with a woman as they slow danced.

'He doesn't waste any time, does he?' Mya grunted, before hiding in her drink. Polly and Paige caught each other's eye at Mya's surprising reaction. But before Polly could say anything a waiter appeared holding a huge silver tray. She bent down and proceeded to put chip barms on the table.

'Sophie has the best contacts,' Bailey said in Polly's ear, his warm breath making her spine shiver.

Turning to whisper back into his ear, she held onto his broad shoulder. 'She really does. I've never needed a chip barm so bad in my life.'

Bailey stood up. 'It would be my honour, would you like it with red sauce or...'

'Only if they don't have hot sauce.'

Bailey grinned. 'Right answer.'

Paige quickly jumped up and took Bailey's place next to Polly almost landing on her knee.

'What you up to, Pol?' Paige asked.

'What do you mean?'

'You know what I mean. You wouldn't be messing with our poor Bailey's heart, would you?'

'Huh? You're not making any sense.' Polly shrugged and tried not to fidget under Paige's intense stare.

'Oh, I see. Oh well, in that case, go have fun. Maybe even show him some of your burlesque moves.' Paige jumped back up and took her original seat.

Polly shook her head none the wiser from the weird conversation she'd just had with Paige. Paige, who was now whispering, well as much as one can in a nightclub, into Mya's ear. Euan shouted Sophie, Marcus and Smithy back to the table. Before long everyone was eating the food of the gods and chatting about the day's events. Apparently, the laser tag had been great, but the whisky tasting had been even better. They had called in somewhere for a quick drink before the nightclub but they didn't say where exactly. Once the food had been demolished, Smithy jumped up.

'OK, well, it's not a sten without shots. Sambuca all round, yeah?' Smithy started walking towards the VIP bar ready to gather drinks. Mya surprisingly followed after him.

After their shots, more Prosecco, more whisky, and more laughs, Bailey stood up and shouted, 'Right, come on everyone let's go dance.'

'No, wait!' Sophie shot up, ever so slightly unsteady on her feet. 'We should show you what we learnt today. Come on, girls.'

'I'm not so sure—' Polly felt that familiar sharp tug of the insidious vines starting to take root, aiming for her newly blossoming confidence.

Sophie moved over some tables and was stood in what was a clear-ish area. Mya had already jumped up. But Polly wasn't sure she was quite drunk enough for this. Didn't this qualify as performing in public? That thing that makes her feel physically ill. That's what the uncurling, stretching vines in her stomach would have her believe.

'We can't do it without you, Pol. You were the best one.'

Bailey leaned back on the sofa, he was still sat close to her side, and for a crazy moment, she thought she'd quite like to see how Bailey would react to her burlesque dancing. Suddenly that one errant thought, along with the alcohol, the music, the lights, the empowerment that she was rocking, as well as the feel, smell, sight of Bailey, was making her tingly. The vines were being pushed back as her confidence returned, burning away the vine roots until they had all but disappeared. Sod it. They were all drunk, no one would remember and it wasn't like the rest of the nightclub was going to stop what they were doing to watch a bunch of drunken girls try and dance burlesque. But you know what, so what if they did? She felt herself stand. A decision made, albeit drunken. Polly stood, confidence spreading like wildfire, laughter and joy in its wake. Why the hell not? With that, she moved towards the rest of them.

'You know what, I'd rather watch. I wasn't that good anyway. Take it away, girls.' After helpfully finding three chairs, Paige sat down as the rest of the lads joined her.

'OK, Pol. Lead us through it,' Sophie said.

Shit. The air had completely escaped his lungs and he had momentarily forgotten how to fill them again. His spine was tingling, his cock aching behind his zipper. He was going to have to look away at least for a minute so as not to embarrass himself, but he was damned if he was missing a second of the sexiest thing he had ever seen in his life. Sure the other girls were fine, at a guess, Bailey wouldn't know he hadn't looked away from Polly and she hadn't broken eye contact with him either. Whilst it was driving him wild he wasn't sure if she was being deliberately sexy for him or just looking for support as she performed in front of others. Oh God, with the hair flicks. It just made him think about Polly doing that whilst she rode him. The leg split thing, holy fuck. What's with the sexy smile she was wearing? Like she knew and loved the effect she was having. It wasn't just the burlesque although, good God, it was Polly. She was on fire. She had him in the palm of her hand, well he wished she did, but at this moment in time he was transfixed, completely spellbound, he would do absolutely anything she wished, and he desperately wanted her to tell him what to do. Oh God, she was getting off the chair now, Bailey both wanted and didn't want her to bend over. With the break in eye contact, he had a moment's reprieve before she bent over and her shorts hugged her closely. He watched transfixed as she slowly straightened up, her back on display thanks to her top, before a final hair toss and the moment was broken, at least for the girls as they all whooped and laughed as they hugged each other. There was a small round of applause as the people nearest had stopped to watch the show. Bailey found that he had to cough to try and get his tongue from the roof of his mouth. Marcus had shot up and taken Sophie off to a dark corner somewhere. Paige was grinning, Mya was now stroking Calvin's arm and Smithy looked cool and collected except for his clenched jaw. Until finally, Polly slowly made her way back to Bailey.

'I cannot believe I just did that. I need a drink.'

Bailey had almost jumped up to get her one when he realised that he would need another minute or two before it was safe to stand up, and prayed that Polly didn't look down. It was dark enough that it was probably safe, but he didn't need much more encouragement at the moment. He was having a hard enough time as it was, literally. Luckily she had one already, which she downed.

'I had no idea you could dance like that, Pol.'

'Neither did I until today.'

'That was seriously something else. It was the sexiest thing I have ever seen.' Bailey grinned as Polly blushed. He could've denied it, but it was the truth.

'Is it karaoke time now?' squealed Sophie.

'I've already done my performance for the night. I'm not singing too,' Polly said grinning and winking at Bailey. 'Maybe we should go dance instead?'

'I need a brew. Do you want one?' Polly asked.

'You have a brew after a night out?' said Bailey.

'Yeah, don't you? I might even make some toast. Yes or no, Bailey, what do you want?'

Oh, he knew what he wanted, but tea and toast weren't quite it, but it would do. 'Yes, tea and toast. I'll sort the toast, you sort the brews. I'm too drunk to be around boiling water,' Bailey pointed out.

For a minute they busied themselves with their tasks before Polly turned around, her back to the worktop. 'Do you think everyone enjoyed themselves? Was it a good sten?'

'I'll tell you what I think,' he said as he walked closer, standing next to her, and putting his arm around her shoulders holding her closer. He was drawn to her and he was powerless. They'd touched a lot more tonight than they had before, unless you include the fake kissing, of course. Their thighs had been pressed together when they were sat down, she would grab his thigh under the table whenever they shared a private joke, and when they had danced together, it had been borderline dirty. Phenomenal, but definitely not entirely platonic. Either way, her body called him now and he was addicted. Trying his hardest to keep at least a little platonic he kept it at just one arm, and held her close, his hand stroking her bare upper arm. She shivered a little, and Bailey grinned before he continued, 'We managed to arrange a kick-ass sten. Well done to us. Everyone had a great time. So great that we outlived them all.'

Polly laughed. A noise in the lounge had them both turning their heads, but hearing nothing further, Bailey moved towards the toaster as it popped up. As they quietly moved around the kitchen, Bailey enjoyed every heartbreaking minute, thinking of it as an insight into what their lives could be like if they ever actually got together. The sex would be extraordinary, he had no doubt, but also the living in each other's worlds, looking after each other, he wanted the whole thing. They sat at the breakfast bar, eating their toast and drinking their brews.

'So you honestly make a brew at the end of each night, no matter how much you've had to drink?' Bailey asked.

'Yup. Every time. You're clearly not as hardened a tea drinker as I am. You're a lightweight.'

'Yes but I think you might be onto something.'

'I know I am.' Polly sighed as she finished her brew. They

sat there quietly, he couldn't be sure what was going through her head, but he didn't want this moment to end. Tomorrow the sten would be over, and she was still with Darren and his mum still had cancer, but for one blissful day he had felt like he had the world and it was hard to try and go back to normal.

A comfortable silence fell again as they finished up.

'Thanks, Bailey, I really couldn't have done any of this without you.'

He'd barely had a chance to register the small kiss she had placed on his lips before it was already over.

'We make a great team. I couldn't have done it without you either. I guess it's time to go to bed now though, huh?'

The sigh that Polly exhaled seemed to reflect his own thoughts.

'Yeah, I guess. Night, Bailey.'

'Night, Polly.'

This time Polly lent in for the hug first, and his heart stirred so much he was sure she would be able to feel it. She was petting him, raising her hands up and down his back. Reluctantly he let go. They walked into the lounge and they both froze at the sight before them.

'Shit. Calvin wake up. Euan, come on!' Bailey leapt over and practically shook his mates, both of whom just snored and turned around.

Polly was chuckling. 'Only you could get kicked out of a room that wasn't technically even a room.'

'What the hell is going on?' Bailey strode down the hall. Listening outside the bedroom door where Euan and Smithy were supposed to be sleeping. Polly followed, her eyes going wide when they heard the noises of what was happening behind the door.

'Who's in there?' Polly whispered.

'If I had to guess Smithy and Mya.'

'What? I thought she didn't like Smithy? OK, so who's in

Mya's room?' Polly asked as they made their way further down the hall. They leaned on the door, their faces next to each other. Polly giggled as she heard snores.

'That's got to be Paige, right?' Polly whispered.

'Got to be,' Bailey whispered back, unable to stop himself from laughing with Polly. Looking down the hall, Bailey nodded. 'And we don't need to guess what Sophie and Marcus are up to.'

'Gross, you're right, but gross. But you're bed-less and sofa-less. Where are you going to sleep?'

'I'll find a corner somewhere or a blanket or the bathtub, it won't be the first time and it won't be the last. Don't worry. Night, Pol.' Leaning down he kissed her cheek staying for a moment or two longer than was necessary and turned around. Until a hand grabbed his wrist.

'There's space in my bed.'

Chapter Twenty

Bailey wasn't awake, but neither was he asleep. He was wrapped up, warm, another's limbs curled in his, the silky feel of skin pressed against his skin, the sound of someone else's soft breathing, a scent in his nose that had him wondering if he was in fact dreaming. It was perfect. He moved his hand slightly and felt himself rise further towards consciousness, as it occurred to him, that he was lightly stroking a hip. But that would mean... but no... surely? He both did and didn't want to crack open an eyelid to see what was going on. On the one hand, he wanted proof that he was where he had dreamt of being for two years now, but on the other hand, this wasn't the first time he'd had this dream only to wake up stiff and hard with nowhere to go. He was stiff and hard all right. Choosing to cling onto the dream for a moment longer, he stayed exactly where he was, breathing deeply. His hand just on the hip of the waistband of her shorts, able to feel skin with some of his fingertips but not all. She was warm and he was closer to her than he had ever been before. His erection, which couldn't be helped at this point in time, pressing into her, if she moved just a bit, snuggled closer, it would be almost exactly where he wanted it. Oh shit. Sure enough, she'd done exactly that, she was stretching into it, rubbing against him. It was the sigh that made his eyes fly open. The sigh wasn't his.

His breath momentarily stopped, keeping everything as quiet as possible to see if he could hear it again. Either he was still drunk, or somehow he was in bed with Polly. His mind raced, whilst his body stayed statue still, unable and unwilling to break the spell. He didn't want to spook her, didn't want his actual real-life dream to end. But neither did he want to take advantage whilst she was asleep and that was the reason for the control. He took another deep breath and tried, in his mildly hungover head, to memorise the feeling and the scents and the heat into his brain so that he would never forget. With every breath, the fog in his brain cleared a little more, and he finally recalled how he had ended up in this situation. Polly let out another sigh, before turning around in his arms. His hand skimming the soft skin of her waist as she turned, but now she was lying on his arm, and her face, her eyes closed, right there in front of his. At least his mini Bailey no longer had anything to grind against, well not unless she moved her leg any higher up his thigh.

Closing his eyes he snuggled in closer until his head was just above hers and his arm that she was leaning on closed around her back, and his other hand retook the position on her other hip, both on and off her skin. Bailey had never felt so relaxed and so tense at the same time, it was a strange combination of never-ending peace, with soul-crushing longing.

The room was lighter when he woke up a second time, but that wasn't what had woken him. Polly was stirring, firmly pressing into him as she did so. One hand holding tightly to the arm that she had been resting on, her other hand lying on top of his as it was lying on her hip. Whilst they had dozed she had turned back around again and now her spine was stretching into his chest, her hair in his face, catching slightly on his beard as she slowly ground into him. His hand on her hip moved as directed by Polly's hand, stroking her sides lightly moving slowly up and down, hitting a sensitive spot she shuddered into him, and Bailey had to close his eyes, her hand remained on top of his, although it clung tighter as she continued guiding him along her body. Each stroke getting higher, now pushing up her T-shirt and travelling underneath, on the next stroke his fingers just brushed the edge of her breast, wondering how high she would take him on the next round, his hand finally back down at her hip bone, they began their ascent—

It was a combination of a door slam, conversation and a text message chime that broke the moment straight down the middle as Polly moved away and stretched, opening her eyes and smiling softly.

'Oh hi, Bailey, is everyone else awake? What time is it?' He watched as she bent towards her phone on the bedside table. 'Shit it's nearly eleven, we need to get ready to clear up before kicking out time.'

Bailey looked at her for a moment, trying to see something, anything, in her eyes. Was she embarrassed, did she know? It was hard to believe that she had been sleeping throughout all that. So what was she thinking? For one horrifying moment, he wondered if she knew she was waking up with him, or if she thought that she was waking up with Darren. It was that last thought that did it. He felt sick to his stomach and he knew it wasn't the hangover.

'Yeah, yeah, of course.'

Polly stretched again before jumping out of bed. 'I'll go make sure everything is OK. Do you want a brew?'

'Sure, please.'

Polly jumped out of bed and out the door. It was his worst and best morning after the night before. He desperately tried to keep a hold of the wonderful things that had just happened. But they were tarnished now. If he had to guess, he would say Polly knew what had happened and was embarrassed because she thought she was waking up to her boyfriend and not him. It fucking sucked. He groaned, glad for a few minutes to get his head on straight, his other head having automatically calmed down at the realisation.

He turned onto his side, but that made it worse because it smelt like Polly. Staying in this bed was torture. He had to get up. He had to put on his happy face. Soon they'd be out of here, he could drop his mates off at the train station and then just crash for the afternoon, not think about anyone or anything.

Turning to his phone, he realised it wasn't his that had

gone off. Perhaps Darren had been texting Polly. Shit. Sitting up in the bed he dragged his hand over his face, hoping to get a grip on things, but inside he felt destroyed. It had happened quickly and without mercy. As if he had filled with highly flammable happiness, that when it hit flame, burnt out quickly destroying everything in its wake. Grabbing the jeans that he'd had on the night before, he put them and his trainers on, before glancing at his face in the mirror. He could do it. He knew that. He could do what he had been doing so much of lately. He could put his game face on, he could say the right things and ask the right questions, and that way no one would be able to get near him. Yeah, it sucked to do that, after he had been able to be so open and honest lately, but what else could he do? He'd do it until he was on his own, then he wouldn't need to pretend. It was a plan, albeit not a great one, but a plan right now felt better than walking around like a zombie, and that was all his instinct was offering. Smiling at himself, game face on, maybe not fitting completely, but on, he walked out of the room, grabbing his T-shirt. It lasted all of three seconds.

'What the hell, dude?' Marcus loud whispered at him.

'Jesus, what's the matter?' Bailey had been met with Marcus his arms crossed over his chest, and a stern look, ah, the big brother look. This should be fun given where his headspace was and where his head had been not five minutes earlier.

'Why are you walking out of my sister's room half-naked?'

Bailey looked down at himself. He was in boxers and jeans, he was literally only missing a T-shirt, which he was in the process of putting on.

'Because our dumbass mates were on the sofas and there was nowhere else to sleep. Why?'

Marcus raised an eyebrow, and Bailey watched as if from above, his mind disassociating from his own body, as a torrent of emotions, none of them good, took over.

'Would it really be the worst thing in the world if I was going out with your sister? Do you really think that badly of me?'

'Dude, no.'

'Also, what difference is it to you who your sister goes out with? This isn't the eighteenth century. Besides, you know as well as I do that she's seeing that prick, Darren. Are you trying to imply that I'm worse than he is?'

'No, God of course not, he's an insufferable—'

'It's none of your damn business, but Polly let me sleep in her bed last night as there was nowhere else to go. End of.'

Bailey shrugged off Marcus's arm and walked off towards the kitchen, his head down. He needed to get out of here pronto before he said or did something that would later come back to bite him on his ass. Paige and Mya were sat on the bar stools in the kitchen sharing some toast. They both took one look at him, a quick glance at each other, and immediately jumped up. Bailey slouched off not knowing where to go but not able to stand still, the small amount of anger he had just thrown at Marcus had used up the reserves he needed for his game face. If he thought he was destroyed before, now he was barren.

'Bailey, come with me outside. I have to show you something.' The bi-fold doors were open, presumably to let some of the hangover skank out and get some fresh air in. He followed Paige as she led him down the small path towards the picnic table. Thankfully it was too cold for most people so they had some privacy. Bailey was grateful for it, the cold biting through him, giving him something to feel.

'Paige, I'm fine I just don't want to talk right now,' Bailey said, his voice low.

Paige nodded, and grabbed his arm. 'I know. I'm here purely to throw out anyone who might want to interact with you. I'm your shield.' She led him to the picnic table.

'Here you go, Bailey. I'll keep everyone inside occupied.'

Mya dropped off a brew and his hoody and disappeared just as quickly.

'If you want to talk you can, but I'm just going to sit here quietly and drink my brew with you.'

Bailey threw on his jumper and held the warm brew to his chest, looking out at the hills that faced them.

Taking a deep breath, his shoulders dropped, and he realised that nothing had changed. His world had only shifted temporarily and for forty-eight hours it had been amazing, but the weekend was over. Real-life had gatecrashed. He sighed and dropped his head onto Paige's shoulder. She gently put her hand on his thigh and patted his leg.

'It's all going to work out OK, Bailey. I guarantee it.'

'Is that a Paige guarantee? Those things are worth their weight in gold,' he mumbled.

'I'm definitely back to my usual self. You can take that guarantee to the bank.'

'I wish I could believe you. I'm just done. This unrequited shit is exhausting.'

'Bailey, don't give up yet, OK? Just give me until the wedding. If it's not done by then, I'll double-check my crystal balls.'

He couldn't help but smile. Paige's quiet confidence, the belief in herself, could be heard in her voice, and it made him want to believe her too. But he was a sap, and he knew it. He was still happy to cling on to any and all hope he could find and what did that say about him? The question was could he wait a couple more weeks? What were a couple more weeks, when it had been years already? He was addicted to Polly, she was the one for him and he knew it. But right now it was agony and for the first time ever he wished that she wasn't.

Chapter Twenty-One

The last thing she wanted, the absolute last thing was to go round to her parents' house when really, what she wanted to do more than anything, was to curl up in bed, put on one of her favourite playlists and clear her head. Instead, she was sat looking at the TV in the lounge with her dad, whilst her mum finished putting together the Sunday roast. Her hangover had disappeared at about two o'clock, which she was very grateful for. Her emotional hangover, however, was still in full force two hours later.

Up until the last hour, and maybe the first few hours on the first night, it had been a brilliant weekend. She'd honestly never felt better, she'd made monumental decisions, she had the most fun, been the bravest she'd ever been, and discovered she owned a shit ton of confidence. She could do anything. Anything, except be honest with Bailey it would seem.

She had tortured them both, and for what. To completely pretend that it hadn't happened straight after. Where would it have gone if they hadn't been interrupted? She longed to find out, maybe they would've crossed the line, done what they both clearly wanted, crossed it and left it for dust, never to be seen again. At least as far as she was concerned, but then she didn't know how he felt, not really. Was she just another to add to his number, a specific itch he needed to scratch? Ugh, that wasn't fair on him, if for no other reason than he could very well be thinking the same thing about her. But if they had, what then?

Well, she'd technically be a cheater for starts. Cringing, she knew that it was only the fact that they hadn't kissed, that was her saving grace keeping her at the border of Cheaterville, even if it was by the very tip of her toes, and Polly felt incredibly unbalanced. She held close to her heart the fact that she had already known she was going to finish with Darren. That surely added a little space, between her and Cheaterville border, right? Probably not. In fact, if you included the fake kisses, which she very much didn't, and if you were to look closely, which she didn't want to, then she would be able to see what she already knew. She was stood on the line, and it would depend on your point of view as to where she was placed. Darren, for example, would be able to see that she was clearly over it. But then maybe that was because he was already over there himself?

'Polly? Polly? Are you OK? You've not listened to a word I've said have you?'

'Sorry, Dad, I was miles away.' She looked at her dad. He got up and sat down next to her on the sofa.

'What's the matter, darling?'

It was the exhaustion of the sten weekend, it was everything she had on her mind, it was the look on Bailey's face when she left the room that morning. She leaned into her dad and one small tear, the only one she would allow herself to shed right now, fell free. She felt her dad hold her close, and it was nearly her undoing.

'I don't think I know what I'm doing, Dad.' Sniffing into his shoulder, she felt his arm reassuringly move in circles on her back. He had always done that, and that was probably why she had always gone crying to him. It wasn't that she preferred him over her mum, it's just that of the two he was the one that, to her at least, could be the most sympathetic. Her mum, on the other hand, was forever practical, and would always try and solve a problem before properly listening and understanding one.

'Does anyone know what they're doing, darling?'

'I can't see straight. I keep making the wrong decisions. I think I'm hurting people in the process.'

'Hmmm. Do you want to tell me about it?'

Polly shook her head. She didn't want to admit how

terrible a person she was, how much she might be hurting two people, how she was keeping important secrets from all of them, how her heart ached because it was currently pointed in the wrong direction, at the wrong person. She didn't want to unpick all of that with her dad. They sat quietly instead, the reassuring circles continuing, as she leaned on his shoulder. Focusing instead on her breathing, keeping it under control so that she wouldn't cry any further.

'Do you want to stay? I can talk to your mum if you want to just go?'

Polly sat up at that. 'You don't mind?'

'Of course not. I'll just tell her that you felt a migraine coming on and that you're not to be disturbed so that you can sleep it off. What do you need? Two days?'

'Thanks, Dad. A night should do it. She can bell me tomorrow. I know she'll want to.' If for no other reason than to get the gossip on the sten, it had been why her mother had invited her over, after all. Gathering her coat, scarf and handbag, she quietly and efficiently got everything on and ready.

'Can I give you one small piece of advice?'

'Anything, Dad.'

'Take it from someone who has been at death's door.' Polly shuddered, she didn't need to be reminded of the two heart attacks her dad had had. She prayed every day that he wouldn't have a third. 'You do whatever you need to do to be happy. The only question you ever need to ask yourself is, am I happy? If not, then make a plan to get there. Your mum and I have your back, whatever you decide to do, there's no pressure from us. So go make a plan. You might feel better.'

Hugging her dad tight, Polly held onto his advice, eager to try anything. 'I love you, Dad, I'll be fine. I'm sure I'm just hungover.'

'You don't have to lie, darling. I just hope that whatever this is, it passes soon, and if it doesn't, come and tell me. We can always figure out a plan together. Love you.'

Nodding, instead of speaking, her throat too tight to say anything further, she snuck out of the lounge to the hallway, quietly sliding out of the front door and closing it behind her. Headphones on, playlist on, she walked back home.

The next morning, as her favourite song by Sia gently woke her, she was surprised to discover that she had slept all night. The ache in her chest had nearly gone altogether. It had been the second night that she had slept so well, her stomach twisting in guilt for Bailey as she remembered the night before. She thought about what else was missing, and she winced as she realised she'd put on the same pjs she'd had on the night before, as she caught the unmistakable scent of Bailey. She allowed herself a moment or two to breathe it in. Then she looked over at her makeshift desk, at the list she had made yesterday afternoon. Forcing a deep breath she found, if not resolve, then something close enough to fake it. After all, she had a plan, and that plan began today.

First things first, she knew she had to break up with Darren – and fast. Then she would be free to see what, if anything, could happen with Bailey. Her heart sped up at the possibilities that lined up in her head. It wasn't just sex for her, although she had no doubt that would be out of this world, it was the rest of it. Pottering about together at the cottage this weekend had cemented that. She needed to break up with Darren and she needed to apologise to Bailey about yesterday morning. She cringed again when she thought about how he had looked at her as she fled from the room. She should've been honest, the fact that she didn't want to cheat the only reason she wasn't. Bailey was better than that, and he deserved – well he deserved everything, if she was honest, no longer shocked at the depths of her feelings for him, now that she was full of newfound clarity.

Nervous energy propelled her out of bed. Choosing her clothes with care, they were calm confident 'I'm finishing with you' clothes. And although she would rather not finish with Darren at work, it was that or drag it out, and lord knows she didn't want to do that, it wasn't in the plan.

Sitting at her desk, she logged on to Darren's calendar to see if he was free at all.

'Shit.'

His diary was full. But whilst she had it open she looked to see what exactly was in there that had forced him to leave the sten so early. All that was in was 'meeting prep' but upon closer inspection it would seem that he had been invited to that, looking at the bottom of the screen it had last been modified by Stacie Hodgkins. OK, another click onto the corporate phone book confirmed her suspicions that it had been put in by one of the juniors in his department. That didn't tell her anything as if it was a junior in his department then it really could be legit. Searching through the calendar she saw that there were an awful lot of 'meeting prep' calendar appointments, and not all of them coincided with any meetings whatsoever, and they were put in by various people, but more often than not it was one of the PAs.

Going back to today, she could see that after 'meeting prep' he had a team meeting, and some other generic thing, certainly nothing that would've taken the whole weekend to prepare for. But there was a distinct lack of 'break up slots' available, and Polly worried she'd have to drag this out another day. She needed to make sure she did it right so that there would be no repercussions. Turning his calendar off she picked up her phone, something needling in her brain. Uploading the dating apps that she had been regularly frequenting she tried to remember which one she had met Darren on. There. She opened it up and in no time stared at Darren's profile. For a start, it wasn't deleted but then, his profile picture. WTF? Wasn't that the same shirt he'd had on at the sten, wasn't that the actual farmhouse she could make out in the background? Polly calmly turned her phone off. Just in time, as it happened.

'Hey, Polly. Just wanted to let you know that the policy change for office relationships has been approved and some comms will be sent out later today informing everyone of the changes and the link to the policy. This should, hopefully, free up some time for us to focus on the recruitment drive when we're not dealing with unsubstantiated gossip.'

'Sounds good, thanks, Leanne,' Polly said, trying to force her face into a smile.

'It was a really good piece of work, well done.' She ducked a little closer. 'I think you're in a really good position for this promotion, you'd be a Head of Service equivalent, Polly. I'll let you know as soon as I hear any more.'

Polly watched as Leanne walked away. She supposed she should feel proud that she had done a piece of work in a short timescale that was corporately approved. But really, it was a document with some precisely worded text on it that utilised just a portion of her HR qualification. It really wasn't anything she felt particularly enthused with. The potential promotion didn't feel like anything worth celebrating either, if she was honest.

The song she had wriggling around in her brain, however, that was exciting. It had the feel of a love song, maybe even a song for Bailey. Whether or not she'd ever play it for him remained to be seen. If she could maybe finish early she could get home and get the melody straightened out. The way it was in her brain at the moment, it wouldn't take long. Maybe she could even perform it tonight? Then again she could also do the song she'd written about Sophie and Marcus. She liked that one too, it was sweet. The one for Bailey was already feeling more slow and heavy and well, sexy, if she was honest. It would work really well to a burlesque dance. A quick glance around to make sure no one could see her screen she decided to spend some time writing the lyrics, and maybe looking for local burlesque classes.

Chapter Twenty-Two

Standing at the edge of the stage ready to go on, she still wasn't sure which piece she was going to perform. The ode to Sophie and Marcus, not that they would ever, ever hear it, or the passionate plea for Bailey. She hadn't seen Bailey tonight, so maybe she could practice it. Then maybe, when she had finally finished with Darren tomorrow, she could play it for Bailey. It would tell him all the things she wanted, without her actually having to say it to him.

'Please welcome to the stage, Miss Polly.'

Polly walked on, feeling more confident than she had ever before. The lights were bright on the stage, and although she couldn't make out the distinguishing features of the audience, she could tell they were there from the expectant hum, the near-silent hush of people waiting in anticipation. Her nerves wobbled just for a second as she sat down on the stool. She had both pieces of music, shuffling them she decided to let the fates decide. OK, the sweet love song for Sophie and Marcus it was.

Turning, she addressed the crowd, something she had never done before. 'I have a new piece tonight that I have written with some friends in mind. I hope you enjoy it. Thank you.' She took a deep breath and began. The song flowed underneath her fingers and her eyes closed as she sang. Her soul lapping up the performance as if it had been starved, as if the vines had been covering it somehow but now, the sound of the piano, the lights beaming down on her, all had the effect of transporting her somewhere beautifully serene. She was getting her fix. She needed it and she knew that she would always keep coming back for it.

He'd just managed to get a seat when she walked onto the stage. She looked different tonight, more purposeful almost.

Taking out his phone, Bailey decided to record her, not that he would ever show it to anyone, but he could watch her at her happiest, at her most talented, whenever he wanted, whenever he needed it, like tonight.

His head had been a mess after Sunday morning, and as such he had no intention of coming tonight, but once he had found out that his mum had taken a turn for the worse, he'd felt compelled to come and see Polly perform, to get his own ease, however temporarily. Looking at his phone as he recorded, so that he could keep an eye for any text alerts, he took a deep breath as he listened to her. Her voice calming him slightly note by note, helping him forget that his mum was seemingly having a bad reaction to her latest round of chemo. They'd been told to keep a lookout for signs of infection. She'd been closely monitoring her temperature, knowing that if it went up she'd have to go to A&E. He'd seen her earlier, but then she sent him out to watch Polly, and although he hadn't wanted to leave, she'd forced him to go, her temperature wasn't up, but there was a feeling that it was 'yet' as she coughed more and more, and tried to take deep breaths after each one. Maybe he could ask Polly if he could share the video with his mum, she'd love to see it. She'd have been here tonight if she could've. Polly probably didn't realise that she'd gotten herself another fan. Keeping his phone steady as she sang he realised that it was a love song for Sophie and Marcus. That she would create something so beautiful for her friends and then never share it with them was both heartbreaking and selfless. As the song came to a close he recorded the thunderous applause. He wasn't sure that Polly was even aware of the reaction she got.

'Thank you.' He watched as she nodded and smiled, and for the first time, she seemed to bask, just for a moment, before standing up and hugging the MC and then walking off stage. Quickly turning his camera off but putting it on the table in case any updates were received, he looked up to see Polly approach. It took a while as she conversed with the regulars on the way to his table.

'Hi, Bailey. I wasn't expecting to see you here.' Did she sound a little anxious to him?

'Really, why not?' He watched as she just shrugged and sat down and busied herself opening the bottle of water he'd got for her.

She was quiet and unsettled. He was desperate to ask her about what happened on Sunday morning, but he wasn't sure he wanted the answer. He still felt ravaged by the whole experience, but with his mum now possibly having to go to the hospital again, he'd found even greater depths of despair, and Polly remained the only thing that calmed him. His frustrations currently had nowhere to go, so they curled viciously at the back of his head, causing a headache he wasn't sure he would ever be without.

'Was that a song for Sophie and Marcus?' Bailey asked, watching her face, waiting for her eyes to meet his.

'Yeah.' Her eye contact didn't last long enough.

'It was beautiful, Pol. It's a shame that they'll never get to hear it.'

'Hmmm. Anyway, how are you? Are you OK? Recovered from the weekend yet?'

'I'm alright. But, erm listen, my mum's had a bad reaction to the chemo. She, erm, she's struggling to breathe and they're worried she might have a chest infection.' Said out loud, it hadn't helped and Bailey suddenly realised how worried he was, how worried his family was, and how much he was barely holding it together. The scrape of the chair leg pulled his gaze from his hands as Polly took a step towards him and waited. Moving his arms she plonked herself on his lap and then cradled his face into her neck. His arms instinctively moving around her back.

'I'm sorry, Bailey. I'm sure... If there's anything I can do you just have to ask, you know that right?'

Of course, his phone vibrated at that moment. They both saw the text.

Billy: They're taking your mum in. I'll call you when we get to the hospital x

Bailey closed his eyes, every bone in his body was tired and every muscle tense. The sinking feeling in his stomach that had been there ever since she'd had the diagnosis had opened up into a cavernous fire pit, spits of flame striking his head. Soft lips pressed gently against his, his eyes shot open in shock. Polly's arms were tight around his neck as his were around her waist. They weren't drunk, they weren't pretending, they weren't asleep. Polly had kissed him, with no excuses, no alternate reason, except, presumably she wanted to comfort him and, at that moment in time, for just a brief moment, he took the haven that she was offering and let himself be looked after, unable to recall a time when he'd let anyone do that for him before. His eyes were watering as she gently pulled away and hugged him again.

'Go and see what's happening. Let me know, OK? I'll keep my phone on loud, call me if I can do anything at all.'

With that, Polly stood up and Bailey's real-world problems overwhelmed his feelings about the kiss. He grabbed his car keys and his wallet, his phone already to his ear as he strode out of the Speakeasy to find out which hospital his mum was going to.

Chapter Twenty-Three

Back to the crap sleep again. Well, it had been nice whilst it lasted those two nights. Polly had no choice but to go to the staff kitchen and make the strongest coffee she could handle. She'd been worried about Bailey. But also worried about breaking up with Darren. The apprehension made her feel sick, she hated confrontation but it had to be today. She'd kissed Bailey last night. With no way of covering it up as to why. She'd been sober, they weren't acting. It had been real, and amazing, as always.

'Hi, Polly. You OK?'

'Hi, Jorge, yeah just tired. You?'

'Yeah not too bad. Well done getting that policy straightened out. But seriously who is the douchebag making his way through the staff? There must be at least a couple of people playing about to get the number of calls that we've had. Hopefully, things will calm down now though, hey?'

'Yes it should. Do you really think that someone is that stupid though?' Polly took a sip of her too hot coffee and winced.

'I don't know, but given the vagueness of the complaints, it wouldn't surprise me if it was someone in management or someone of a high level at least. They're untouchable because they've never been specifically named. All we ever seem to get are managers pulling their hair out because staff are too busy either getting busy or being dumped. I wish we knew who it was though.'

'Hmmm. Well, if you find out let me know. See you later,' Polly said as her skin prickled, and her nausea worsened.

'See you, Polly.'

Polly grabbed her thermos cup and slowly made her way to her desk. If Jorge was right, then she needed to do some digging. With a deep sigh and a sense of foreboding, she started looking through the complaints to see if there was a common theme.

'Bailey you don't need to be here. Shouldn't you be at work or something?'

'No, Marcus is covering for me. I don't need to be anywhere else.'

'Bailey.'

He looked up at his mum as she sighed his name. He hated the tubes coming out of her nose. Her oxygen levels had taken a dive last night; she was battling a chest infection, her weakened immune system just not up for the job of fighting it off on its own. He held her hand as they watched *This Morning* on the tiny TV. Billy was sorting things out at their house, and unbeknownst to his mum, his siblings were making arrangements to free up their time so that they could get here too. The doctors were due to make their rounds soon, and then they'd all know where they were up to. He wasn't watching the TV, he was holding his mum's hand and thinking of all the struggles she'd faced, especially as a single mum. It hadn't been easy. But if she could get through all of that then, she could get through this now.

'How's Polly doing?' his mum asked, interrupting his dark thoughts.

'She's OK.'

'Just OK?'

'She's…' He ran out of words to accurately describe what she was. At the moment she was a puzzle; another man's girlfriend, a best mate, a brilliant singer-songwriter. The one thing she wasn't was his. But maybe the kiss last night was an indication that things might change. Or maybe it was a mate consoling another mate who just had some really shocking news. Maybe, just maybe, he was overthinking the whole thing.

'You really love her, don't you? Bailey, that makes me so happy.' He looked at her then, she was smiling, beaming in fact as she squeezed his hand. 'Why do you look so upset about it?'

'It's complicated.'

'These things always are, and at the same time aren't.'

'Huh?'

'You love her, that's the hardest bit, now you have that figured out you'll find that the rest of it will all start to make more sense.'

'Hmmm.' Bailey had no choice but to be non-committal about it. It wasn't like he could tell her everything that was going on. Then he'd have to admit that he'd lied. His mum was poorly enough already, she didn't need that.

'How was she last night?'

'Amazing. She's written a song for Sophie and Marcus. It's really good.'

'I wish I could've been there. When I'm better I'm going to make her let me sing one of her songs. She's really talented, Bailey.'

That wasn't just a mother saying nice things about her son's girlfriend. Bailey remembered how his mum had had very little in the early years, but her choir group got her through so much. She paid that back by helping out with the youth choir whenever she had a chance, although obviously not as much lately.

'So will she play it for them? Maybe at the wedding?'

Bailey shook his head. Then remembered the video that he had taken on his phone. Looking at his mum, he hoped that Polly wouldn't kill him for what he was about to do.

'Here, watch this, but if Polly asks you know nothing, OK?'

'Bailey, if you filmed her without her knowing I'm going to have to tell you off. But I'll do that after I've seen it. Give it here.'

Bailey loaded up the video and handed it to his mum. He

didn't need to see it, he'd seen it about ten times last night after he'd left the hospital. He felt his bones relax a little as the soothing tones of Polly's voice crept out into the room. He looked at his mum and saw her eyes close, a smile on her lips and she started to gently sway to the music. There's no way that the Polly he knew would ever have discouraged this. She might have massive performance anxiety but ultimately she would do anything she could for her friends, and anything to give people who were hurting a moment of peace.

As the last few notes died off and the thunderous applause started, his phone beeped a text interrupting the applause.

'That was Polly asking how I am.' She handed the phone back over to him. 'It really is such a shame that she isn't able to do more with that talent. I'm guessing Brenda doesn't know about her singing either?'

'No one does. We're in a very select group.'

Denise paused and looked up to the ceiling, nodding slightly as if she was listening to it again in her head. Eventually she was humming the melody. 'Are you going to message her back?'

'And say what? That my mum is hooked up to tubes, but she loved your song?'

'Bailey Christopher Johnson. Just because you're taller than me doesn't mean you get to use that sort of sarcasm with me, mister. Just text her and see if she's free tonight. She can come to see me, if she doesn't mind? I'd love to see her. If she's hospital phobic though I quite understand.'

'Really?' Bailey asked shocked.

'Why not? She's family. Or at least she will be soon enough. Text her now.'

Bailey: She's ok, she wants to know if you want to come and see her tonight? She also said that if you're hospital phobic you don't have to x

'What's she said?' His mum was interrupted as a group of white coats and one in scrubs came into the room.

'Mrs Williams, I'm Doctor Carmichael, Oncologist and these are my students and this is Michelle, our senior nurse. I'm going to get your chart.'

Bailey looked at Michelle as she smiled warmly before turning back to the computer she had wheeled in. Bailey grabbed his mum's hand and held on tight; it didn't escape him that he was holding her hand for support and not the other way around. He was a mummy's boy, always had been and right now he was scared.

'Michelle, can you get me the results from the last lot of tests, please? Stats look better, oxygen has increased. OK team, what are your thoughts?'

'Respiratory infection, most likely a side effect from the AC Chemo treatment. Suggest abx IV continues for another twenty-four and re-test.'

'Anyone else?'

'Potentially look at other chemo drugs that may work better?'

'OK then. Michelle?'

'They're here.' Michelle smiled and made some room. With that Dr Carmichael and the team all stood around the computer. It took probably less than a minute, it's just that the minute itself felt like an hour to Bailey. His back in spasm at his awkward angle in the plastic chair as he held onto his mum but watched the medical team at work.

'Both suggestions seem fine to me.' Dr Carmichael picked up the chart and wrote something in it, passed it to Michelle who wrote something down, and they began to file out.

'Wait, so what's happening? How's my mum?' Bailey asked.

'Mrs Williams is recovering nicely. Twenty-four more hours on an IV of antibiotics and fluids should really take the edge off the mild chest infection. We'll try taking you off the oxygen later. When you have your clinic appointment with Doctor... erm...' he checked his notes '... Doctor Nielson, she'll do the usual checks and discuss options with regards to chemo moving forward. It might be that she continues with the treatment plan that you are on now, or she may swap it. But first, she'll need to know that you are healthy enough to have your next treatment. From what I can see, whilst understandably this is unpleasant for you, it's relatively common and if you continue to recover as you have been, you'll be back on track again with no problems.'

'OK, thanks,' Bailey said quietly as the white coats walked out and he tried to digest everything he had just heard.

'Denise, you're OK, there's nothing to worry about right now, and I'll nip back after rounds and we can chat then, OK?' Michelle said, wheeling the computer back out again.

'Thanks, Michelle,' Denise said with a smile.

'No problem, Denise, I'll see you later.' Michelle smiled again before closing the door behind her.

Bailey let out the breath he'd been holding tight in his lungs. His ribs stretching.

'Oh good I can see Polly later and I won't have oxygen wires coming out of my face. Did she text back? What did she say?'

Bailey's mind had gone a little blank. Was his mum really OK? Well, OK, for someone with cancer, but she was alright? Right? He looked down at his phone.

Polly: Sure. What time is best? Should I bring anything? x

'Tell her seven would be brill and she doesn't need to bring anything.' Had he read that out loud?

Bailey: Mum says seven and don't bring anything just yourself x

Bailey sat back in his chair as he studied the x on the end of the message. He added them to every message he sent. But it got him thinking about last night again. Lifting his head he watched as his mum called or texted everyone to tell them she was OK and would be home tomorrow, hopefully.

'Billy's coming back this afternoon. Duncan will call tonight at some point, and your sister is going to hang out

182

with me tomorrow. I've never seen so much of you all. Bailey, why don't you have a little rest? You look awful.'

'Shouldn't I be telling you to rest?' Bailey asked, feeling his body weigh down heavily.

'Family nap?'

'Family nap. Yep.'

Seeing Bailey's mum later meant one thing. Pretend relationship. Enough was enough and if she could have it her way she'd get rid of the pretend part. Speaking of getting rid. This was how Polly found herself striding towards Darren's office. She'd heard him tell people on more than one occasion that he had the corner office. He sort of did, in so much that technically it was a corner, but there was not a lot of point having a corner office that had only one window. It didn't even really have walls, it was an office in the very loosest sense of the word. Luckily she'd had the forethought to book the conference room.

'Hi, Darren. Can I have a quick word with you please?' She tried to keep her face calm, wanting to look professional.

'Erm, sure, I can try and see if there's a meeting room free.' He looked harassed. Like Polly was putting him out and his face had greyed at the mention of needing to book a meeting room. Figured. She'd heard that another one of the admin team was going to hand her notice in for some vague reason. Although she strongly suspected the reason was the man in front of her.

'No need. I booked the conference room. It won't take a minute.'

As they walked the few meters to the, thankfully, soundproofed conference room, Polly tried desperately to get into her burlesque Polly headspace. Not that she fancied giving him a dance, but because she needed to feel like a queen. She needed that extra bit of confidence to do this, and do it right. Her throat was tight though, and she felt really warm, as her fierce emotions threatened to take over. Angry tears were so not the look she was after right now. Once Darren had walked past Polly into the conference room, Polly made sure the door was shut behind her.

'What's up, babe?' He raised an eyebrow and patted the table, and Polly tried not to retch. What a prick. What had she ever seen in him? She'd been thinking about that a lot and all she had was that he was the best of a bad bunch and that maybe she'd not been in the best place to demand something better. Or, if she were really honest, her head had still been a little out of place from the first fake kiss with Bailey, and perhaps maybe she had overcompensated. Whatever the reason, it was irrelevant, she could control what happened next and that's what she was going to do. And so Polly waited and didn't say anything, she wanted to see what, if anything, he would come out with first. He didn't speak but his expression changed, he was giving off a stony poker face. That must be his contract negotiating face, thought Polly. This was enough to flip her switch. Taking a breath, she started, her voice barely louder than a whisper, 'Exactly how many people in this company are you sleeping with?'

Polly put her hands into the pockets of her skirt, amazing as they were already by just existing, it also meant that her pose was one of bored confidence and so she stood taller. It also meant that that way her knees were locked and less likely to give way, and he couldn't see that her hands were shaking, plus it stopped her from playing with her watch. She carefully studied him as she waited for his response, and saw his jaw clench. Here it comes.

'Babe, what are you talking about? I would never! Where's this coming from? Is this from Terry, because I only hired Jackie over him because she was the more qualified? I knew he wasn't going to let it go. What did he say?'

'How's your new PA working out for you? She's the third one since you started, isn't she? Your door pass seems to show you spending a lot of time on the second floor too. Seems that you are conducting a lot of business within a particular server room? What contracts could you be negotiating in there, I wonder? Oh, and you almost got caught out in the ladies toilets a couple of months ago. Did you know that? I have every single complaint against your door pass, your calendar and I guess, if I ask the right people, I'll even get confessions. So how many people exactly are you shagging at this office? You seem to be struggling with basic maths so let me make it easier for you. It's one less now.'

'What... The... How...' Darren spluttered before slamming his palms down on the table. Polly tried not to jump back as she saw something unpleasant in his eyes as his face transformed yet again in front of her. 'Oh, please, don't come all innocent with me, as if I didn't know what was happening with you and Bailey. You're hardly a saint. You spend all your time with him, is it any wonder I had to go looking elsewhere? Besides, you were hardly doing it for me, if you know what I mean.'

Polly wanted to walk away and she wanted to knock him out at the same time. Knowing that one would undoubtedly cost her her job, she took a quick breath.

'You're pathetic.' And before he could say anything further, Polly walked to the conference room door and pulled it wide open. 'Whilst I am happy to discuss HR issues with you, Darren,' Polly's voice was raised, 'you don't need to ask me the best way to inform your girlfriend you have super gonorrhea! That's massively outside of my area of expertise!'

Polly walked along the corridor towards the lift, knowing full well that every eye was on her. She prayed to the shoe and feet gods that she didn't stumble. She wanted to strut. She added a little sway in her hips and stood up tall once she'd pressed the button for the lift. She held that position as the lift doors closed and she continued to stand tall throughout the journey, her head looking forward with a cool calm facade, even as she exited the lift and got to her desk and grabbed her bag.

'Off to lunch, back in a bit.' Until finally she was out of the building, she walked as far as she could until she found herself sat at the bench overlooking the park, the trees now beginning to burst with buds more and more as they made their way towards April. She took a deep breath and let out everything she had been holding. The tears began pouring down her face and she just let them. Until finally, she wiped her face using the edge of her scarf, feeling cleansed. As horrible as that had been, she was free now. The worst part was over. Her phone went off, a notification in her girl group WhatsApp.

Paige: My spidey senses are tingling roll call.

Sophie: All good

Mya: Same

Paige: Polly?

Looking down at her phone, Polly smiled.

Polly: Just broke up with Darren, so all ok now x

Paige: 🫠 Good for you x

Mya: 🙌 Thank God x

Sophie: Yasss x

Polly: Wow tell me how you really feel guys x

Another beep went off and she saw that Mya was sending her a private message.

Mya: I'm really glad that you finished it with that douchebag Pol. I didn't know how to tell you, but he came onto me at the sten. When I said no, and threatened to rip his testicles clean off, I figured that was why he legged it. I wanted to tell you but didn't want to ruin the sten xx

Polly sighed, as residual anger churned in her stomach.

Polly: I'm sorry Mya x

Mya: You have nothing to be sorry for. But if I see him again, he'll be safe for people with allergies xx

Polly: Huh?

Mya: He'll be nut free xx

186

Chapter Twenty-Four

'Hi, Denise, how are you doing? Or is that a stupid question?' Polly had been walking around the hospital for ten minutes trying to find the right room, whilst trying to not feel guilty that Denise wanted her, the fake girlfriend, to visit during what must be personal, family time. The familiar shudder of guilt about lying to his sweetheart of a mother lasted for all of a second when she saw Denise lying on the bed. She knew that they were doing it from the right place and for the right reasons, even if it was still a little bit wrong.

'Polly. There you are,' Denise said, smiling up at her.

'Hi, babe.' A quick hello kiss with Bailey and Polly had to remember to open her eyes and regain her equilibrium when he stepped back. 'Sit here, I'm going to go and get another chair.'

'So how are you?' Polly asked again.

'I'm doing better now that I have fewer tubes and wires. Still got this pesky thing but I think with the right accessories I can jazz it up a bit.' Denise pointed to her IV.

'How much longer do you have to have that for? When can you go home?'

'Hopefully tomorrow, all being well.'

Denise's eyes weren't as bright as she was used to seeing and it shook her to the core. She glanced at Bailey, walking back into the room holding the statutory orange plastic hospital chair, and gave him a quick appraisal. The same brightness was missing in his eyes too. His honey tone looking a little less honeyed and more sallow. He wasn't eating, at least not properly she could bet money on it, and almost definitely not sleeping well, again understandably. It really sunk in at that moment how much Bailey had going on. His head was bound to be up his arse, she just hoped that Marcus would pick up the work so that Bailey could have some time to adjust to what would be, at least temporarily, a new normal. Her stomach dropped as she realised that perhaps now wasn't the time to look at starting a relationship. It wouldn't be fair to add the responsibility of her onto his plate. Whilst she considered herself low maintenance, a relationship would still require maintenance of some sort. Polly reached for her bag to focus on why she was there.

'I know you said not to get you anything but, well… erm.' This was awkward, even with her new confident kick-ass self.

'You weren't supposed to get anything at all,' Denise grumbled.

'Well, you might not like it. I took a bit of a gamble, but now I think it's a little egotistical. So if you don't like it, that's totally fine.'

'Pol, you're rambling. You OK?' Bailey put his arm around the back of her chair and it was all she could do not to sink into it.

Polly began biting her lip, her hands locating the gift in her bag. She didn't want to make a big deal out of it but for her it was substantial. It had been fun to make, but perhaps she had given more of herself away than she ever had before and the choking sensation in her throat tasted like vulnerability.

'Here.' It was an old iPod shuffle. 'Sorry, it's not a new iPod but I just happened to have that one lying about. It's what's on it that's the main thing.'

Polly dropped her head watching through her eyelashes as Denise put the headphones in. It only took a couple of seconds for Denise to realise what it was. She watched as Denise gasped in shock, and immediately skipped through all the tracks on there, to see what there was. Denise's eyes teared up and Polly felt a whole new level of discomfort – yup definitely awkward.

'Just don't let anyone else listen to it OK?' Polly asked.

'Polly, oh my God. I can't believe this. This is a million

times better than grapes.' Polly felt her hand get grabbed and looked up to see Denise smiling. 'Thank you, this means a lot.'

Polly just shrugged, her eyes wandering back over to Bailey.

Bailey had a small smile on his face. 'What did you do?'

'It's just a small compilation of some songs I thought your mum would like.'

'Except she's performed them, and there are some original compositions in here too, right?'

'Maybe. I just thought if it was me in here, I'd need music now more than ever. Whilst you probably have loads on your phone or Spotify, I can guarantee that you won't have these as nobody does.'

'I love it, Polly, thank you.' With that, Denise put the other headphone in and began listening in earnest.

'Polly. You didn't have to do that.' There was something in Bailey's voice, something nearly tangible, that she longed to hold onto.

'I know that. I'm just glad she liked it. It would've been really awkward if she hadn't.' She laughed, but even to her own ears, it sounded off. She looked down as Bailey's hands clasped hers. His thumb rough as it stroked her knuckles. The faint smell of the alcohol hand sanitiser helping to remind her where she was, and how inappropriate it would be to think about his rough hands on other parts of her body.

'It's really lovely and thoughtful and you've put the rest of us grape buying idiots to shame.'

'I just wanted to help in my own little way.' She watched as his shoulders tensed slightly and he sighed. He entwined his fingers in hers, letting go of her other hand and relaxed back into his chair. They both quietly watched Denise as she smiled along to the music. Polly's phone buzzed and holding onto Bailey's hand she carefully got her phone out of her skirt pocket. She could have let go of his hand but she didn't want to so instead she had to lean into him to reach the pocket at her side. They both saw that the text was from Darren. As surprised as she was, she had no inclination to read it at that point. Instead, she locked her phone and wedged it between her and the side of the chair.

'Everything OK?' Bailey asked, his voice slightly harsh.

'Yep. How's work?'

'Marcus has picked up some of my jobs this week, and it's starting to quieten down now anyway as we wait to get the final approval on a huge project, but it's looking good.'

'That's amazing, Bailey. Well done.'

He winked. 'Thanks, Pol.'

She stared into his eyes and marvelled at the man he was. She felt a longing in her heart that for now at least their timing was still off. Maybe their timing would never be right. But the pull towards him was there and it was stronger than ever. It probably had something to do with the fact that Polly considered herself all in, and she had found a new sense of calm with that. Polly wondered at how bizarre it felt to be so happy to love someone, even though it may as yet be unrequited. Oh, she had no doubt that it would get hard if that was the case, but for now at least she felt really good, her mind and her heart finally singing from the same hymn sheet. Every cell of her knew that she loved him. She just didn't need to tell him that right now. It could wait, and hopefully when the time was right, then maybe they could be together for real. She wasn't an idiot, she knew he was interested to some degree. Their chemistry pulling at each other with every fake kiss, and their real friendship deepening with every conversation.

'OK I'm going to stop being rude now, but, Polly, this is amazing. Thank you,' Denise interrupted her thoughts.

'Oh here's the charger too.' Reaching into her bag she felt her phone go off again. Putting her bag back down after passing the charger over, she quickly glanced at it.

Darren: Last chance.

Huh? What the hell was he talking about? She didn't need a last chance, she'd binned him already. She felt the familiar beat of anger in her gut again. Anger at the betrayal, at his skeevy antics, at his dating apps, but also at herself. How could she have fallen for it for as long as she did?

Her phone buzzed again, this time continuously. Now what? Looking at her phone she saw it was her boss.

'Sorry I have to take this it's work.' Polly stood up and quickly walked into the hallway, her hands shaking and a feeling of dread slicked its way over her skin. Leanne never called her outside work. Ever.

'Hi, Leanne, is everything OK?'

'Hi, Polly, I'm really sorry to call you in the evening but, well... erm, something has come up. I shouldn't really be ringing you at all, I could get in trouble for this, but I've been made aware of an issue. I'm calling to warn you that you'll be asked to attend a meeting first thing in the morning about the policy you wrote. I can't say more than that, but I wanted you to expect it rather than go in blind tomorrow.'

Polly had been walking down the corridor unable to stay still as she processed what Leanne was saying.

'It doesn't sound like it's going to be a good meeting. Are you sure you can't tell me more?'

'I can't, I'm really sorry. Maybe I shouldn't have called you at all, but I couldn't not warn you. I'm sorry, Polly.'

'OK, well, erm, thanks, Leanne.'

'See you tomorrow, bye.'

She still had her phone to her ear and could hear the beep indicating that Leanne had hung up. What the hell was this all about, it sounded like she was in trouble for something but what had she done wrong? Pulling her phone away, it lit up showing the texts from Darren.

Darren: I can't believe how badly you overreacted. Are you feeling alright? I think we should talk, see if we can't figure this out, I don't want you having any regrets about us. I think that our relationship deserves more than that don't you? xx

What the actual fuck?

Darren: You've left me with no other option. Please call me before I do what I have to do xx

Darren: Last chance

What the fuck has he done now? Shit. Walking back into the hospital room, her legs shaking, she plastered a smile to her face as she sat back down, her knees shaking.

'Everything OK, Pol?'

'Yeah. Yeah, everything's fine. She was just ringing me to remind me about a meeting in the morning. It's fine.'

'Hey hey hey, we're here.' Seb and Duncan walked in at that point, and Polly felt saved by the, well not bell, but by the family. There wasn't a lot of space and she'd delivered her get well package. She could legitimately go.

'Hi, Seb. Hi, Duncan. No, no sit here. I have to go now anyway. Denise, it was lovely to see you, although next time I hope it's with even fewer wires.' Polly instantly lent forward and hugged Denise, relaxing when she felt Denise's arm hold her tightly.

'Oh no, are you sure you have to go?' Denise asked, releasing Polly's arm.

'Yes, I have to prepare for a meeting at work tomorrow.' Ain't that the truth.

'Thanks again, Polly. See you soon, love.'

'I'll walk you out,' Bailey said.

'See you.' Polly hoped that her smile would work.

Bailey grabbed her hand and handed over her bag. 'Back in a minute.'

With that, Polly walked down the corridor in a stupor, stopping only to put on her coat, scarf and hat.

'Are you sure you're OK, Pol? You look a little shaken.'

Polly opened her mouth and nearly told him everything. She would do if it were about anything else. He was her 'go-to guy' for all things, and it made it really clear at this moment just how much she needed him in her life. But what was also clear was just how much he had going on. She'd wait for him, of that she had no doubt. But she also couldn't tell him what was going on, it wasn't fair. Besides there might not be that much to tell anyway. She'd know more tomorrow. Using every ounce of energy she had she stood up taller, held his hand tighter and smiled properly.

'Yes, everything is fine. But you need to make sure you eat something healthy soon, OK? Otherwise, I'm going to come round and cook for you, and I wouldn't wish that on anyone. Not unless you like everything covered in hot sauce?'

'I do as it happens. You should just move in it would be easier.'

'Ha, no chance, you just want a housekeeper. Anyway, I've got to go, if I can do anything for you just let me know, OK?'

'Sure, Pol. Are you really alright though?'

'Yes, absolutely. See you later.' She didn't hesitate, she couldn't afford to. So she marched towards the bus stop, looking back just once to smile and wave, really sell the fact that she was fine. When she honestly wasn't sure if she was. What the hell had Darren done? One thing was for certain she wasn't ringing him to find out.

Chapter Twenty-Five

Polly looked at herself in the mirrored lift. She'd been torn between smart comfortable and smart confident. She'd gone comfortable and had on her brown flat knee-high boots, over her wool tights, her burgundy skirt and emerald green shirt. Confident would've been very similar but with more red or maybe black, and a heel so that she could tower over everyone. Shifting her body weight from side to side, she hummed her song for Bailey. Well, she tried to, she had a lump in her throat that was constricting her breathing, humming was hard. Taking deep breaths and studying herself to see if she looked as nervous as she felt. Yep. She re-arranged her scarf to hide the anxiety rash that was spreading up her neck. Then she began clicking and un-clicking the fastener on her watch. She looked up in dread as the annoying ding indicated that she was at her floor. It was time to face the music. Walking up to her desk, she had only enough time to take off her coat and scarf and put her handbag down.

'Polly, I'm sorry but would you mind coming into meeting room three, please? We need to discuss something with you.' Leanne had avoided eye contact. Her tone overly professional. It was the only confirmation she needed as she followed her down the corridor.

'Thank you, Polly, please sit down.'

Polly did as requested, and was reminded of when she interviewed for her first job with the company, as she faced the panel of three in front of her. Sat opposite her, Leanne, her boss, Raj, Head of Service and his colleague Jackie, Head of Recruitment. Jackie was known for being a bit of a hard-ass but she'd always been pleasant to Polly, and she would've been the one to formally offer Polly the promotion, but from the look on her face, she knew that was no longer an option. It was Jackie that spoke first.

'Polly I'm not going to beat around the bush. It has been brought to our attention that you were having a relationship with Darren Selby, Contracts Manager on the third floor.'

Polly was mute, the only person who could have informed them was Darren himself. They had no proof that there had been a relationship and she'd been very clear that they didn't do anything at work. There weren't even any playful emails that would give them away.

'The reason that this is problematic for us is because the new policy restricts this, as you know.'

Polly was still dumbfounded and looked at Leanne, who was just looking at the floor and shifting uncomfortably in her seat.

'I'm not sure I understand. Even in the new policy it states that relationships within departments need to be declared to managers. Whether or not Darren and I had been in a relationship, it would've been from different departments.'

Jackie sighed. 'Polly, I don't want to have to request access to your emails but I will if I have to. I don't want to make this any more embarrassing for you than it already is and besides Darren has told us everything.'

'What do you mean everything?' Polly asked, her insides turning icy cold.

'Really, Polly? You want me to go into detail about your sexual practices with a Contracts Manager that took place within this building?' Jackie asked.

'Nothing took place within this building. With me at least. I found out that he was screwing multiple other people within the building but I can assure you that I was not one of them!'

'So you're saying that you weren't in a relationship with him?' Raj quietly asked, with an almost hopeful look in his eyes.

'I was in a relationship with him outside of work, yes. I ended it yesterday when I found out that he had been sleeping with numerous people within the company. I have no doubt that he came to you immediately after that. Would the timings be right?'

The silence from the panel confirmed everything.

'I have the evidence, it's in my folders on the OneDrive. Please feel free to get access. I also have nothing to hide in my emails, access them as well. Do whatever you need to. Will that be all?'

'Polly. I'm sorry but you're suspended,' Raj said.

'*What?*'

'Suspension is a neutral act so that an investigation can take place. I wouldn't have to come down so hard, but this has come from the Senior Management Team and, Polly, you wrote the damned policy. Why didn't you just declare your relationship?' Jackie asked.

'I... I... I... You're suspending me?'

Raj nodded. Polly felt like screaming, she hadn't declared it because it was already over. She was in love with someone else. Suspended? Fuck.

'So presumably you'll be suspending Darren as well then?'

'That decision will have to be made by the Board,' Jackie said.

'So it's because he's a man. He can get away with it? Or is it because he's bringing in money and I'm just an HR bod?' The fire in her veins was toxic and it was taking over, the anger within was providing all of her verbal and non-verbal responses right now.

Jackie looked away too at that point. Now no one was looking at her, and Polly was furious. She felt like she would simultaneously vomit, throw the desk into the wall, and curl into a ball and sob. Instead, she felt her mouth get tight, she sucked on her own tongue trying to curtail all of the things she wanted to say but that she couldn't get past her throat. She took a breath.

'So what happens now?' Her voice tight her windpipe contracting against her vocal cords.

'You'll be assigned a contact in HR, they will stay in contact with you throughout the investigation. But until then you are suspended. You are not allowed to come into work or communicate with anyone from work aside from your assigned HR contact. You'll need to pass your fob and your ID to Leanne.' With that Raj stood up and Jackie followed.

For a minute Jackie looked like she wanted to say something further, but decided against it. Instead, she followed Raj as they quietly walked out of the meeting room.

'Shit. Shit. Shit. I cannot believe that asshole has done this to me. Leanne, I wasn't making anything up. All the investigations, links to his fob and where he was in the building, it's all on the One Drive.'

'I'm sorry, Polly. I'll give you a minute to compose yourself, then I'll walk out with you.'

It was a really nice way of saying escort you out of the building but Polly got the drift. She just wished that she didn't have to walk past everyone. This would be the talk of the company for a long time. Leanne closed the door, and the silence in the room was temporarily cathartic. She bathed in it, trying to slow her brain down and process everything that had just happened. Suspended. Fuck. Not a great career move. All thoughts kept coming back to dickhead Darren. First, she'd had no idea he was cheating on her with half the company, then she'd had no idea that he was so malicious and cold that he would do something like this. Had she ever really known him at all? Obviously not, but how had he managed to be so deceitful? Why oh why had she slept with him? With that thought came the desire to vomit again. But then her rage returned and she never wished she had punched someone more in her entire life. At least then it would've been worth the suspension.

Polly clenched her jaw fighting back the urge to puke and the want to cry. She could do both at home, in fact not only could she do both things at home she could do them for as long as she wanted. After all, she had nowhere else to be.

Leanne walked back into the room. 'OK, I got your stuff for you.'

Polly mumbled a thanks as she put on her coat and took her bag.

'Oh, you'll want these, won't you?' Passing over her ID and her fob she let out a sigh.

'I know it doesn't mean much, but I'm going to tell the team that I sent you home because you were poorly. I will make sure that the worker assigned to you is discreet. I want this all to be over and you back here as quickly as possible and I'll do what I can this end.'

'Thanks, Leanne. Just watch out for Darren, he's more of a dick than I thought.'

They walked through the office towards the lift. It might not seem important, but the fact that Leanne was happy to tell people she was sick, really did make her feel better. Much better that people thought she was ill, rather than... well, what would they think? That she was an incompetent whore, or that she just had bad taste? Shame pressed down on her shoulders. Once outside Leanne gave Polly a quick hug, before turning around through the glass doors. Polly walked to the bus stop, not even bothering to put her headphones in. Grateful for the fresh wind that was swirling past, taking the thoughts from her head with it. Looks like it was going to be a pj day today, and tomorrow, and who knew for how long? That was fine, she didn't want to be anywhere but in bed anyway. Another blast of cold air and the numbness spread, and Polly was grateful for it.

Chapter Twenty-Six

'There's a new bar opening across the road,' said Paige as she sat down in the seating area around the firepit in Mya's gorgeously landscaped garden. The same garden that had brought Sophie and Marcus together in the first place.

Bailey, Marcus, Polly, and Mya all looked at her, waiting for more, but that was it apparently.

'So? You're doing great business. Weren't you talking about opening up a second bar? You're not worried are you?' Mya asked as she messed around with the fire currently roaring.

'No. Not yet. The new owner may have called in today though.'

'And?' Marcus asked. 'Are they nice? Are they going to be a problem?'

'They seemed nice enough, but I'm not sure.' Paige sighed. 'I can't tell.'

Ah, thought Bailey there's the problem, her spider-sense was playing up again. It was almost funny to watch her squirm, having to deal with life sneaking up on her, as it does the rest of them. Life hadn't been sneaking so much as running up to him, he couldn't believe that the wedding was just a few weeks away.

Before anyone could add anything further, whirlwind Sophie walked down the path and slammed her wedding planner down on the walled border. They'd all seen her latest vlog and knew that there was a new wedding drama. Sophie had been recommended a wedding planner, an actual person, and apparently, she was worth her weight in gold. So far, of the issues that Tatiana had helped resolve, there'd been a mix up with the wedding flowers, potential loss of venue exclusivity, and an issue with who was and who wasn't invited. Fortunately for Bailey, Seb had been amazing and had sorted out all of the designs for the invitations, place settings etc. and apparently one or two other things, that weren't disclosed. He had been a little worried that his sister might not take it seriously, but, by all accounts, Sophie had already gotten Seb a load more clients, so she was understandably thrilled. She'd been telling them all about it at his mum's the other night, and he was pleased that he'd been able to help and to be able to give her something positive to focus on. Sophie even suggested that she could be a mentor to Seb with regards to brand and visibility for her business. His mum was better and rested and ready to go back in for her next round of chemo next week. Everything was starting to calm down a little as they all adjusted to what was their new fragile normal. They met more regularly for family meals and catch-ups, and he found that he was looking forward to them more and more. Polly had even been invited a couple more times but in the last week or so, she'd not been able to come. She'd said she was too busy helping with the wedding stuff, so much so that she hadn't even gone to the Speakeasy on Monday. He was worried about her, and with a deep breath, he realised that for once an additional worry didn't weigh him down. Instead, it felt more normal, like he had more headspace, more room to breathe. He knew it was only temporary, but he would take it, and gladly.

'I'll be back in a minute, but first I desperately need a drink.'

Bailey watched as Sophie all but ran to the kitchen. Marcus got up, presumably to check that his beloved was all right. Bailey looked over at Polly. She was quietly sipping her drink, looking devastating as usual, as she stared into the fire, and avoiding eye contact with pretty much everyone. He wasn't sure if anyone else had noticed, but he had. Then again, if he was being honest, he had noticed everything about her these last few days, well, months, well, year – OK fine, years.

'So we have a problem, a potentially big one,' Sophie announced as she and Marcus returned and sat down. Now that she was here they had the quorum, it was one of the last full team meetings before the big day, and with the weather finally starting to improve they needed little excuse to enjoy the garden. Bailey was more than happy to see his and Marcus's work being utilised. Especially considering the state the garden had been in before, and not to mention the love that had blossomed from it.

'Are you going to tell us what's the matter, or are you going to be dramatic for a bit longer yet?' Mya asked as Marcus put his arm around Sophie.

'Well pretty much everything is sorted, but the wedding planner—' There were groans from Paige and Mya, who rolled their eyes at each other. 'Anyway Tatiana's just been in touch to tell me that the wedding singer can't be there, apparently she's on doctor's orders not to sing.'

'So, just hire someone else.' Mya's eyebrow raised as if this was as easy as changing a pair of socks. Bailey had to agree, it was that easy surely? Apparently not.

'It's not that easy. I wanted her, she was going to sing a solo piece whilst we signed the register and then again with the band after the wedding breakfast for the first hour until the DJ.'

Bailey looked over at Polly. It was so obvious that she could be the one to help out. He knew that this put her in an awkward position. She would immediately feel like she should help, but would also hate the idea of performing. As it was, she was twirling the bottle of Becks around, picking at the label. She was doing a fine job of looking like she had no course to offer assistance. Then again, she also looked like she wasn't listening. He cursed himself for not getting here sooner, he could've been sat next to her.

'So what's Tatiana saying?' Paige asked.

'She's looking high and low for someone similar that can

perform for us. Worst-case scenario we'll do something else like a string quartet and then just have the DJ start an hour earlier.'

'So it's not really a problem then?' Mya said, doing nothing to hide the bored look on her face.

'You guys suck.'

'Come on, bridezilla, this is nothing to worry about. Not having a dress, a ring, or an official to do the ceremony, those are major problems,' Mya said.

'Or not having a venue,' Paige added.

'Wait, why, what do you know?' Sophie asked hurriedly.

'Nothing, I know nothing,' Paige groaned.

Sophie sighed and rolled her eyes. 'There's just so much that could go wrong, so much outside of my control. I can't take it.'

'It's just a wedding,' Paige said as the rest of the group sat back, expecting Mount Sophie to explode. Bailey jumped in, ready to take the grenade and save everyone else.

'Come on now. Cut her some slack. Look, Sophie, I can do it. I mean I sound exactly like an Adam Sandler wedding singer, but if that's what you want?' Bailey started singing, 'I live in my sister's basement.' Everyone sang along and then promptly laughed harder, except Sophie who was giving daggers to everyone and Polly who just looked up and softly smiled.

Polly definitely wasn't right, and Bailey was desperate to find out what was wrong. He both hoped it was, and wasn't, that smug boyfriend of hers. If it was then maybe he could whisper in her ear that she would be better off without him. No, he wouldn't do that to her. She'd figure it out on her own soon enough, or at least he desperately hoped that she would.

Bailey nearly jumped in his seat when he realised that if his mum had another reaction to the chemo like last time and ended up in the hospital, there was every chance that he might not be able to make it to the wedding either. Shit. Presumably, the best man was an important part of the wedding too? He'd have to speak to them about it. He didn't really want to broadcast his problems, but it wouldn't be fair to them if he let them down last minute. Then again, the idea of watching Polly and Darren throughout the wedding made him feel physically sick and uncharacteristically violent. Even if his mum was fine, well as fine as she could be, he could use her as an excuse to get out of it. Nah, he'd never do that, he loved Marcus and Sophie too much to do that to them.

'Oh, that reminds me. Tatiana wants some of the sten pictures, the ones that are PG at least. She wants to do a slide show. So pass me your phones I want to go through them all and send myself the ones that I like.'

'Sophie, I have to go. I'm sorry. I'll send over all my pics later, OK?' Polly stood up slowly.

'Are you OK?' Sophie asked, standing up to hug her.

'Yeah I think I'm just coming down with something, but I'm sure it's just a twenty-four hour thing. Don't panic.'

Sophie pulled back moving away from Polly like she had the plague.

'I love you, Polly and I hope you feel better soon, but please get the hell away from me. I don't want to catch anything before the wedding.'

'Bridezilla,' muttered Mya and Paige.

'Yeah, sure. See you later. Good luck getting a singer. Let me know if I can do anything.'

Bailey watched her carefully as she put on her jacket and scarf and walked up the steps. Bailey jumped up and threw his phone on Sophie's planner unlocked. 'Go for it. I just have to check something with Polly before she leaves.'

'Sure you do,' Paige whispered, and Mya grinned.

She was just at the back door of the house when he caught up to her.

'Polly, what's wrong? You know you can talk to me, right?'

She opened her mouth to speak, but then closed her lips again before nodding. 'I know, Bailey. I'm OK, really.'

She clearly wasn't by the way she leaned in and hugged him close. He held her and willed his unreciprocated love out of his pores and into her. It didn't matter to him that it wasn't returned, he just wanted her to feel it somehow. Reluctantly she let go, and for a brief minute he forgot himself and went to bend slightly to give her a kiss goodbye, but she'd already moved away.

'Take care, Pol,' Bailey said, the scent of her shampoo still in his nose.

'Thanks, Bailey. Bye.'

'I'll text you later.'

Walking slowly back to the table, he didn't like not knowing what was wrong, but he wasn't about to force her into talking. He just hoped she'd tell him what the problem was whenever she was ready, and whatever it was he knew without a doubt that he would do anything he could to help. Sitting back down, Marcus leaned over.

'How you doing, dude? How's your mum?' Marcus asked.

'She's doing really well again, for now. She's got her next round in the next week or two.'

'I've told Sophie. She said to tell you that under no circumstances are you to worry about the wedding and that your mum comes first.' Bailey raised an eyebrow. He loved Sophie but there's no way she said that.

'It's not what she said at first, I think her first words were "God no that's awful", but then it was immediately followed with the rest of it. She might be a bit bridezilla-y but she still loves you, you know.'

'I know, man, I'm sorry. I'm just not going to know until nearer the time but it's one day, or at worse it's a few hours, we'll make it work don't worr—' His train of thought was interrupted as he heard the sound that he had been listening to non-stop since he had originally recorded it. He was happy for a good three seconds before he felt his brain fall down to his feet, taking his stomach with it. Fuck. Fucking fuck.

He leaned over and snatched his phone back but it was too late. Of course in the laws of the universe, you can never ever simply just turn off your phone when there is something on there you don't want people to see or hear. That would be too fucking easy. So Polly kept singing for another ten seconds whilst he fumbled with his phone and eventually got it locked and back in his pocket.

'What... the...' He looked at Sophie as she stuttered, and hoped that somehow she might not have noticed it was Polly. Or maybe she had temporary deafness and hadn't heard her sing.

'Polly's a *singer*?' Sophie cried.

Nope, no such joy. He'd officially outed her. His headache returned, he hadn't realised that it had gone until this point, but now his eyes stung, and he groaned as he shut his lids and dropped his head to his hands. Whatever shit Polly was going through, he'd made it ten times worse.

'Was that Polly? She sounded amazing.' Mya's face lit up in wonder.

'No way was that Polly. I'd know if she was a singer.' Marcus shook his head. 'It must be someone else.'

'That was Polly,' Sophie stuttered.

The only quiet person was Paige. Figures.

Bailey lifted his head, and opened his eyes and knew that they were all staring at him, waiting for more. What could he say? He could deny it. He could confirm it. He could ask them to lie and say that they hadn't seen what he hadn't been permitted to record. Shit.

'I can't say anything. I need to talk to Polly.' Bailey tried to stand but his brain and his stomach were still on the floor.

'You need to talk to Polly? Hell, we all need to talk to Polly. Why would she keep this from us? We've got her back. We said she was wasted in HR. Why wouldn't she tell us? No, seriously, why? Why has she kept this part of her life from us? Are we not good enough to know? How did you find out?'

Bailey had been watching as Sophie's face changed throughout her speech from bewilderment to annoyance. He shrugged, powerless to add anything more. Great, they were hurting too and this was his fault as well. He clearly couldn't be trusted. The only thing ringing through his head, with any great volume, was that he had accidentally betrayed the woman he loved and there was no way of getting through this without causing her more hurt. He'd have to let her know what he'd done. It had been accidental, sure, he hadn't meant for anyone to see the video, but he had deliberately chosen to record her. This was on him. He was a fuck-up just like he always had been. He honestly thought that he had changed over the last two years. Turned over multiple leaves literally and figuratively. There'd be no way she'd ever want him after this, and there was no way he would ever be worthy of changing her mind.

Chapter Twenty-Seven

Facedown in her bed still fully clothed with her boots and coat still on, Polly was absolutely shattered. Which was funny considering she'd been in bed pretty much all week. She'd tried to get out of going tonight, but having already bailed on a number of meetings with Sophie she knew she had to go to this one. But getting dressed, going out to Mya's and pretending that her world wasn't falling apart because she'd had the strange idea that getting together with Darren would be a good thing, had been shattering. She'd put her phone onto airplane mode, and listened to music on the twenty-minute walk home but that hadn't helped. The bracing wind had propelled her to her front door. After utilising the last of her will power to drag herself up the stairs, the bed was where she had landed and she wasn't sure if she would ever be able to move from this spot.

Her eyes were hot and she held them firmly shut so that no tears could escape. She didn't want to cry, that would just take even more out of her. Also, she didn't want to give in, she was afraid that she might not stop. It wasn't just the Darren thing and the work thing, it was the Bailey thing, and the general life thing. She'd been peddling along quite amenably, but now it felt as though the whole world had stopped spinning and she had fallen arse over tit with no ground to catch her. She really needed a cup of tea.

The realisation that she couldn't summon the energy to go and make a brew was what tipped her over the edge. Regardless of how tightly shut her eyelids were the tears found ways of escaping. She had honestly thought that dumping Darren would make everything right. That she could be happy, free, with Bailey, and maybe even a little more confident about her music, maybe even tell her friends and family. The whole burlesque / breaking up with Darren / bearing her soul on her old iPod for Bailey's mum thing were huge strides for her. She was starting to own it. Now just over a week later and she owned what exactly? Nothing, and nor would she ever, she was going to lose her job after all. Then what? Sell her keyboard and guitar? Move back in with her mum and dad?

Curling on to her side in a foetal position only helped marginally, in so much that her face wasn't hot on the pillow and now her tears had somewhere to land.

The banging on her door made her jump. It was too late for visitors. Suddenly bolting upright, shit what if it was Darren? She no longer knew him, his behaviour abhorrent there was nothing stopping him from just rocking up. Shit. Grabbing her phone she went to dial 999.

'Polly it's only us. Please, can we come in for a minute?'

What the—? Why the hell was Mya outside her house? Us? Does that mean they were all with her? Was Bailey there? She didn't have the energy to deal with them, especially not Bailey, she'd had a hard enough time pretending in front of him for five minutes. Staying still and breathing as quietly as possible, she figured that maybe they'd go away.

'Please, Polly, we need to speak to you.' Sophie's turn. So maybe there was another wedding emergency. Her heart dropped a little, feeling ashamed of herself. It was an important day for Sophie, she wouldn't belittle Sophie's experience however out of proportion it might feel to Polly at this moment in time.

When was the last time they'd been to her house? It had been ages ago. She'd not had to hide her instruments for a long time. Another reason they couldn't come in now. She had no time to hide all of her music stuff. Her guitar was lying casually on her sofa, instead of a dining table she had her piano keyboard and desk where she wrote and recorded her music. Even up here she had some music paper scattered about, and she always had pen and paper in the bathroom, because as corny as it was she always thought up the best lyrics when in the bathroom.

It had gone quiet again. Hoping they had gone away she re-assumed the foetal position as she looked down at her phone still held within a death grip and realised that it was still on airplane mode. Taking it off, in case there was some indication on there as to why they were stalking her, she foolishly forgot to take it off silent. There was a symphony of beeps and alerts. Multiple missed calls, most of them from Bailey. Some texts and some WhatsApps.

There was a click and then she heard footsteps. Crap. The spare key, which meant that Marcus was with them, and given the amount of missed calls from Bailey she guessed he was here too. Great, she hated an audience at the best of times, looking like, and feeling like absolute shite was bound to help that no end.

'Polly. Are you in here?' Mya shouted.

'Polly it's just Mya, Sophie, and me. We just want to check you're OK.' Paige's voice sounding more gentle when compared to the others.

'No we don't, we want to know why she lied,' Mya hissed.

Lied? Lied about what? Polly was at a loss, her lack of energy meaning she had no desire to go downstairs, but also knew that if she stayed quiet they would come and find her. She couldn't even think about hiding, that would involve moving, which brought her back to the lack of energy thing.

'I'm up—' Polly coughed her voice barely a croak and tried again. 'I'm up here. What's going on?'

As the herd of baby elephants made their way up the small staircase, she prayed that they hadn't lied. That there was no one else with them.

As she had curled up into a tight ball facing the door, she watched as one by one they tumbled into the room and then stopped abruptly, and Polly knew that there was no escaping.

'What's the matter, babe?' Mya asked, her tone of voice doing a full one-eighty.

That was it, the main reason she had been avoiding all of them. She hated crying but there was no stopping it now. Everyone piled in and climbed on her bed. Mya getting in behind and spooning her. Sophie somehow getting higher up the bed and stroking her hair. Paige at the bottom of the bed taking off Polly's boots. The crying had turned into full gut-wrenching sobs now.

'Tell us what's wrong, Pol. We can't do anything unless we know what's going on.' Now that her boots were off Polly curled even tighter, snotting with no delicacy whatsoever into her duvet.

'Oh, I know.' Paige disappeared, and everyone just continued the strokes and shhhh noises. Sophie got up and quickly re-appeared, toilet roll in hand, and began gently dabbing at Polly's face. That was true friendship right there. It wasn't about holding each other's hair back when drunk and throwing up, or swapping clothes with each other on a drunken night out, or stepping in to save a bad date. It was wiping snot off another person's face without heaving or wincing. The thought made Polly smile slightly, which in turn gradually de-escalated the crying back down to rapid tears rather than the animalistic grunts and full-body shakes, from just a few seconds earlier.

'Thank you,' Polly whispered as her breathing evened out and the tears slowed down further.

'Sit up, Pol. I have something that will make you feel better.' Paige re-appeared and Polly slowly sat up and everyone around her got comfortable but still held onto her wherever they could.

'Thanks, Paige.' But Polly couldn't take the cup of tea that was offered, as it just set her off again. Putting the cup on the bedside table, Paige reached over.

'Does it have something to do with that douchebag Darren?' she asked.

Polly slowly nodded and got her breathing under control once again. Finally able to speak she said, 'The cheating arsehole got me suspended at work.'

'Bastard.'

'What?'

'How the fuck did he do that?'

Polly looked at the horror and anger in her friends' faces, her tears slowing once more. Reaching over she took the brew and cradled it in her hands as she relayed everything that had happened over the last week. It took a while for everyone to process the information. Sophie immediately got her phone out and started typing something. Paige looked like she wanted to kill somebody. Mya grinding her teeth for a minute before she spoke.

'OK, well, you don't know for sure that you will lose your job, right? Is it paid suspension? Actually, you know what that doesn't even matter. Here's what you're going to do. You're going to come and live with me. You'll be safe there. Darren doesn't know where I live. I could use the company as it's not the same since bridezilla moved out. I can offer you really cheap rent because my work is going really well at the moment and then you could quit your job and maybe try your hand at being a singer-songwriter.' Mya spelt out the plan of attack.

'What?' Polly nearly dropped her cup of tea.

'I think that makes a lot of sense,' said Sophie, looking up from her phone to nod her approval.

'That's a great plan. We'll all feel better knowing that you're safe,' said Paige, nodding.

'Why didn't you tell us about all of this sooner? Wait, you weren't going to tell us at all. Why not?' Mya asked.

Polly swung her head back and forth looking at them all. 'No, wait. Everyone wait. How do you know about the singing?'

'We'll get to that. First things first, do you agree with the plan?' Mya said.

'No. I'm not just gonna up sticks and move because of some ex. No.'

'Polly.' Sophie spoke just louder than a whisper and grabbed hold of Polly's hand. 'When you first got together with Darren did you have any idea whatsoever that he might cheat on you?'

'No, of course—'

'Did you have any idea that he would try and get you sacked from your job?' continued Sophie.

'No not—'

'So you have no reason to believe that he isn't capable of coming round here and doing something dangerous. Even if it's only for the short term you should stay at Mya's. It's not safe for you here. Then when you've moved in there, and once you're settled we are each going to take it in turns to yell at you for not telling us sooner, and potentially putting your life at risk. But we will hold off on that for now. Yes?' Sophie's grip on Polly's hand tightened, and Polly could see that her friends were genuinely worried for her safety.

'OK, fine. Mya, thank you.' Polly felt her shoulders drop. 'Thank you. But wait, why were you here in the first place? Did you know that I was in a bad way?'

Paige shook her head. 'No, I'm not firing on all cylinders again. I blame the new bar owner.'

'So why are you here?' Polly watched as they each passed a look from one to another, clearly not sure how or who should begin. Whatever was coming wasn't going to be great news, that much was clear.

'It's not Bailey's fault.' Paige had started but by the looks of things she was hoping to pass the conversational baton to whoever would take it.

'He passed me his phone to look at the sten pictures, right before he went to talk to you before you left.'

Polly was lost. So what. Bailey was the only one who knew. He hadn't told them, so then what?

'We saw the video. I'm sure it wasn't on purpose. In fact, Bailey looked horrified.' Mya also spoke with soft tones.

Polly looked up at the ceiling as if there would be some clue as to what was going on or at least some sort of sign as to how to proceed, but her lampshade was not forthcoming. 'What video?'

'The video of you singing that love song, on the stage,' Sophie said.

'What?' Polly's voice had dropped an octave, hitting the bottom end of her range.

'Shit,' Paige muttered.

'Oh God...' Sophie broke off and started pacing.

'Bailey had a video on his phone of you performing at some club. Whilst letting Sophie look through his sten photos she scrolled too far and saw it,' Mya explained.

'I only saw like half a minute, if that,' Sophie said.

Polly's phone chose that moment to sing. Bailey was calling her. Polly just stared at it for a minute before launching it across the room. How could he do this to her? What the hell was happening? Was it crap all over Polly week? No, maybe it was 'shit blokes wear brilliant disguises' month. Bailey. How could he? He knew. She closed her eyes and let out a breath and with it went everything. All the hate, the anger, the bitterness, the confusion, the love. Everything. Her song had finished and there was no applause.

Chapter Twenty Eight

'Come on, pick up, pick up.' Bailey wanted to hurl his phone across the dashboard, but as that would only break his phone, the phone he desperately kept ringing Polly on, he instead jumped out of his car and slammed the door. Nope, that didn't work either. She wasn't responding to any of his calls, texts, WhatsApps, Messenger or anything, how the hell was he ever going to make it right? Could he even make it right? Holding the title of Mr Fuck Up for so many consecutive years had him believing it was unlikely, but he would continue to try.

Bailey was about to slam the front door shut, having no recollection of how he had even got to his mum's house. The hushed tones of music playing in the front room, the smell of his family home, the medical folder on the hallway table that the MacMillan nurses were using, stopped his temper in its tracks. Instead, the quiet just made the thudding at the back of his skull even louder. So he softly closed the front door instead.

'Bailey is that you? Is Polly with you?'

'Yes, it's me and no.' Bailey threw his coat towards the vicinity of the coat stand and tried not to think about kissing Polly in this hallway. Or how much further they might have gone if they hadn't been interrupted. God, that was ages ago now, and by all accounts not likely to ever happen again. He trudged his way into the front room towards the sound of his mum's voice.

His mum was sat up, a blanket around her legs messing about with Polly's iPod, Billy was sat next to her reading his Kindle. On the surface, it would appear relatively normal, but Billy was sitting close to his mum and not in his usual armchair. The music was on but it was quiet and no one was dancing or singing along. The place was clean but from lack of use rather than everything just having been cleared away. There was a quietness, a stillness. They were counting down until the next lot of chemo. Just waiting to see what adventures await, will it be another life-threatening trip to the hospital again?

'Hi, darling, you OK? Where's Polly?' Denise asked.

No fucking clue because she won't speak to me and it's been days and I feel like I've lost my best friend, no offence Marcus, was what he wanted to say. But he didn't.

'She's busy, Mum, sorry.' Close enough.

'What's up, kid? You don't look good,' Billy asked as Bailey sat down in his armchair.

'You don't need to worry about me. I'm fine. How are you both?' Bailey took a breath.

'Fine,' Denise said, smiling, her eyes twinkling. 'What about you, Billy?'

'I'm fine too,' Billy said, with a smile.

'Neither of you is funny you know that right?' Bailey looked at his mum.

'Darling, I am feeling good and rested, in the best possible place for more chemo. But, Bailey, you're obviously not fine. Did Polly find out about the video?'

'Huh? Why would you say that?' Bailey asked, surprised that she would hit the nail on the head.

'Billy, love, would you mind getting us a drink, please?'

'Of course.' As Billy stood up, he gestured for Bailey to take his seat next to his mum, and also gave his shoulder a quick squeeze on the way out.

'I have never seen you look happier as you have these last few months. Why do you look so down now?'

'You're right. I've done something stupid. It was a complete accident, but yeah, Polly not only knows that I recorded her but she knows because the rest of the group saw it. So I recorded her and outed her. That's some stellar boyfriending right there, huh? Anyway, Mum, I'll figure it out. You just focus on you, OK?'

The irony of asking Polly to be his fake girlfriend in order to help his mother's recovery, and now explaining that he had hurt his fake girlfriend and therefore causing his mum additional stress was not lost on him.

'Hmmm, stellar boyfriending indeed. So can you figure it out or not?'

'She won't answer my calls...' Bailey sighed and shrugged, he hadn't meant to let on how bad it was.

'Have you asked Marcus or Sophie?'

'I really don't want to get them involved. I also don't want to disturb them as it's not long till the wedding. They have enough on.'

'Well you love each other, I'm sure you can figure it out.' Denise smiled softly.

'Hmmm.' What more could he say without laying it all on the line?

'You don't love her?'

'Of course I do.' He didn't hesitate, not even for a second.

'I know, sweetheart, I can tell. Let me tell you that I think she is perfect for you, and I am sure that she loves you too.'

Bailey just grunted. No. She probably didn't now, and he didn't know if she ever had. She had a boyfriend after all. A real one, one that wasn't him. For a second he thought about coming clean and telling his mum everything but what purpose would that serve? In fact, hell, why was he here at all? He was so selfish, he hadn't thought it through. He was upset and wanted to see his mum, it had been that simple. But now, now she was asking questions that he couldn't answer. Now she would be worried that his relationship was in trouble, the fucking issue that started this whole thing was her worrying whether or not he could even have a serious relationship. Well, it would seem he couldn't even keep a fake serious relationship, she was obviously right to be worried.

Maybe he should go back to what he was good at, he was far better at lots of short-term relationships after all.

'Do you want some help figuring out a way to make this right?' Denise asked quietly.

'I don't know, Mum.' He could feel his mum's eyes staring into him and it was a little while before she spoke.

'Well, if we can fix your fake relationship then maybe it can turn into a real one. Then you wouldn't have to keep pretending to make out with each other, you just could,' Denise said.

'What?'

'Hahaha. Billy you were right, I owe you twenty quid!' Denise called out, laughing.

'Seriously what?' Bailey stared at her.

Billy walked in then holding a tray of hot drinks and chuckling softly. 'Sorry, son.'

'You knew?' Bailey asked, gobsmacked.

'Of course we knew. The timing was a bit suspicious, don't you think? I tell you I worry about you having a serious relationship then boom you're in one? Jokes on us though right, because you actually fell for each other whilst you were busy pretending and you didn't even notice.'

'I did, she didn't, I don't think. Before you think badly about Polly for lying, it was my idea and I talked her into it.'

'That's just it though, sweetheart. Neither of you were lying. You just didn't know it. Now stay for tea, we'll figure out a way to make this right. Shall we call Duncan and Serena?' Denise asked, her arm around his shoulders.

'What are you making, Billy?' Bailey asked.

'My famous toad in the hole.'

Bailey's stomach rumbled and he realised that he hadn't eaten properly in a long time. 'No, we don't need to invite them.'

'Right, OK then, let's come up with a plan,' Denise said.

'I'm just not sure what will work, Mum. Maybe we should

leave it, even if I fix this mistake there's every chance I'll mess it up again. I've not exactly got the best track record with relationships.'

'Bailey Christopher Johnson. Yes, that's right I full named you. You haven't got a history of long-term relationships, that was the whole reason I was worried in the first place. All of your other little shenanigans don't count. A relationship is hard work and you will undoubtedly mess it up many times over, as will she. But no son of mine is lazy. You are a hard worker, and sometimes that's what a relationship needs. You two are perfect for each other. Now let's get it sorted.'

'Did I just get told off?' Bailey asked, unable to stop the grin from spreading across his face.

'Yes, and if you're not careful I will ground your ass.'

Chapter Twenty-Nine

'So what's this new event of Paige's? Why is she even bothering?' Polly readjusted the shoulder strap on her bag as she walked next to Mya.

'I don't know what the event is specifically, I just know that Paige is freaking out about the new bar opening up and she wanted to try something a little different.'

'Ohhh. I hope it's a psychic night or a gin night,' Polly said.

Mya grinned. 'I'm so happy you moved in, Polly. I miss having company.'

'I've not moved in, I am staying temporarily to avoid a very unpleasant ex. Besides, it's only been two days. You don't know what you've signed up to yet.'

'Hmm, we'll see. Polly…' Mya hesitated. 'Can I ask you about your singing?'

'What about it?' Polly ducked her chin into the scarf relishing the warmth of her own breath.

'Why the secrecy?'

'Pah. You're one to talk, you won't tell us what you do for a living so how am I any different?' Polly replied.

'It's complicated.'

Polly turned to look at Mya, well as much as she could as she walked down the busy street into town. It was the first time Mya had said anything at all about her career that didn't involve her joking around.

'Whatever it is you're doing, you're safe though, right?' Polly asked, her tone serious.

'Polly, come on. I'm indestructible. But yes, I'm safe, silly. But I was asking about you, stop deflecting.'

'I don't know. I've been thinking about it a lot lately. It's mine. It's my yoga, my meditation. I need it. At first, I didn't want to share it because I needed it. Then I had a couple of bad experiences that knocked my confidence but the desire to write songs and perform remained. I don't know and I don't expect you to believe me but I was just getting to the point where I was going to tell you all. I just, I guess I felt like I needed to learn more first. But now I think that maybe none of that mattered. I just needed to get out there and do it but at my own pace. It's not like I could've not. I'm addicted to songwriting and when I do perform, or at least when I do it at the Speakeasy, in front of people I know have my back, then it's electric. It's the greatest feeling in the world. But terrifying at the same time. I'm rambling I know. I'm sure I'm not making much sense.'

'It makes sense to me. I understand what you mean, honestly, you have no idea.'

'But you're still not going to tell me what you do?' Polly searched Mya's face.

'No. It's against my brand.'

Polly shoved Mya as they walked.

'Thanks for letting me stay. It means a lot.'

Mya linked her arm with Polly's. 'We all have your back, Pol. You know that, right?'

'I do now.' Polly grinned, the love for her friends warming her bones.

'I have another question for you, though you might not like it,' Mya said.

'Oh God, this walk to the bar is taking forever,' Polly feigned.

'You and Bailey? What's happening there?'

'Nothing.' That came out a little too quickly to her own ears.

'Nothing at all?'

'No. You may have forgotten but I was with Darren until recently,' Polly said matter-of-factly.

'Hmmm. But you like him though, don't you?' Mya asked, a sense of caution in her tone. Understandable, she didn't want to get her head bitten off.

'Bailey, yes. Darren, absolutely not.'

'And he likes you so why haven't you got together?'

'First of all I don't know that he likes me, second if he did or does, he knew better than to record me singing. Thirdly, the timing was always off. I was dating, he was dating and it was never going to be with each other. Now, it's too late.'

'Why is it too late? You could just let him apologise you know? It was a genuine mistake; he never would've shown it to us. His head's up his arse with all that his family is going through,' Mya pointed out, causing Polly to pause, mentally and literally.

'You know about that?'

Mya stopped until they were facing each other. 'Yeah he told us that afternoon in my garden after he couldn't get through to you. I really feel for him.'

Polly sighed. 'Me too.'

They walked the last few minutes in silence, allowing Polly to try and filter her way through the thoughts in her head. Polly was grateful for the quiet. She had lost her own emotional bearings. Her anger at the betrayal by Bailey had been sustaining her in some way. That and songwriting at Mya's. Without the anger, all she had left was to question her own ability to figure out if a person was good or not. She didn't know any more. She'd lost her way, putting herself in the company of people who would turn around and betray her. She'd still not heard from work yet, other than to be informed who her contact was in HR. She knew, having been the person that would normally assist in the investigation, that these things take some time. Still, she'd worked so hard in that company, she'd been steadily promoted and now, as far as she knew, probably couldn't get an HR job anywhere if she were to be dismissed. She just hoped that they would offer her the chance to resign first.

Polly had been so lost in thought that she hadn't really been paying attention to anything until she was at the bar and Paige was looking at her expectantly.

'You with us, Pol? What are you drinking?'

'Erm, parma violet gin and tonic, please,' Polly said.

'You alright, babe?' Paige asked, her stare penetrating.

'Will be. You?'

'Yeah, I'm excited for tonight. We've got a big crowd in for a Wednesday.'

Polly was about to ask what was so special about tonight when she looked around at the customers and recognised more than one or two familiar faces. Wasn't that Lesley of *Cats* fame? What was she doing here?

'I might have to do this as a regular thing. We'll see how it goes. Here's your drink, it's on the house. This once.'

Polly smiled, before reaching up on her tiptoes to give Paige a hug over the top of the bar. As they pulled away Paige smiled. 'It's all going to work out, I promise.'

'Yeah?'

Paige nodded and moved to serve another customer. Polly looked around trying to find Mya. She was sat at a table talking animatedly to Sophie and Marcus. As she approached, they all stopped. One by one they jumped up and gave her a hug.

Marcus held onto her arms. 'Pol. I'm sorry that Darren was such a dick and if I ever see him again I'm going to rip his head from his neck.'

'Woah, OK, bro, chill. It's alright. I made a mistake, not the first time, might not even be the last.' Detaching herself Polly went to sit down.

Polly watched as Marcus sat back down next to Sophie, who was clearly moved by what he had said, as she curled towards him and promptly started making out with him. Gross. Lovely, but still, gross. The only person missing was Bailey. On instinct, she went to get her patched up phone to text him before she remembered that they weren't exactly talking.

It hit her then like a great big slab of concrete from the sky.

Her anger subsiding, in its place, she felt the loss. She missed being able to contact him day and night, about everything and nothing. She wanted to know how he was getting on, how his mum and the rest of his family were. She just wanted him near. It had been an honest mistake, and really in the grand scheme of things, losing her job weighed significantly higher than being outed as a singer. She could almost laugh at the absurdity of it. Almost. It still hurt that her secret had been let out, but she knew Bailey. He wouldn't have done it on purpose. At least she thought she knew Bailey. But at the moment nothing was making sense, she didn't know if she could trust that he was 'good'.

Shaking her head she looked at Marcus. 'So only nine more sleeps. How are you feeling?'

Marcus grinned. 'I'm so excited.'

'Ahh, babe.' Another two-minute interlude, they were like teenagers.

Mya leaned over and whispered, 'Don't mention it again unless you want to be brought in as the wedding singer. I don't think they've been able to find anyone yet.' Mya winked and held her finger to her mouth.

Polly grinned. 'Thanks for the head's up.'

'I'm sorry that you're having such a shit time. For what it's worth, I didn't think that Darren was such a massive idiot as he turned out. I mean sure when he came on to me I knew he was a dick, but not like this.'

'Ladies and gentlemen, thank you for coming to Barberella tonight.' The lights dimmed and the crowd whooped. Polly was dumbstruck. What the hell was Mike doing here?

'It's Barberella's first ever Open Mic night. So here are some ground rules. Please respect everyone that has the balls to get on this stage. So when someone is performing, there's no talking, no getting up to go to the bar or the loo, there will be plenty of chances for that throughout the night. You have to cheer, and if invited, you can join in. It's all about having fun.

So if you want to try your hand at singing why not? Come find me at the front and we'll go through the song choices. Whether you want to play an instrument, we have those, or you want to do it karaoke style we have it all. It's going to be a good night, I can tell. So I already have a few acts lined up. We'll get started in fifteen minutes, then after the first fifteen minutes we'll have a break, and so on and so on until everyone that wants a go has had one. Let's have some fun.'

The crowd cheered and Polly could feel that tingle that she got when she was at the Speakeasy. This crowd were happy and ready to celebrate with every performer.

Polly looked away from the makeshift stage that they had so conveniently sat directly in front of and turned towards the rest of the table.

'What is going—?'

'Before you start you need to know that there is no expectation for you to sing tonight. None at all. This is simply a business idea for Paige,' Sophie started.

Paige appeared from nowhere and stood over her, her hand on Polly's shoulder. 'That's right. I figure you could let me know if it works or not from your previous experience at the Speakeasy. I can see if it works from a financial point of view. That's it. Just enjoy yourself. But should you want to sing then, of course, you can do.'

Everyone was grinning, she looked around at them all, they were all so happy. She felt her shoulders relax. If she took away the performing side of it, she could just have a fun night. In fact, she could have a brilliant night. It suddenly occurred to her, that she didn't have to worry about how much she drank either. She could safely walk home with Mya and it wasn't as though she had work to worry about tomorrow. Polly laughed to herself.

'Regardless of whether or not you're going to sing, I am!' Mya jumped up and practically ran towards Mike and his famous clipboard.

Polly grinned.

'Oh well if she's going to do it.' With that Sophie jumped up too and ran towards Mya screaming, 'A duet! We should definitely do a duet!'

Polly smiled at Marcus and Paige before standing and walking over to the bar.

'Alright, Pol, what can I get you?' India asked.

'Can I have a row of Sambuca, please? I think we're going to need it.'

'Sure thing, Pol.'

'So how's it going, India? I haven't spoken to you in ages.'

'All good. Actually, I think I'm seeing someone,' India said as she gathered the drinks.

'You think?' Polly asked, leaning on the bar.

'Yeah. We've had a few dates, well quite a few actually. We're about to have THAT conversation you know. I'm freaking out.' India grimaced, whilst lining up the shots.

'He's not called Darren, is he?'

'No, why?' India looked puzzled.

'Just checking. In that case, go for it.'

'Thanks, Pol. Here you go.' India put the drinks on the bar before catching Paige's eye. Paige nodded and rolled her eyes. 'They're on the house too. She's in an extra nice mood tonight.' India laughed.

'Thanks, India. See you later, come sit with us if it gets quiet, yeah?'

'Will do, Pol. See you in a bit.'

Polly carefully walked back to the table the tray of shots intact. As she placed the tray down she knew that at some point she was going to have to ask about Bailey. Reluctantly she let go of her lip that she had been biting. 'Erm, so where's Bailey tonight?'

Marcus shrugged, his eyes on his wife-to-be as she and Mya deliberated with Mike about what song to sing. Suddenly Polly was worried that something had happened and she cursed herself for cutting Bailey off so abruptly. She really should've spoken to him. It had only been a few days, but it had been too many. Getting her phone, she wrote a quick message.

Polly: I'm sorry I haven't spoken to you. I hope you're ok. We're out at Barberella if you're about? x

Taking a deep breath she figured that he would either rock up and maybe they could talk, or maybe he was pissed at her. Worse case something could've happened with his mum. She just hoped whatever it was that she would find out soon. At that point, Sophie and Mya walked back, grinning.

'I figured we might all need these.' Polly gestured towards the shots.

'Thanks, Pol.' Sophie took a shot and necked it immediately.

Mya shrugged and followed suit.

'Now that I've signed up to do a song, I'm so nervous. Shit. Pol is this what you feel like?' Sophie asked.

'Yup probably. Except I'm always sober when I perform.'

The lights dimmed again as Polly's phone vibrated in her pocket.

Bailey: See you soon Pol xxx

What did he mean by that? Was he on his way or what?

'OK, ladies and gentlemen we are ready to begin. So like I said at the start nothing but cheers, and no talking whilst acts are performing. First on the stage tonight we have Bailey, please make him feel welcome.'

Mike clapped as he walked to the side of the stage. Polly looked in amazement as everyone at her table stood up cheering and yelling. Polly just sat there, her tired brain stalling, trying to keep up. Not Bailey, not her Bailey surely? Well, not HER Bailey but...

'Erm, hi everyone. First-time performer so please be gentle.'

'Whooooo go Bailey!!!' Mya screamed.

'Thanks, Mya. If it's OK I'd like to dedicate this one to Polly.'

226

Suddenly Polly felt nervous as if she was the one performing, her heart was in her throat, her palms clammy as she rubbed them on her skirt. Her crossed leg jingling up and down. She'd never really heard Bailey sing before. Had he really done all of this for her? How else would Paige have gotten in touch with Mike?

He looked so vulnerable on the stage all by himself. She wanted to go up there and help, she wanted to stay where she was and see what it was he was going to do. It was silent in the bar, everyone patiently waiting. He looked up at her and winked, holding the microphone in his hands, a small shy smile on his face, his weight shifting from foot to foot. He was getting more nervous, what were they waiting for? Suddenly the song started, there was no introduction with a baseline, or a beat, or even a piano.

Bailey was gripping the microphone as he softly sang, 'We'll be singing, when we're winning. We'll be singing.' His soft tone was beautiful to Polly, she didn't have long to ponder that before he released the microphone from the stand and jumped around the stage.

'I GET KNOCKED DOWN, BUT I GET UP AGAIN. YOU AIN'T EVER GONNA KEEP ME DOWN.'

Polly burst out laughing when she realised that in true Bailey form he was putting on a tubthumping show. He was stomping around the stage shouting in the microphone and the crowd went wild. Suddenly on the higher parts, Denise appeared on the stage, and someone quickly wolf whistled as she sang. Looking behind her Polly saw Billy stood up, clapping along. A further glance and she realised that she was the only one sat, everyone was dancing around and cheering. When the instrumental kicked in, Bailey jumped off the small stage and shouted, 'Everyone join in!' Before running around the audience until everyone was singing Chumbawumba.

When the song finished everyone was screaming and cheering, and Bailey got back on the stage grabbed his mum and the pair of them bowed for everyone. Polly was clapping as she watched them. Her heart still pumping heavily in her chest as Mike walked over and took the mic.

'Wow, what a start. Thank you, Bailey. Normally we try and finish on something like that but Bailey was insistent that he went first. Anyway let me get set up and then I'll introduce the next act.'

Denise was first to get to Polly, and as Polly stood, she simply took her into her arms and gave Polly a big hug, which she immediately returned.

'Don't be too hard on him, Pol. But don't let him get away with anything either.' She felt Denise kiss her cheek and then went to sit at the table behind and to the left with Billy. Bailey came up next. He moved closer and opened his mouth to speak, then she watched as he turned his head. 'Guys? Come on!'

All of their friends including Paige were stood staring at the two of them, leaning forward to hear what he was going to say.

'Polly, can I have a quick word with you, erm, privately?' he said, frowning at their mates.

'Sure.' Polly smiled at him, and she saw his face transform into a grin. He grabbed her hand and led her out through the door. His hand at once warm, comforting, rough, and tingly, and oh God she'd missed him.

'I'm glad it's starting to warm up a bit, but don't worry I won't keep you out here for long. I just wanted to tell you how sorry I am. I wanted to make it up to you and I figured that the only way I could do that was putting myself out there on stage like you do. Well, not like you do, you're way better.' He grinned.

'It's OK, Bailey. I'm sorry I overreacted.'

'You didn't, Pol. You really didn't. I should've asked your permission before recording you on that stage. I just couldn't help myself. But I really am sorry because, Jesus, that's terrifying. My heart is still racing.'

Bailey put Polly's hand that he was still holding on to his chest and sure enough his heart was going for it. She could feel it through the soft cotton of his T-shirt pressing into his firm chest, and passing back down again into her hand and up her arm, travelling all around her body until she was no longer aware of anything else at all.

'Did you do all of this for me?' Polly asked.

'Well I knew that Paige wanted to try something new, and I knew that I had to make it up to you. It was more a case of putting the right people in contact with one another, in case you were thinking I went all out and organised every detail.'

'Bailey, you didn't have to do anything. It's OK, honest. I was upset at first, but I knew you wouldn't do anything like that maliciously. I'm fairly certain that you're actually a good guy. Right?' The question wasn't hypothetical she needed the confirmation. She needed to hear him say it, to listen for any lies, any hints that he wasn't what he seemed.

'Always for you, Polly. For you, I will always try and be the best.'

Her radar had been off, but his words, carefully chosen, rang with sincerity and Polly smiled.

Chapter Thirty

Keeping Polly's hand at his chest, he looked into her eyes and hoped to see something in them that would indicate she would forgive him. He'd known for quite some time that his feelings for Polly were deep. But the last few days without any contact, he felt like he'd lost a part of himself. He was functioning but only basically, and it wasn't as nice as having her there to text or call upon or hang out with.

'It's OK, Bailey, really. I promise. Let's forget all about it, alright?'

Bailey let out all of the breath in his lungs, which wasn't a lot because for the last week he hadn't actually been able to take a full breath. They were standing so close and staring into one another's eyes. He had to physically hold himself back from kissing her. He needed her to realise that Darren was an idiot, and dump his ass sooner rather than later, but until then he wouldn't cross that line. Instead, he gently pulled her into a hug and was rewarded when Polly stepped into it fully, pressing her body against his. He marvelled at their height and loved that in heels she was only an inch or so shorter. It meant that he had no choice but to breathe in the scent of her. She wrapped her arms around his neck and held him close, and he could feel with every second passing that his soul was mending. There was a weird sense of relief in figuring out that everything else was outside of his control. He couldn't make his mum better, he couldn't make Polly finish with Darren, he couldn't do a lot of things. All he could do was wait, and actually, whilst that was hard at times, waiting was something he could do. Slowly he released his arms and took a step back, again to stop from throwing himself at her. 'We should get back inside before the next act starts.'

'OK sure.' He was looking in her eyes and saw

something cross them briefly before she looked away. Was it disappointment? He didn't care how rude it was, if she wanted to stay out here with him, he would stay out here all night. Before he could say anything further, Polly was leading them back into the bar. He waited until she was sat down and then pulled a chair so that he could sit next to her.

Why were his mates all staring at him, with small sappy smiles on their lips? He looked behind him and saw his mum, she blew him a kiss and then Mike started.

'OK, ladies and gentlemen. Next on the stage tonight we have Belinda, she's singing the classic 'Piano Man'. Let's hear it for Belinda.'

Seeing his mum and Billy had reminded him. 'Oh, Polly, I—'

'Shh. Tell me after.'

Belinda had started singing, the crowd were swaying with their phones lit up into the air. Bailey left his arm along the back of Polly's chair, the ends of her hair tickling his arm, unseen by the rest of their group as everyone faced towards the stage. When the song finished, Marcus was nodding at Bailey and then nodding towards the bar. Getting up he followed his best mate to a quieter more discreet area.

'Look. I just want to say I'm sorry. It's, erm... it's OK with me, not that it needs my permission, I get that, but I'm not going to be a problem, OK?'

Marcus punched his arm and then all but ran back to Sophie. Bailey stood trying to figure out what the hell that was about. He suspected that it was Marcus's attempt at telling him that he wasn't going to be a problem if something happened with Polly. But if that was what he was saying, well that would be easy enough to say considering that Darren was still in the picture. Glancing at the girl in question he saw that his mum was talking to her about something. He was still puzzling over Marcus as he made his way over there but he was too late, his mum was already walking off.

'Everything alright?' Bailey asked, casting a quick glance towards his mum, as she approached Mike.

'Yes. I've just agreed to something incredibly nerve-racking,' Polly said.

'What?' Bailey asked, taking his seat next to Polly.

'Your mum has just asked for permission to sing one of my songs. She said that she's been practising at home and wants to sing it tonight.'

'Wow, and you said yes?'

Polly nodded her eyes wide. 'I've never heard one of my songs performed before. I feel like I'm letting my baby out into the world for the first time.'

Bailey grabbed her hand to stop her from whittling her wrist away by her watch strap. Friends held hands, right? That wasn't cheating, was it? He didn't want to let go so he carefully put their hands so that they were under the table. He didn't want to give their mates anything more to gossip about. Polly held on tighter, and Bailey tried to not think about how happy it made him.

'I think I'm going to throw up,' Polly whispered in his ear, the feeling of her breath against his neck, her lips so close to his ear, made him breathe deeply.

'Just let me know and I will clear a path for you, OK?'

For a second Polly stroked her thumb across the inside of Bailey's palm and the heat of that one stroke swept through him and a flash of fire worked through his entire body. It didn't help that she left their hands on her thigh. Well, that was it, he could barely think straight, his body was freaking out at the contact, and the nearness of places he was desperate to get to.

'OK, ladies and gents, next on the stage we have Mya and Sophie. After that we have a favourite of ours from the Speakeasy, it's Lesley. Then we will be having a small break, after which Denise will be singing a very special song indeed. But for now, let's hear it for Mya and Sophie.'

Bailey grinned and laughed out loud when he noticed their faces drop just before the song started, as they realised how daunting it was up there with all the faces looking out at them. At the same time, he felt Polly gasp and lean forward as if she could somehow help them. Then the funky ABBA beat of 'Knowing Me, Knowing You' kicked in and they just went for it. They were awful but hilarious. They did a relatively good job of keeping Bailey's mind out of the gutter, as Polly moved their hands to the beat each time landing back on her thigh, letting go only to applaud. Then it was Lesley's turn and after a few stray meows, everyone eventually got into the swing of Lesley's version of 'Memory'.

Quickly standing up when the song was over, Bailey made his way to the bar to get another round of drinks in. Of course, it was the break, and the bar was three deep. When he finally made his way to the front, Paige was already getting the drinks ready, and chatting away as she did so.

'So are you and Polly a thing yet or do I still have more work to do?' Paige asked.

'What do you mean? What are you talking about?' Bailey asked.

'You and Polly? I know it's none of our business but this thing has been building between the pair of you for so long, we're all invested. We're totally shipping you two.'

Bailey's jaw dropped. He'd kind of figured that by now everyone might have an inkling but to suggest that something happen between Polly and him whilst she still had a boyfriend was just way off.

Paige gasped. 'Oh shit. You don't know.'

'Don't know what? What the hell is going on?'

'Here's your change. The bar's too busy, I can't get into it now, but Bailey, she's not with Darren. Yes, please, what can I get you?' Paige moved to the next customer at the same time as Bailey felt his heart kick in his ribs.

Grabbing the drinks he made his way back through the

crowd at the bar, using his elbows and his shoulders to his advantage so that he didn't spill or drop any of them. He sat down in his seat. Polly had gone over to Sophie and was chatting to her presumably about their singing, or maybe wedding stuff. He didn't really know because, at that moment in time, his head was buzzing. Shit. Was she really single? What did this mean? He suddenly felt like a schoolboy with his first ever crush. Thinking about sending a note over saying that he liked her.

'You OK?'

'Hey, Mya. I think so,' Bailey replied.

'So you and Polly...?' Mya left the end of the sentence to hang there, a huge grin spreading across her face.

Bailey rolled his eyes. 'What about us? I've literally this second found out that she's broken up with Darren.'

'You didn't know? Oh, yeah I guess, how would you? Well, this isn't going to make your situation any better because he screwed her up good. She can tell you the story, but, Bailey, this might take time. I don't know, there's a chance you might have to wait it out.'

'Of course,' Bailey said, shaking his head.

They had nearly kissed outside. Before. At least she was going to, Bailey had pulled away. Maybe she had imagined that they were getting closer? Maybe it was all one-sided. She didn't know what to do. It's not like they'd met on a dating app or at the bar. How do you ask a mate out?

'OK, ladies and gentlemen, take your seats, our second part of the evening is about to begin.'

Shit, Polly's nerves were on edge tonight. First Bailey, then Mya and Sophie, and now this. Although this was something else entirely. The applause would be for her and Denise. Shit. Standing up she squeezed past Sophie to get back to her seat as quickly as she could.

'Wait, Polly. Hang on.' Mya's hand on her arm stopped her.

'You OK?'

'Yeah listen, you need to know that none of us told Bailey about Darren,' Mya said hurriedly.

'Huh? I just assumed you—'

'Yeah, I figured. He doesn't know any of it, OK. I thought that you needed to know.'

Polly mumbled thanks and sat down in her chair.

'You alright?' Bailey asked.

'Yeah, are you?'

'Yeah.'

Talk about awkward. Polly was stunned. She'd just assumed that he'd known about the whole Darren thing. How did he not? Well, he wasn't there when she told the girls. She hadn't exactly been speaking to him either. All good enough reasons. How in the hell did she tell him that not only was she single, but that she fancied him? Nope, they weren't in school. Adored him? Well, it was true but probably a bit too heavy. Loved him? Again she suspected that the truth might be a bit strong. The lights dimmed and Polly's heart sped up as she watched Mike hand over to Denise. Before she realised, her hand was high up on Bailey's thigh as she leaned on him to get inches closer to the stage. She gave herself a second to feel the heat and strength of Bailey underneath her fingers before it dawned on her that she didn't know which song of hers Denise was going to sing.

'I got permission to sing this song tonight by the incredibly talented and wonderful Polly Bowman who has written this beautiful song, called, "For You, Today". Thank you.'

There was the polite smattering of applause and cheers from the crowd but everyone on her table was staring up at Denise at the keyboard as if she held the secret to immortality. You couldn't have torn them away. Paige and India were sat with them too, and Billy had brought his chair over to sit with them, every single one of them leaning forward waiting to hear Denise. Polly was no different, although her eyes were closed. She heard better that way and most often performed that way too. She both could and couldn't wait to hear what Denise sounded like singing her song.

It. Was. Magnificent.

Polly had never been higher. Sure she felt the need to perform, but that was always outweighed with the nerves of actually performing. This was the best of both worlds. She didn't have to feel as nervous, mostly because Denise had pipes, her range soaring higher than Polly ever could, taking her song to new places but she still got the high that she got with her own music. When the song finished, Polly opened her eyes and was the first to jump up and cheer, closely followed by Billy and then the rest of their table. So what if it was a little egotistical to applaud her own song, Denise had made it something else altogether.

Walking off the stage as though she was flowing, Denise took Polly into a hug for the second time that night. Polly had no way of ever thanking Denise for what she had done. Polly hadn't known that was what she had so desperately needed. Someone with such a soulful voice, taking something she had created and making it real. It was as if Denise had handed her a gold cup, a gold star, a well-done sticker, and a record contract in one go. Polly didn't want to let go, her eyes full of happy tears she didn't want unshed. When she did finally let her arms drop, Denise was beaming.

'It's a beautiful song, Polly. It would sound even better at the actual wedding for the couple it was written for.'

'Ladies and gentlemen, another big round of applause for Denise. And for those of you that have travelled from the Speakeasy tonight that song will sound familiar because our very own Miss Polly wrote it.'

With some applause, Polly got flustered and sat back down. Eventually, she lifted her eyes and looked at her friends. Sophie, in particular, who was crying in earnest, kissing Marcus's hand as she held it tightly in her own.

'Sophie are you OK?' Polly asked.

'Was that song about me and Marcus?' Sophie asked, letting go of Marcus and wiping her tears off on her sleeves.

'Yeah. Of course.' Polly was blushing, she could feel it on her cheeks to the roots of her hair. 'Before you say anything else, if you still need one, I guess I could be your wedding singer. You'll have to get someone else to sign the register though because I assume that will be the bit where you will want me to sing?'

Sophie jumped up, crying harder now as she hugged Polly over the table. They didn't get a chance to say anything else because the next act was starting. Quickly making another decision whilst still in a songwriting high, she subtly got her phone out, looking around to make sure she wasn't disturbing the act too much.

Polly: We need to talk. Can we go outside when this song is over? x

Bailey: Of course xx

Polly had to sit on her hands, she couldn't focus on the song at all and she felt marginally guilty, but everyone else was joining in so she figured she wouldn't be missed, just this once. Her butterflies were going crazy and she could feel her sped up pulse in the back of her throat. Her body fizzing everywhere. It was just a chat. She just needed a quick catch up with Bailey that was all. But what she was to say was going to change everything. She couldn't sit still. The song finished and she applauded but her limbs weren't quite cooperating as they should. The sound was muffled, and her heart was pressing tightly against her chest as it raced. Oh God. What if this was a mistake? She felt her stomach twist and turn as she stood up and made her way outside, leaving Bailey to make an excuse for his own disappearance. But was it the right time? Then again, would it ever be?

'Hey, everything OK?' Bailey smiled, but his eyes searched her face with concern, and Polly could only look into his blue eyes. 'You said you wanted to talk?'

Looking at Bailey she drank him in, looking for signs that this was the right thing to do. He was studying her too, and she felt like she was the centre of his universe. He'd stood out with his back to the road, acting as a barrier and she knew that he did it instinctively. He quickly raised his arms putting them through his hair as he re-tied it back. The action causing the muscles on his arms and neck to bulge, and Polly thought she might have stopped breathing. Quickly trying to regroup, she'd completely lost her ability to function. As his arms dropped to his sides, he changed course and put them on her hips.

'What's wrong? You're worrying me.'

'I think that, erm, I think maybe we've done enough talking. Maybe I could try something else?'

'Sure but what are—?' She didn't give him a chance to say another word, she'd heard a yes and that was all she needed, following her instinct she allowed her butterflies to propel her forward. Her hands gripping his neck as she dragged him towards her. Their lips met gently for the tiniest of moments, before the fury, the waiting, the passion was unleashed. Polly felt her body pulled closer until it was pressed against the length of him. Polly's hands moved until they were holding his face angling him perfectly, her tongue pressing against his, her chest crushed as he pulled her tighter. The same explosion that always happened when they kissed, possibly would always happen when they kissed, lit up throughout her entire body. He was her fuel and she wanted it all. Her body driven by instinctive desires she hungered for all of him, the soft feel of his neat beard under her hands, the feel of his roughened hands somehow on her skin at her hip, and at her back. Circling, feeling, wanting.

She moved her hands until she could feel the width of his shoulders, feeling the tight muscle beneath her hands all the time keeping him close and pressing him closer, until her legs were parted with his strong thigh pressing between hers and nearly every inch of their bodies touching. His mouth moved as it kissed, licked and bit her neck. His hands, moving too now, one caressing her back the other holding the back of her head keeping her exactly where he wanted, the power exchange swapping back and forth between them. She groaned, the sound breaking through her passion, re-anchoring her, reminding her of where she was. Pulling her hands back up to his shoulders, not having realised she had moved her arms in a lock around his neck, she moved away slightly. Bailey slowly lifted his face until their heads were touching as they panted. Polly closed her eyes, it had been amazing, but she was no clearer into figuring out what was actually happening between them.

'Polly, I really hope that was for real, but I also need to tell you that we don't have to pretend for my mum any more. Billy had us figured out from day one.'

Polly laughed. 'Seriously?'

'Yeah.'

She had no choice but to lay it out on the line, her hands stroking his face, the need to touch him completely let free. 'It was for real. I wasn't pretending, I wasn't drunk, I wasn't pretending to be asleep. It was real.' She desperately wanted to ask him what he felt, but what he might say had her biting her swollen mouth. Polly felt the rough texture of Bailey's hand as he lifted her chin so that he could look her in the eyes.

'Polly, I have wanted you for a long time. I would love nothing more for this to be real. Are you sure though? I mean you've only just broken up with Darren.'

'I'm sure. Just promise me that you're good, right? You're a good person.'

'I am a good person, you know that. But I can also be very bad.' Bailey kissed her lips biting slightly at the bottom one, pushing into her until she was pressed against the wall, his thigh still between her legs. Her hands dropped to his sides as she completely gave herself over to Bailey. Giving him free rein to do what he liked, whilst she savoured everything about him. The sound of their panting, the scent and taste of Bailey everywhere, the hunger of the kiss built up again until a delicious feeling of anticipation started building in her stomach and she realised she had been grinding herself on his thigh. She'd have been embarrassed if it hadn't felt so good, oh and if he didn't have one hand on her bottom coaxing her to move on his leg.

'Shit we can't do this here. Can we go? Should I be playing hard to get? Shouldn't we be taking this slow?' Polly's mind was racing as fast as her bloodstream, and she was grinning.

'I've waited two years, Polly, but if you tell me I need to wait longer I will, but you should know that I'm yours. Just yours, for as long as you'll have me. So take your time.'

Polly laughed. 'Let's go.'

'Do you need anything from inside?'

Patting her pockets would have been easier if Bailey had left any room between them. Feeling him up as she felt for her phone, yep there it was. Ohh was that Bailey's phone or… going by the way he hissed through his teeth she had an idea that it was more likely the start of something else. Tearing her hand away before she did something that would surely get them arrested for public indecency she pushed him away and straightened her clothes.

'I have my phone and keys. Are you parked close by?' Polly asked looking at him through her eyelashes.

'Just down the road.'

'OK then, let's just go.'

Practically running to the car she eventually got in and dug out her phone.

Polly: I'm not coming back in but you need to know I'm safe. See you soon xx

Mya: I'll keep hold of your coat and bag shall I? Give my love to Bailey ;) x 🍆 xx

Chapter Thirty-One

The drive back to his apartment had taken too long and no time at all. They had spent the entire twenty minutes, taking it in turns to grin at each other. Now, Bailey held onto Polly's hand tightly as they made the way through the lobby towards the lifts. Bailey desperately wanted to kiss Polly but he knew that once they started he wouldn't stop, and he wanted her all to himself, and in private. Finally, they made it into his apartment, the front door locked behind them.

It was dark for a moment before he reached the switch to turn the light on, covering the open plan living space in a warm glow. All the while still refusing to let go of Polly's hand. Unable to shake the feeling that for all the build-up, for all the years he had waited for this moment, something was going to interrupt them. He led Polly around until she stood facing him.

'Can I get you a drink or anything?' Bailey asked, before Polly stepped closer and leaned into him, shaking her head. Still refusing to let go of her hand, he used his other to stroke the side of her neck, as he stared into her eyes. He felt burnt. Her brown eyes searing into him as he leant down to place the softest kiss on her lips.

Refusing to move away, Bailey spoke their lips still touching. 'Polly, we don't have to do this. We can wait, I can take you out for dinner or something first?'

Polly laughed. 'We've been fake boyfriend and girlfriend for weeks, I don't want to wait any longer, for anything else to get in our way,' Polly pressed closer, 'and neither do you.'

He didn't. He really didn't.

Polly closed her eyes as Bailey's mouth and tongue took over the rest of the conversation, somehow managing to be both hesitant and persuasive. She let go of his hand to wind hers around his neck and up into his soft hair, grabbing lightly as she lost herself in the sheer heat of Bailey.

She moved back for the second or two it took for her to take off her jumper and vest top in one move. The look in Bailey's eyes made her knees weak and when they kissed again all hesitancy was lost, as pure demand took over.

She squealed as he lifted her up, and she wrapped her legs around his hips, feeling his hardness against her, causing her to grind involuntarily. He stopped moving forward for a second as he leaned against the wall, helping her ride him further with the firm hold he had on the backs of her thighs. She gasped into his mouth before he moved to kiss, lick, and bite her neck. She ground down on him harder, frustrated at being so close to what she wanted, to what they both wanted, but still so far. She clung tighter still as Bailey all but ran to his bedroom and she landed with a soft thud onto his bed. It was Bailey's turn now and she lent up as he removed his long sleeved T-shirt, revealing inch after tortuous inch of his mouth-watering body. Not waiting for a second, Polly reached forward and began to lick at his six-pack, feeling the definition of his muscles with her tongue, having wanted to do that exact thing for months. It was delicious and it made her own stomach clench in satisfaction. Bailey's scent had always made her body react and now she was surrounded by it and it was addictive bliss.

It was dark in his bedroom, neither of them stopping to turn on a light, brightness coming from the hallway outside, and the lights of the apartments opposite coming in through the window, but it was more than enough to make out what she wanted to see. T-shirt removed, Bailey's fingers were in her hair tugging her back until once again she was on the bed. Immediately surrounded by the scent and heat of Bailey. He kissed her lips, below her ear, all over her neck. Polly grabbed at Bailey as she undulated, feeling his hot heavy body pressing her into the duvet. He propped himself up one arm whilst the other went to her bra strap gently pushing it down her arm, kissing and licking as it went. He switched arms and did the same with other side, and Polly shivered in anticipation, moving her arms through the straps. She had expected this to be fast and frenetic given how long they had waited, but waiting a little while longer, just meant that her lust was furling tighter and tighter, and she thought she might explode with the slightest of touches. Making his way back to her mouth he thoroughly kissed her again, their tongues diving and parting, the only sound their panted breathing and sighing.

Using one arm he held her spine lifting her a few inches off the mattress, his other hand undoing her bra. Polly raised an eyebrow smiling at his deftness and was awarded with a wicked grin that shot fire through her entire body. Keeping hold of her weight he removed her bra, looking down before grinning again. That wicked smile of his was going to be her undoing. But then he began his torturous licking and biting towards her breasts and Polly couldn't help but think that maybe it wasn't his grin that was the specific problem, but his mouth. Giving herself up to him, she fell back onto his arm, letting him take the weight, her neck dropping backwards as her breasts were pushed forward and Bailey quickly took advantage. Then he began moving his jaw around her nipple and she thought she would pass out, all her breath held in her lungs until she was as much on fire inside as she felt on the outside. His beard was abrasive against her tender breasts, the friction making her squirm. Until he rolled her nipple in his mouth and she no longer had the ability for thought as she held onto his arms, feeling the huge muscles tensed beneath her hands. He must have sensed she was getting close because he pulled away until she was flat against the bedding once again and Bailey began licking down her stomach. He undid the button of her jeans, and jumped back, quickly removing her shoes and socks until he could pull down her trousers, and then he was there, kissing her inner thighs. Polly looked down as Bailey made himself comfortable, kneeling on the floor he moved her until her hips were on the edge of the bed, and her thighs over his shoulders.

Polly's breath caught in her throat at the realisation of her fantasies coming to life. Then Bailey began pulling down her knickers until they were gone too, and he moved her legs back where he wanted them, his movements precise and confident. He left her with no question as to what he wanted to do, and there was no way she was going to stop him.

He gently held her open with his hands, as he explored her with his mouth, all the while looking at Polly, the wicked gleam in his eyes pushing her further forward, and she had never felt hotter and more desired in her entire life. His mouth was hot as he slowly licked his way over her clit, his chin moving so that his beard gently scratched all over her. Polly couldn't take any more, she tried to keep eye contact but it was too much, he was too much, the feeling too much, the wait had been too much, and with a squirm and a cry Polly gave in.

Bailey rose to stand, watching Polly in a post-orgasmic state as he straightened. She was magnificent. Her red hair spread out all over his duvet, just like in his dreams, the taste of her still on his lips. Until her eyes opened again, and her smile grew wide. Now Polly was kneeling on the bed, pulling his face down towards hers where she kissed and licked his lips, his jaw, his chin. Pulling away Bailey removed the rest of his clothing, and then gently moved Polly further up the bed so that he could lie down on it. He picked her up at her hips until she was sat on the tops of his legs. She grinned, clearly happy to be moved wherever he needed her to be, and he needed her everywhere. Keeping one hand stroking her thigh, Bailey reached over to the bedside table with the other, brushing the lamp to turn it on as he reached into the drawer for a condom. When he fell back into place, his eyes studied all of Polly in the light. She was the most beautiful thing he had ever seen. Did she realise that she had his heart? Did she realise she was making his dreams come true? That everything he had wanted for over the last two years was in reach. At least he hoped everything he wanted was, he really didn't want this to be a one-night thing. His thoughts were derailed as she rested her hands on his chest, casting a look at his hard length before looking up and grinning, and starting to scoot backwards. He grabbed her hips to stop her moving further backwards, the naughty sparkle in her eyes making her intentions clear what she was about to do.

'Polly,' Bailey whispered as he leaned and their lips touched, 'if you do that now, this is all going to be over embarrassingly quickly for me, and I have a much better idea.'

Polly chuckled kissing him once more before quickly straightening, sending her long red hair flying. Bailey was reminded of the burlesque and hoped that maybe later he would get a private dance of his own. He opened the package and unwrapped the condom onto himself. Before he could say another word, Polly was grinding and sliding herself all over his cock and Bailey's eyes closed of their own accord, as Polly gasped and sighed. Forcing his eyes open not wanting to miss anything, Bailey reached down holding himself up and watched mesmerised as Polly slowly, tortuously slowly, lowered herself onto him. She lent on his chest as she raised herself gently up and back down again, taking more and more of him each time, until finally she had him all. Licking his thumb he pressed it towards her clit, and Polly really began to move as she cried out.

His control snapped and the next moment he pulled Polly down closer to his chest and from there he had control once more as he began thrusting, harder and harder feeling Polly tighten around him, hotter and tighter. Their bodies covered in sweat, as they clung onto one other until finally, Polly collapsed on top of him, and Bailey was trying to catch his breath, his heart racing, and thudding into Polly's as his arms held her tight against his chest, not ever wanting to let go, and only praying that she would let him hold on forever.

Bailey was a beast and she hungrily stared, watching his body as he made his way back into bed, next to her. She kept the duvet low so that she could explore what was the most sculptured body she had ever had the privilege of exploring. He lay down on his back and held her to his side, his hand possessively drawing circles on her bottom. He was just magnificent. He was covered in the defined muscle that made her think he could be an advert for Calvin Klein. He had tattoos that ran up both arms and across the top of his chest and she found herself lazily following the patterns with her hand, and then those that she could reach with her mouth she was kissing. His hair loose and just touching his shoulders, she ran her hands through the silky strands. Then he said the words that would forever seal his awesomeness. Something that no man had ever before offered her after a sexual workout. Something that made her believe beyond a doubt that she was with the man of her dreams.

'Let me just get the feeling back in my legs and then I'll make you a brew. Then we're going again.' Polly sighed as he turned and nuzzled into her neck. 'What time do you need to be at work in the morning?' he asked, grinning as her hand began stroking lower and lower.

'Oh yeah about that. The good news is that I don't. The rest of it I'll tell you over breakfast. There's something I want to do first.'

Chapter Thirty-Two

Polly woke up with a grin as she stretched in the bed, savouring the way her body felt, she was wonderfully sore everywhere, beard rash everywhere. Her eyes opened, and the smell of Bailey, the heat of Bailey, the possessive touches of Bailey. She couldn't believe it.

Quietly slipping out of his bed, she nipped to the bathroom, once she had finished with the necessities she stared at herself in the mirror. A huge grin, eyes shining, lips swollen, burlesque Polly stared back at her and she still couldn't believe everything that had happened in the last twenty-four hours. Leaving the bathroom she was torn between getting back into bed or making a brew. The pause also gave her a moment of panicked thoughts. What happened next? He'd said he'd been waiting for her for ages. Waiting for what, a one-time hook-up, or something more? Now that they had gone at it pretty much all night, was that it? Is that what she wanted? No. Absolutely not. Her heart ached, she'd adored him twenty-four hours ago, and what she felt now was indescribable. Feeling vulnerable and not just because of her nakedness, she crept back into Bailey's bedroom. Finding the long-sleeved T-shirt he'd had on last night she pulled it over her head.

'Morning.'

Oh God that voice, that sexy croaky morning, bed yummy voice. 'Hey, sorry I didn't mean to wake you,' she whispered back.

'You weren't planning on leaving, were you? You've had your wicked way with me now so are you just going to throw me away?' Bailey laughed, but Polly felt more nervous, her own concerns reflected. Bailey sat up.

'What's wrong?'

Before she could say anything, Bailey leaned further upright until he was knelt on the bed in front of her, the bed sheet long gone.

'I think we need to talk,' Polly stuttered, her eyes unable to look at anything except his body as it graciously prowled closer, his abs contracting and the muscles in his wide thighs overwhelming. Reaching across he pressed the smallest of kisses on her lips, his hands moving low on her hips.

'Are you sure? We could do something else and then talk after? I'm not going anywhere.'

Finally, she looked up and saw Bailey's grinning face as he bit his own lip, she felt her nerves disappear once more as he gently dragged the T-shirt off. They could talk after. He was right. They had a lot of time to catch up on.

He'd never wished that he could hear another person's thoughts so bad in his entire life. He sat himself up higher in the bed moving all the pillows until the headboard was super soft and he could lie into it. Gently, he tugged on Polly's hand, until she fell backwards covering him in red strands that tickled wherever they landed. Moving his arm until she was resting on his shoulder, he traced patterns into the skin on her back. Taking a minute he wondered at how this had finally happened, and, of course, wishing to know what Polly was thinking. Taking a deep breath, he couldn't control the smile as he scented Polly everywhere, he tried to figure out what to do. His immediate go-to would be to make her laugh and to charm her into staying for as long as he could get away with, whilst hoping against hope that it would be forever. Or, against his first reaction, he could just be honest. Without humour, without the banter, he could just lay it all out there. It was terrifying, but, he realised, Polly deserved the whole truth. She needed to know what he was hoping for. If it was just a one-night thing for her, it would kill a part of him but he needed to know. Maybe. No, he definitely needed to know.

He felt her relax further into him, and as she sighed, he couldn't stop the smile on his face from growing. He looked down at her and really took in every moment, just in case, what he was about to say would mean that this would be their last.

'Polly—'

'Bailey we need to talk.' They both spoke at the same time.

'I was just about to say that. Do you want to go first or…?' Bailey asked, noticing that Polly wasn't looking up. 'I'll go first. I wasn't kidding last night. I have wanted you for over two years now. I tried not to, thinking about how awkward it might be, but…' He moved his arms re-tying his hair whilst he thought about the words he wanted to use.

'I don't want to freak you out. I just think you should know, that I am crazy about you, Polly. I'm all in, I—'

Bailey's ringtone was loud and shrill and it made them both jump. Leaning over Polly he reached for his phone on the bedside table.

Silencing it, he responded to Polly's bemused look. 'It's just Marcus, he can wait… Oh, apparently he cannot wait. Sorry, hang on. Dude, what is it? Are you OK?' Bailey sat up.

'There's been a problem with the wedding suits. I need your help.'

Slouching back down and tucking Polly back against him, Bailey said, 'OK when and where? What exactly can I help with?'

'Sophie's going to kill me if Tatiana doesn't get to me first.'

'Not to freak you out, but with their collective organisational skills they could have you dead and buried with no one the wiser in about an hour.'

'Jesus just come over when you can. Sophie's out, you can't tell her that there are any problems, OK?'

'Dude, I'm not going to say a word. But is it really so important? Can't it wait till tomorrow, or later today?' Bailey asked desperately.

'Bailey this is Code Arrow.'

Bailey winced. 'Shit, OK hang tight.'

Well damn, there goes his amazing plans of spending all day in bed with the woman of his dreams, her brother unknowingly cock-blocking. Well, actually he didn't know that he might have just done it himself telling Polly the truth about his feelings. He groaned as he threw his phone back on the nightstand.

'Pol, I'm really sorry but I have to go. Marcus just called in an Arrow Code.'

'Say no more. I totally understand I—'

This time there was no ringtone just an incessant hum. It stopped and then it started again. He watched as Polly jumped out of bed, and found her phone.

'Hi, calm down, what's wrong? What do you mean your mum is trying to wear white? What?'

Bailey watched as Polly crawled back into bed and put the cover back over her legs, and settled back next to Bailey as she listened. For a moment Bailey felt smug. Yes real life was coming crashing in but the fact that Polly had put herself back next to Bailey in bed to deal with it, meant the world to him and he clung on tightly.

'Right, OK. So what can I do? You're kidding, right? Ten-foot and bargepole... Oh, you did not just pull that card on— right. Right. Yep. Fine. I'll be there soon.' Ending the call she looked at him.

'I'm sorry, Bailey, I think all the wedding dramas are about to hit at once. Sophie needs me. Apparently her mum wants to change the colour of her mother of the bride dress to a white gown, and there's an issue with the band.'

Bailey's jaw dropped. 'She doesn't? Anyway, Marcus needs me too. Go jump in the shower, I'll drop you off wherever you need to go.'

'No it's OK, apparently Tatiana, the organisational wizard that she is, has already booked me an Uber. It's no secret where I am, apparently.'

'Did you want it to be?' He felt nervous.

'No, I just—' Polly looked down at her phone again. 'Oh great, apparently it's already outside. They're going to have to wait.' Leaning forward she kissed him, her hands holding his face gently before she pulled away.

'I really am sorry. Call me later, OK?'

Bailey nodded and watched as Polly flew around his flat like a whirlwind. Until finally a quick peck on the cheek and she was gone. They'd have to have 'the talk' at some point, right?

Chapter Thirty-Three

'I don't think I can sleep,' Sophie whispered.

'You need to. Otherwise, no amount of make-up will help you, and you'll be the ugliest bride there ever was.' Polly smirked in the darkness.

'Thanks, Pol, no pressure then, hey?'

Polly yawned, her mind as exhausted as her body. 'You're the celebrity make up vlogger, not me.'

'I'm so nervous and so excited at the same time. What if I fall over on my way down the aisle? What if I make a complete tit of myself when the live feed is on? What if I have forgotten to invite someone important? What if my fans all leave me now that we're married? What if Marcus doesn't turn up? Help me, Pol, my mind is going a million miles an hour. Please?'

Even in the darkness, Polly could make out that Sophie's body was practically buzzing. Understandable the night before the big day.

'Turn around,' Polly ordered.

Sophie turned onto her side and Polly curled around her.

'If you trip and fall then you will be human, it might even increase your subscriptions. You're not going to make a tit of yourself, Tatiana wouldn't allow it. All the most important people are going to be there. Anyone else you can always get to them first and ask why they didn't show. Just pretend you posted the invite and then never heard from them. Your fans aren't going to leave you, at least not until after the first pregnancy announcement anyway. I think if it was up to Marcus he'd be camping at the venue overnight and if not, then Bailey will make sure he gets him there in plenty of time. You're going to have an amazing day, surrounded by everyone that loves you. Not to mention your kick-ass wedding singer.'

'Thanks, Pol,' Sophie whispered. 'I mean it. Thanks for everything. How are you feeling about singing at the wedding though? You know I never would've forced you, right?'

'I know. I also know that I have to focus on the things that make me happy in the long run. Whilst it is nerve-racking I still love it. Although I think I love writing songs more than I like performing them. Denise really blew my mind when she sang your song. Just know that I won't be quite as good as that, OK?'

'OK. But thank you. Really. Are you alright with the list of songs to sing at the reception?'

'Yes, I've been practising. I've never sung with a full band before so that should be fun. Again, scary, but fun.'

'Once you've done your bit I'll make sure to get you a big drink, then you can just party the night away whilst the DJ takes over.'

'I know, Soph, we've already gone over the plan a million times. Everyone knows what they are responsible for throughout the day. We all have the Trello app, detailing the timings and the responsibilities. There's nothing that could ever stop you and Tatiana.'

Polly stroked Sophie's head, somehow managing to navigate around the giant curlers.

'Soph?' Polly hesitated, now definitely wasn't the time to be bringing this up, but she wasn't sure she could contain it.

'Yeah?'

Polly paused giving her brain a second to simmer down and register that this was not the best time. 'What do you think of Bailey?' Never mind.

'What do you mean?'

'I mean, he's good right?' Polly asked, immediately before holding her breath.

Sophie turned around until they were facing one another. 'Are you worried that he will pull a Darren?'

Polly exhaled. 'No. Well, not exactly like that. I just, I

don't trust my instincts at the moment, that's all. Forget I said anything.'

'Polly, that man adores you. And you adore him. But if you go into this thinking he's going to turn on you, then you're not going all in. You stand more chance of ruining something amazing before it's even begun. You need to speak to Bailey.'

'I know. I've not really had a chance to see him, not blaming anyone, in particular, cough cough, but after I ran out of his apartment last week we've not really had a chance to spend more than ten minutes together. We haven't had "The Talk", you know. It's awkward because we're so close already there's no build-up. I know it's coming, I'm just worried about what I'll hear. It's hard to explain.'

'Look, Polly, I'm really sorry that this last week or so has been so mad. I really, really appreciate all that you have done. In fact, my original plan was to have you be my maid of honour so that you'd be forced to spend more time with Bailey, not less. But I might have killed my mother if you hadn't intervened, and the rehearsals you've been doing with the band, I'm so excited to hear you perform.

'Anyway, he will tell you that he adores you and that he wants to be with you night and day, I'm sure of it. All the girls are and, if not, and it's a huge if, then we'll figure it out. But really you need to work out how you feel, because if you're just stringing him along then, frankly, we're all Team Bailey.'

'My God, no. I love him, Sophie, I really do and that's why I'm so scared.'

'Yup, it's terrifying. Also, you've made me feel a million times more nervous about tomorrow and I was just starting to calm down, so thanks for that.'

'OK sorry, sorry. Now turn back around your breath is banging.' Polly chuckled as Sophie turned around, Polly continuing to stroke her head very softly, humming the melody to their wedding song. Great. Polly had been shattered and now her mind was going a mile a minute.

'Love you, Pol.'

'Love you too.'

After a few minutes and making sure that Sophie was snoring soundly, good luck with that Marcus, Polly turned and grabbed her phone.

Polly: I'm really sorry that I've not been able to see you properly. I guess we'll see each other tomorrow, well later today now. Hope this doesn't wake you, I just wanted to txt. See you soon xx

Polly knew that what she really wanted to add on the bottom of the text was 'love you'. But that would be ridiculous. Right? Luckily he replied before her fingers did the talking.

Bailey: Goodnight gorgeous I can't wait to see you tomorrow/later, and pretty much every day thereafter. In case I haven't been clear, I would very much like to be stuck with you for a very long time xx

How did he always know the right thing to say? She sighed, the little butterflies taking off again, she couldn't wait to see him.

Polly: Night Bailey. See you tomorrow xx

Polly wasn't nervous: between the stylists, the official photographers, as well as managing the bride, bridesmaids, mother of the bride and Tatiana, she hadn't had time.

Checking herself out in the full-length mirror again before topping up everyone's Prosecco, Polly made sure everyone was OK. They were all made up and in their dresses, and every one of them could be caught guiltily checking themselves out in the mirrors of the bridal suite, as she'd just done, even Paige.

Sophie kept closing her eyes and taking deep breaths. Sophie's mum was the life and soul, but she also managed to keep everyone away from Sophie when she could tell her daughter needed a minute to compose herself. Their earlier fall out forgotten, now that she was wearing pistachio green. Polly's mum had said that she would wait with Marcus and Bailey at the venue. Sophie's sisters had arrived and were now sat with the rest of them and all was right on schedule.

Sophie sat in the chair facing the mirror.

'I'm so honoured to be doing your make-up, Sophie. You're going to look so beautiful.' Patrick Handley, make-up artiste extraordinaire and winner at last years vlog awards was gently touching up Sophie's make-up.

'Patrick the honour is mine, thank you so much.'

Polly opened her phone to check that everything was on schedule. Not that she needed to when Tatiana was managing everything, full headset and clipboard, and iPad in hand.

Once Patrick had finished it would be time to get Sophie into her dress and then show time. Deciding that now would be a good time, she quickly messaged Bailey.

Polly: How is everything your end? xx

Bailey: My end is missing you xx

Polly: Oh God that was awful. You know what I meant xx

Bailey: All good here. I miss you xx

Polly: Miss you too see you in a bit xx

Bailey: You'll be fine today so don't worry ok xx

Polly stared at her phone, and sighed, a smile on her face and Bailey's reassurances settling her nerves.

Polly: Any news? Is your mum ok? Xx

Bailey: She's probably not going to make the wedding, but she's just usual sick. Not rush into hospital sick. But I'm keeping my phone on. Don't tell Sophie, she's scary xx

Polly: Your secrets are safe with me. I'll keep mine on too just in case they can't get you xx

Bailey: xx

Her shoulders relaxed an inch now that she knew that Denise was alright, relatively speaking. Hiding her phone away in her cleavage, she braced herself to go back out into the fray. Sophie had requested that no one had their phones on in the ceremony. The reason being that she wanted everyone there to enjoy it, she also wanted the photographers to have unfettered access, and finally because she wanted to be the one to share clips with her fans. She didn't want any spoilers, seeing as though her fans had played a crucial part in getting her here. Well, Marcus played a big part, but you know. In the last week, well-wishers had sent cards, and gifts, as well as companies wooing Sophie for a major spokesperson deal, and potentially her own merchandise, it had been unbelievable really.

'You alright, Pol?' Paige was grinning as she came in, rocking her dress and the bespoke Converse that Sophie had had made, looking every inch a badass. She'd kept all her piercings in, only changing the ring in her nose to a sparkly stud. Her hair put in a style that showed off her undercut, the dress also showing off the tattoo that started at her wrist and travelled up her arm.

'I will be at about eight tonight.' Polly ruefully smiled.

'You're going to kick ass. But I will be the first one to offer you a drink when you're done, OK?'

'Thanks, Paige. You look gorgeous, by the way.'

'I know, right? I'm nothing compared to you though, Bailey is going to launch himself at you when he sees how smoking hot you are in your dress.'

Polly heated up, her stomach twisting in ways that were absolutely nothing to do with nerves.

'Right, love, I'm all finished and you are magnificent.' Patrick had barely finished speaking before Tatiana rushed him away.

'Thank you.'

'Enough of that you can thank him later,' said Tatiana. 'Right now we need to get you in your dress, Sophie. Come on, and you, Polly. We've got ten minutes until we need to be downstairs ready to walk the aisle.'

Chapter Thirty-Four

'How are you doing, Bailey? You ready for your best man duties today?'

Bailey shook the hand George was offering, and for a minute looked him up and down, remembering how it wasn't all that long ago he'd stood beside George in a hospital bed. He was relieved to see how well he was looking today.

'Hi, George. How are you? Mrs B is looking absolutely stunning.' Don't think about how much you love his daughter, don't make this weird. Bailey kept repeating to himself over and over.

'You can tell her yourself, she always did have a soft spot for you.' Bailey grinned. 'Listen, before this wedding takes place I'd been meaning to catch up with you for a little while.' George gestured towards the side of the room.

Bailey swallowed, his panic mounting, don't think about Polly, don't think about Polly.

'I know that technically it's not my place to say anything any more but…' Shit where in the hell was this going? 'But I just wanted to tell you how impressed I am with everything you're doing with Marcus on the gardening business. I know that you're partners now, and, well, it just fills me with so much pride to see how much you've both accomplished. It means the world to me that you were able to develop it and take it further than I ever could. I know that it's in safe hands with you and Marcus. Anyway, my soon to be daughter-in-law will be here in a minute so we'd best get back into our places. But I just wanted to let you know that I really am so proud.'

George put his hand out again and drew Bailey into a hug, before turning around and walking back to his seat. Bailey tried to cough away the unexpected lump in his throat. The wind had been taken out of his sails in the best way possible.

He felt a warm tide of relief ripple through him. He hadn't realised how badly he had needed to hear that. Bailey blinked a few times and coughed a couple more. He couldn't fully articulate why but he could have cried at that moment. The relief, the joy, the achievement of making George proud, the love for his best mate, for his soon to be missus, for his family, for his mum, for Polly. Composing himself he made his way back to Marcus and slapped his back. Just in the nick of time. The music changed and there was a sudden noise as everyone stood up, turning to look as Sophie's bridesmaids slowly walked down the aisle towards them.

Watching as Paige walked up the aisle, followed by Mya, Bailey could just make out the music was an instrumental version of Polly's song for Sophie and Marcus. It made his smile stretch a little further until he finally saw Polly. The smile nearly fell from his mouth as it opened in wonder. He was watching Polly walk purposefully towards him and damn if he didn't want to shove Marcus and Sophie out of the way so that they could take over. She was the most beautiful thing he had ever seen, sorry Sophie, but she was. Her gorgeous brown eyes shone brightly as the last bridesmaid to walk up the aisle. He had to tell her soon. It was doing his head in that he wasn't completely honest with her about how he felt. She didn't need to say it back, he just couldn't hold it any longer. He almost forgot to look at Sophie as she came up next, but when he did see her, wow. She looked like an angel as she gracefully walked up the aisle, her father beaming with pride beside her. Bailey turned to look at Marcus. His eyes shone so brightly and he looked absolutely entranced in the best possible way. Bailey couldn't help but feel the love that glowed from Marcus as he looked at his soon to be Mrs. As she finally made her way towards them, Bailey saw that Marcus's hands were shaking as he reached for hers. Bailey felt like his heart was going to burst, he was just so damn happy for his two friends.

Of course his mind went back to Polly and he glanced over at her as the officiant began talking. He watched as she gave him the once over, a small smile on her lips that was all for him, making himself stand a little taller, so that she could really soak in the effect. It worked, he saw, as she licked her lips and winked. He nearly laughed, and knew he was also done for.

When the time came to produce the rings he did so without any drama. In fact, the whole thing was drama-free apart from Marcus getting choked up whilst saying his vows. Sophie spoke hers with a loud confidence that rang out across the entire hall in front of hundreds of guests.

Before he knew it, it was time to sign the register, getting up to the front, he stared at Polly knowing that she would be nervous. When she caught his eye, he let his desire for her show through his eyes, so that as she got her guitar that had been stowed away, she had a moment to think about something else besides her nerves. As she turned to face the audience he was close enough to her mum and dad to hear their reaction.

Her mum stage whispered, 'Oh my word, is Polly going to sing? I haven't heard her sing since school.'

Bailey tried to make quick work of the signing so that he could hold eye contact with Polly, should she need it. He saw her hand tremble a little before she closed her eyes and sang the song she had written for Sophie and Marcus. There wasn't a dry eye in the house.

Finally, after quite a few photographs and a quick bit of live streaming, he was finally stood next to the other half of his soul, and he had never felt more delighted. She walked as close to him as possible, as they followed the bride and groom down the aisle.

'You were amazing and you look phenomenal,' Bailey whispered out of the side of his mouth as they smiled at the rest of the wedding party.

'Thank you. You look incredibly hot in a suit.'

'I think that we're going to need to find somewhere quiet and discreet, at some point today.'

'Oh, absolutely.'

He felt her shiver as he lightly and platonically-ish put his hand on her lower back as they walked.

After they left the great hall, they were escorted into what was affectionately called the Hayloft. It was huge and even Bailey had to admit Tatiana had outdone herself. It had been completely transformed.

Marcus and Bailey had been working closely with Tatiana on the flowers, or plants in the case of the table arrangements and Bailey was pleased to see that they had worked out perfectly. As a nod to both Sophie and Marcus's work each centrepiece was a plant that contained the flowers that had been planted in Mya's garden where their romance had blossomed. Bailey was under strict instructions to pack them away carefully when finished, as they were going to create a flower bed with them all in Sophie and Marcus's new place.

As Bailey sat down and was about to turn and speak to Polly, the toastmaster announced that the new 'Mr and Mrs Bowman' had arrived and everyone stood up to applaud. Then it was his turn to get nervous, but grateful that they had decided to get the speeches done first.

Before he knew it, the speech, an absolute success by the way, was done, the wedding breakfast eaten and Sophie and Marcus had gone to speak with their guests. Bailey finally turned round to Polly.

'How you doing, Miss Polly?' he asked as his gaze took in as much of her as he could, because honestly he never wanted to forget just how amazing she looked right at this moment.

'Nervous.' She was fidgeting and he knew that she hadn't eaten a lot.

'Do you want me to give you something else to think about for a while?' He tried to keep his tone calm and not give away any of the wicked thoughts currently going through his head, but something must have shown, as Polly turned fully in her seat and crossed her legs, revealing the slit in her dress, and more importantly her long leg in nearly all of its gorgeousness.

'Come with me.' Bailey stood up and held out his hand.

Chapter Thirty-Five

Feeling somewhat rejuvenated and more than a little bit wild after a few impromptu minutes with Bailey, Polly made her way through the hidden door and through the other half of the Hayloft, up towards the stage. She stood still and took in the transformation of the room. Yesterday when she had sound checked it had been a very simple room with white walls and beams, a wall of floor to ceiling windows and doors to her left.

Now some of the doors had been opened and she could see in the dusk that the trees had all been bejewelled in fairy lights. The stage had been added, as had the black and white tiles that outlined where everyone should be shuffling their feet. There was another smaller stage to Polly's left where the DJ would be arriving shortly and would be setting up ready to take over once Polly and the band had finished. Two bars had been set up at the back of the room and the bar staff were finishing setting up, ready to serve drinks to the masses. Polly couldn't wait until she had a drink in hand. But honestly, what Tatiana could accomplish in such a short timescale was outstanding.

'Polly are you ready, do you have everything you need? You're due to start in ten minutes,' Tatiana said from the dance floor, iPad in hand.

'Yep.' And that was all she could say, her nerves making it difficult to get words through her throat. Not a great start for the wedding singer, but it seemed to be all Tatiana needed before she took off again.

As Polly reached the stage she said hi to her fellow bandmates for the evening, giving each of them a quick hug before getting to her spot. She'd spent whatever spare time she could in the last week rehearsing, and now, now it was happening. And that was made even more obvious as the walls were seamlessly removed and the room was opened up. Polly's thoughts about the room must have been shared as the rest of the wedding guests let out quite a few ohhs and ahhs.

Oh God.

Polly quickly looked around at her bandmates. It was time, wasn't it? Taking a deep breath she tried to remember what Sophie had told her. She had instructed Polly that the idea was to get people dancing if they fancied it, but mostly it was for ambience, and, frankly, Polly was more than happy with that, it meant that for her first set ever, she could find her bearings, and take it at her own pace. The only thing was that the last song she performed would be for Sophie and Marcus's first dance. Sophie had already asked if they could stream at least some of the first dance, and Polly had said yes, before realising that she would inevitably be heard by Sophie's millions of followers. Oh well it was too late now.

After making sure the musicians were all comfy and ready to go, and making sure that she had the set list nearby just in case, she turned around to her microphone. The problem with the lighting became apparent at once. There was no way of not seeing the audience. At the Speakeasy the spotlights were so bright and the rest of the room so dark, that it was easy to pretend that they weren't there. This was not the case, as was apparent when she saw one of Sophie's family members pick their nose when they thought no one was looking. Not wanting to gag, the vines in her belly pushing up the food to her throat as it was, she quickly looked away. Her hands shook a little as they gripped the microphone on the stand. She looked out at Sophie and Marcus, and she couldn't help but feel the love in the room. Sophie was positively radiant and the way she looked at Polly's brother, made her smile.

Right, it was now or never, but then panic flared. Was she supposed to introduce them, draw attention? Or should she just start? What if the PA system didn't work properly? What if she forgot all the songs and the lyrics? She fell down onto the bar stool that was behind her.

No.

Forcing the vines back into the bottom of her belly, taking deep breaths she recalled all the times she had performed previously. She distinctly remembered the thrill, the complete and utter freedom. She thought of all the incredible things she had accomplished in the last few months. She clung onto the feeling of burlesque, of how powerful she was. Looking down she thought about how sexy she felt in her killer goddess dress, the hint of leg visible. Finally, she focused on love. The love she had for Sophie and Marcus, how she could honour the love they had for each other tonight, and how much she loved the man still staring at her and grinning. She stood back up, her heart racing still, she turned around and nodded. Off they go.

The first song finished without any problems or any technical difficulties. Polly had managed to lose the audience again as she sang with her eyes closed and focused on the beat, the rhythm, the song flowing through and around her. The applause did what it always did, and brought her back down to earth. But this time she was giddy, this time she didn't have to come off the stage and let someone else take their turn. This time she was going again, and again, for nearly forty-five minutes, she could keep getting the high.

'Thank you,' Polly whispered into the microphone before smiling. Her glance unable to avoid the cheers and smiles of her friends and family, even Sophie and Marcus had stopped circulating so they could listen, their arms held tight around each other. Turning again to make sure that the band were with her, she was surprised to see that they were all grinning too. Giving in to it all, she nodded and they carried on.

Thirty minutes later and people were already dancing, none more so than Euan and Smithy who were taking it in turns to strut their stuff and Polly laughed feeling elated, ecstatic, and endorphined up to her eyeballs.

'Thank you so much.' Polly saw Denise and Billy blowing kisses at her and smiling. Polly had assumed that Denise would be too poorly to get to the evening do, but she was happy to have assumed incorrectly. She nodded at Denise and gestured for her to come to the front. Giving only a second to wonder at the confident way she was owning the stage, she waved at Denise again and watched as she made her way over. Walking to the edge of the small stage, Polly grabbed Denise in a hug.

'How are you feeling? Are you maybe up for a quick duet?' Polly asked.

'Are you sure?'

'Absolutely, we were going to perform "All of Me".' Denise nodded, and Polly saw her eyes fill up. Swallowing down her own tears, Polly continued, 'You go first, I'll join, you go high, I'll stay low, and I'll follow you, OK?'

Denise cleared her throat and nodded. Walking back to the centre of the stage, Polly watched as Denise acknowledged the rest of the band. Luke, the guitarist, magic'd up a microphone and handed it to Denise with a smile.

'Everyone, it is my absolute pleasure to welcome on stage Denise Williams. Please show Denise the love.' Polly grinned, as the crowd, and yes it was a crowd now applauded, yelled and wolf-whistled, namely Euan and Smithy. Denise curtseyed a little and nodded at Polly. Polly, in turn, looked at the band and they were off. She had no idea how to do a duet, and she prayed that she didn't mess it up. Keeping her eyes on Denise she let her lead.

The thunderous applause, and it was deafening, was nothing compared to the soaring feeling that was in Polly's chest. She was floating and her blood was thick as it pumped the intoxication around her body – she could feel everything. The hairs on the back of her neck had gone from standing on end to disappearing up into her hairline. She was moved, it was almost spiritual. Denise's arms were clung tightly around her neck.

'Thank you so much, Polly. You didn't have to do that. Thank you, sweetheart.'

Polly wanted to utter her heartfelt thanks in reply but was still too moved, too excited, too pumped to do anything else. Denise smiled and walked off the stage. Remembering where she was and what she was meant to be doing, but not ever wanting to lose that feeling, she quickly walked over to Luke, her mind racing as she thought, why not?

'Luke, would you mind if I borrowed your guitar? I have a small piece that I need to perform before the official first dance. Would that be OK?'

'All yours, Pol.'

Turning back around, Polly looked out over the audience. 'Thank you all so much, isn't Denise amazing?' Polly took a deep breath and waited for the applause to die back down again.

'I wasn't going to perform this next song tonight, but Sophie, Marcus, I hope you will allow me to run over by a couple of minutes.'

'We love you, Pol!' screamed Sophie, in true fan girl response.

Her hand was surprisingly steady as she righted the guitar strap, not quite believing what she was about to do, but knowing that she could. She felt the power coursing through her and it felt incredible. It was her choice. It was up to her. She knew how she felt and she wanted to share it. She'd take whatever came back her way.

'OK then, in that case, I wrote this song about three months ago, long before the intended recipient had any idea how I felt. This song is called, "I'm The One Loving You".'

The feeling was more subtle this time, the song slower, but no less powerful. She sang with everything she had, her eyes closing as she put every ounce of love, every bit of heart into it, until the entire room was full, there wasn't an inch that escaped the resonance of Polly's voice. When the song finished and the applause thundered once more, Polly couldn't look up at the man she wrote the song for. She still had one more song to sing. Giving the guitar back to Luke, she gave him a quick one-armed hug. 'Thank you.'

'Not at all. Polly that song was amazing. You'll have to come and do more gigs with us. Let's talk after, OK?'

'Thanks, Luke.'

Going back to the microphone she clutched it and realised that she was stood taller, her voice more powerful than ever before, and without any hesitation, she spoke to the crowd.

'Thank you so much from all of us up here, it's been amazing, and we have loved every minute. But for now, I am going to have to ask you to clear the dance floor and ask the new Mr and Mrs Bowman take to the floor for their first dance.'

She'd been rehearsing with the band to make Sophie and Marcus's song more upbeat for the first dance, and Polly couldn't help herself as she swayed along to the rhythm. This time she sang with her eyes wide open watching as Sophie and Marcus swayed in each other's arms around the dance floor. It was the most beautiful thing Polly had ever been blessed to be a part of. As more people joined the newlyweds on the dance floor, the song continued, and Polly saw in the corner of her eye that the DJ had finished setting up and was ready to take over.

When the song had finished, Polly made quick work of bowing, before turning and applauding the band along with the rest of the crowd. As she stepped off the stage, real-life came at her fast, in the form of a beast in a suit, his hair tied back neatly, his beard sexy as hell, his grin reaching up to his shining eyes. He held onto her elbow and walked her towards the outside terrace.

Polly chewed her lip as she contemplated what she was going to say. Although really the song said everything, didn't it? Once outside, under the glow of the rosy pink outdoor heating and fairy lights scattered amongst the ivy and trees her whole world stopped as she looked up into his beautiful blue eyes. His hands held onto her waist, and she could feel the warmth of him he was so close. Taking in the sight that was Bailey, his shirtsleeves rolled up, bowtie loose on his neck, waistcoat unfastened, the top button of his shirt undone showing a hint of the black tattoo on his chest, the broad shoulders that blocked out whatever was going on behind them, protecting her from any spring chill. She took it all in and savoured it.

He shook his head, shoulders shrugging slightly. 'I love you too, Pol. I want to be everything you deserve and I am going to try my hardest every single day to be that man.'

His big warm and calloused hand cupped her face gently as he lowered his head and pressed his lips to hers. Polly sighed into the kiss, her body following. Until his arm was wrapped around her lower back, her hands tight around his neck. She'd taken a huge risk, throwing out her heart and soul and hoping Bailey would catch it. That he would cherish it and return it was a feeling beyond measure, and Polly marvelled at all she had received in return.

Chapter Thirty-Six

Polly was back in the lift, one that she wasn't sure she'd ever be in again. She readjusted the handbag on her shoulder and tried to take a deep breath. She closed her eyes and thought of Bailey kissing her as she left, wishing her luck. She thought of Bailey at the wedding and just how devastatingly handsome he was in a suit. She thought of singing at the wedding. She remembered how much of a badass she was now. Straightening her spine she stood taller. It helped that she had put on heels. She was dressed to kick ass regardless of what waited for her. There was a ping and the doors opened.

'Polly, morning. How are you? Would you follow me?' Leanne smiled and if Polly had to guess it was genuine. But that still meant she was none the wiser, so she followed Leanne as she led them through the desks and towards the meeting rooms. Keeping her focus on where they were headed she didn't look at anyone else, but she could feel the stares.

'Just in here, please.' Leanne gestured into the meeting room. There was one empty chair, and once again it faced three other chairs. And just like last time occupied by Raj and Jackie, with Leanne taking the empty one.

'Hi, Polly,' Raj said.

'Thank you for coming in.' Jackie inclined her head before they each looked at the other.

'We conducted the investigation and wanted you to know the outcome,' Leanne began.

Polly took a breath.

'We've decided on a written warning. As you know it will sit in your file for twelve months and that's that. We'd love to have you back from next Monday,' Jackie spoke in a rush.

'What about Darren?' Polly was almost shocked by her own tone, she really was a badass today.

'Yes, well,' Raj began. 'Leanne lead an investigation based on your findings and he has been suspended.'

Polly tried not to roll her eyes.

Jackie cut in, 'He will be dismissed. The findings are conclusive, we're just finishing up the reports.'

'Right and why will he be dismissed exactly?'

'Well, after some confidential conversations one or two complaints were made that we were able to use as the basis—' Leanne began.

Jackie cut Leanne off and leaned forward. 'He was sleeping around with various staff members and there was an issue with his reference from a previous job. It seems he may not have been as forthcoming about the accounts he managed.'

Polly snorted. It was the money and the contracts more than it was anything else. Of course.

'So we'd love to see you back in the office from Monday, Polly, and we can put this whole mess behind us,' Raj said as he stood.

'No, thank you,' Polly started. 'I've done my calculations and I'm owed about two weeks annual leave, and I think it would be fair to say that the way I have been treated could quite easily be called into question. So why don't we say two weeks annual leave, two weeks garden leave and you can consider my resignation effective immediately?' Polly pulled out the letter already typed up and signed and pushed it along the table.

Raj sighed as he sat back down, Leanne looked uncomfortable and Jackie smiled but nobody said a word for a minute. Polly stared them all down and felt the power she held in every cell and with every second of silence the power in her grew and grew.

'Polly, you don't have to—' Raj began.

'Come back on Monday, after one month your salary will be increased by two scales, and in three months you'll be offered the newly created position of "Head of Development",' Jackie countered.

'Why?' Polly asked.

'This Polly I'm seeing now is the one that I knew was there. I need someone confident, in charge, I need someone like you are now, to lead on this.'

Polly kept her poker face, looking cool, calm and collected whilst she thought through the unexpected offer. It was tempting, but only for all of one minute. This company did what any other would be expected to do, they followed the money. Not the staffing issues, or the people affected, it was the money that mattered in the end. The new position would mean more money for her and them, but ultimately it meant more HR and more boredom. More of being trapped to a desk.

Polly pushed the letter further towards Jackie. 'Thank you, but no.'

And with that she stood up, smiled warmly and genuinely at her ex-managers. Putting her handbag on her shoulder she walked out of the office and straight to the waiting lift. She didn't plan on wasting her badass self here. Not when she could be pouring it into her music.

Chapter Thirty-Seven

Three months later

'I've said it before and I'll say it again, we are an exceptional team,' Mya said as she sipped at the Pornstar Martini Paige had just made her, her eyes shining with laughter.

'Let's see it,' Paige demanded as she leaned over the bar. Mya turned her phone over to Paige, who promptly burst out laughing. 'Oh my God, that's even better than I thought it would be.'

'It was Polly that first gave me the idea, then my meticulous ability to stalk online to get just the right picture of that idiot, your legendary photoshopping skills, and Sophie's social media clout. Like I said teamwork.' Mya chuckled again as Paige returned the phone.

'We've probably saved lives with this,' Paige replied deadpan.

'Oh absolutely. It will help those that have possibly been affected, and prevent anyone else from going near him with a ten-foot bargepole.'

The grinning continued as they studied the poster that had already been shared nearly a million times. Dickhead Darren should know better than to mess with them, and now thanks to the power of social media, Darren was the spokesman for the local Sexual Health Clinic, complete with a warning about the effects of spreading genital warts and herpes, as well as full details for the clinic.

'I heard that BBC Manchester wanted to get in touch with him.' Paige grinned.

'Oh, you heard that, did you?' Mya snorted nearly covering them both in Martini.

'Is Polly coming tonight?' Paige asked as she wiped down the bar.

'No, she's having dinner with Denise and then rehearsing with her band.' Mya's smile dropped a little.

Paige looked up. 'How is Denise?'

'Treatment is all finished, and sounds like she won't need anything further.'

'That's amazing news.' Paige grabbed a drink and they toasted to Denise's health.

'So...' Mya sighed, drinking again. 'Then there were two.'

'Don't be like that, Ms Drama. Sophie will be back off her extended honeymoon soon enough, and Polly and Bailey are just in that new couple phase of wanting to spend every minute together.'

'Yeah, I guess.' Mya put her phone down and sipped her martini. 'Have you seen Polly's page on Instagram?' Mya asked.

'Yeah, but I didn't think there was that much...' Paige's voice wandered off as she picked up her phone.

'Her bands' page?' Mya spelt out.

'Oh, let me guess, social media influencer Sophie set her up with one.'

'Yep, the day before the wedding and then live-streamed the song for Bailey off her own social media linking to Polly's.' Mya grinned.

'Wow, is Polly mad?' Paige asked.

'No, not really, because she knew that Sophie was going to stream at least some of it anyway. And she certainly isn't mad now that agents have been in touch.' Mya tossed her hair back over her shoulder.

'Shit, are you serious?' Paige gasped.

'Yeah, our little Polly might be about to become a pop star.' Mya grinned.

Paige stopped what she was doing and shook her head. 'She'd hate it. She'll be a kick-ass songwriter though. I bet she goes down that route instead.'

'Oh you bet do you, or do you know?' Mya asked eyebrows wriggling.

'Ah, don't remind me. I can only bet, my doodah is still off.' Paige huffed.

'Ohhh well if your doodah is still off you should get some vagasil, love!' said Mya, her voice oh so innocently increasing in volume.

'Oh haha. I'd borrow yours but I don't want to touch it, what with you're untreatable clap!'

Mya snort laughed, which just set them off even more as Paige sniggered her way over to serve another customer.

Mya looked around the bar. She was feeling a little mopey, if she was honest. It wasn't that she wanted to be married off or even coupled off, far from it. But changes were happening, they were of an age. Before she knew it she would be Auntie Mya and the late nights out would come to an end. Her phone buzzing brought her out of her melancholy and nicely into a fiery rage.

Smithy: I made it through. I guess I'll be facing you again after all.

Mya groaned. That's what she deserved for whinging about her friends all leaving. Her enemies just got closer.

Mya: Then prepare to be beaten. See you in Vegas.

Thank You

Dear Reader,

It has been a pleasure to be able to create something gorgeous and lovely during what is one of the hardest periods of our lives, admittedly it hasn't always been easy to do. I sincerely hope that this book has given you a little bit of joy, and a small amount of much needed escapism. If you have enjoyed it, and you think that others might enjoy it too, then perhaps you wouldn't mind leaving a review, or telling your friends, I'd be ever so grateful.

I wish you all the best.

Take care,
Lucy K x

About the Author

Lucy Keeling is an author writing fun, sexy, stories with all of the happily ever afters. When she's not typing at the kitchen table, she's arranging and then re-arranging to see her friends for the occasional spot of day drinking. Lucy is currently writing the third book in a contemporary romance series, the first of which was runner-up in Choc Lit's 'Search for a Star' competition which was sponsored by *Your Cat* magazine.

Lucy lives in Greater Manchester with her family.

For more information on Lucy:
www.twitter.com/Lucy_K_Author
www.facebook.com/lucykeelingbooks/
https://www.instagram.com/lucy_k_author/

More Choc Lit

From Lucy Keeling

Just a Boy Friend

Book 1 – Friends

What do mascara wands and gardening shears have in common?

Absolutely nothing! At least that's what wannabe beauty influencer Sophie Timney thinks when her friend Polly suggests involving her brother Marcus in Sophie's make-up tutorials. She needs more views, Marcus needs promotion for his gardening business – in Polly's mind joining forces will help them both. Sophie isn't so sure.

Because Marcus Bowman has a habit of getting under her skin in a way that no exfoliating face scrub ever could. But, as the views and comments on her videos begin creeping up, it becomes increasingly obvious that Sophie's subscribers like Marcus, and what's even worse is that Sophie might be starting to feel the same way …

Visit www.choc-lit.com for details.

Just Friends in Vegas

Book 3 – Friends

Is love always a losing game?

When Mya is with Smithy, it feels like her eyes are constantly rolling. His wheeling and dealing charisma charms everyone but her. Well, that's not strictly true – Mya is only human after all, and there's no doubt the man is hot with his suits and swagger. It's just that Smithy knows Mya's secret, and she's not sure she can trust him to keep it from their group of friends.

As they immerse themselves in the glamorous and mysterious world of 'The Suits', growing closer as a result, Smithy has to question whether his time with Mya is destined to become a case of 'what happens in Vegas stays in Vegas' …

Visit www.choc-lit.com for details.

Introducing Choc Lit

We're an independent publisher creating
a delicious selection of fiction.
Where heroes are like chocolate – irresistible!
Quality stories with a romance at the heart.

See our selection here:
www.choc-lit.com

We'd love to hear how you enjoyed *Just Friends*. Please
visit **www.choc-lit.com** and give your feedback or
leave a review where you purchased this novel.

Choc Lit novels are selected by genuine readers like yourself.
We only publish stories our Choc Lit Tasting Panel want to
see in print. Our reviews and awards speak for themselves.

Could you be a Star Selector and join our Tasting Panel?
Would you like to play a role in choosing which novels
we decide to publish? Do you enjoy reading women's
fiction? Then you could be perfect for our Tasting Panel.

Visit here for more details…
www.choc-lit.com/join-the-choc-lit-tasting-panel

Keep in touch:
Sign up for our monthly newsletter Spread for all the latest
news and offers: www.spread.choc-lit.com. Follow us
on Twitter: @ChocLituk and Facebook: Choc Lit.

Where heroes are like chocolate – irresistible!